D1083285

DEAD MEN
DON'T MARRY

BY THE SAME AUTHOR

Dead Men Don't Give Seminars

DEAD MEN DON'T MARRY

Dorothy Sucher

St. Martin's Press, New York

Design by Karin Batten

Library of Congress Cataloging-in-Publication Data

Sucher, Dorothy.
    Dead men don't marry / Dorothy Sucher.
       p.   cm.
    "A Thomas Dunne book."
    ISBN 0-312-02900-4
    I. Title.
    PS3569.U24D44 1989
    813'.54—dc19   89-4113

First Edition

10 9 8 7 6 5 4 3 2 1

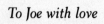
To Joe with love

ACKNOWLEDGMENTS

For many helpful conversations I would like to thank Joyce Johnson, Anita Landa, and Joe Sucher.

I also appreciate the help of Jack Brickman, formerly of the Metropolitan Police Department of Washington, D.C.; Malvin Vitriol, librarian at the Milton Helpern Forensic Library in New York City; Professor Arthur Halprin of the University of Delaware; and the photographer Michael Belenky of New York City.

One

FRAN

One

The red eye of the answering machine blinked at me as I shouldered my way through the door and set my suitcases down on the floor of the living room. It was two in the morning and I was home, and the empty house felt lonely and too big for me. I told myself, not for the first time, that one of these days I was going to sell the house and move downtown, buy myself a condo, and start working seriously on my social life.

I headed for the bedroom, and as I passed the answering machine it flashed again. If I wanted to hear the sound of a human voice, all I had to do was push a button.

I pushed a button.

Abby Rademacher had left a message asking me to call her about a case when I got back—she was a free-lance detective who'd been subbing for me at the agency while I'd been away. There was a message from a former girlfriend who lived in Chicago and had spent a few days in D.C., and who thought it would be fun if we got together, or so she said. I had my doubts, but anyway she was back in the Windy City by now. There were more calls—nothing major. And then I heard the voice of Fran O'Donnell, who'd lived across the street from me as long as I could remember. "Victor, honey, just wanted to let you know I'm getting married next Saturday at the courthouse in Upper Marlboro. If there's any chance you'll be back by then, could you come? It would feel—sorta like having Billy there, you know . . ."

I played the message again. So—she'd actually gone and done it. Funny, I hadn't really believed she'd get married again. Hadn't wanted to believe it, probably. I wondered how long ago she'd left the message. It could have been quite a while, I'd been gone six weeks.

The rest of the calls were mostly routine—a few friends had checked in, a brokerage house I'd never heard of wanted to help me invest my millions, Abby Rademacher had called again—except for a message from a woman with one of those high-pitched, whiny voices that make you start backing away. "This is Elnora Poge, Mr. Newman," she said. "Please call me *immediately!*" The name seemed vaguely familiar, but I couldn't place it. I figured giving her a ring could wait until morning, since she must have called a while ago, and I was about to turn off the machine when I heard the voice of my boss, Sabina Swift. She sounded testy.

"Victor. It's ten o'clock on Sunday, August seventeenth. I assumed I would hear from you by now. Obviously, I have not. If this means your plane has been delayed, do not, I repeat *not*, telephone me later than midnight tonight, as I will be asleep. However, if you are simply skulking about the house 'unwinding,' I expect you to phone the office *at once*. When I granted you leave of absence I didn't expect you to prolong it unduly."

Skulking. Now that's what I'd call a hostile word. Since she was ten miles away and the answering machine couldn't care less, I replied aloud, "I never skulk, my dear Sabina. Have you forgotten that my leave of absence was unpaid, at your suggestion? Also that I handed in my resignation, which you refused

4

to accept?" The red eye blinked indifferently. "Plus, certain things can't be rushed, such as regaining one's health after a bulldozer falls on one." That's what had happened to my cousin Eric, who was a maintenance worker on the Alaskan pipeline. I'd gone to stay with him in his cabin outside Prudhoe Bay because there was no one else he could ask—we're a small family.

Telling Sabina off had given me a nice relaxed feeling and, yawning, I headed for the bedroom. Before I got there, though, I veered toward the picture window and looked across the street toward Fran O'Donnell's split-level, figuring I'd give her a quick call if there was a light in her window, congratulate her on her marriage. But the house was dark. There was no sign of Fran's old Toyota in the driveway. In its place crouched a sleek, low-slung Jaguar, gleaming under the street light. Fran with a Jaguar? It was hardly the image of the Fran I'd known since I was five years old and used to run across the street to play with her son Billy. Was the flashy new car something she'd bought to go with the new husband and the new life? I didn't care for the idea, I'd liked the old Fran the way she was. Pull in your Oedipus complex, I told myself. I knew damn well that's what was bothering me, after all the woman had practically raised me after my mother died.

I drew the blind, went upstairs to my bedroom, and crawled into bed. I told myself that Fran had a perfect right to live her own life. And it wasn't as if she hadn't warned me.

Two

 Something jolted me awake the next morning. Something I'd been dreaming?

No. Something I'd remembered.

Elnora Poge, who'd left the whiny message on my answering machine, was Fran's housemate. The reason I hadn't recognized her name was that Fran always called her "Pudge."

Pudge had been living across the street from me since Fran's first husband had died, but that didn't mean I really knew her. She was just a middle-aged woman I used to see puttering around Fran's garden, followed by a longhaired white cat that needed to go on a diet. Whenever I passed, Pudge would look up from the rosebush she was pruning, or whatever, and mop her brow and let her shoulders sag. I got the feeling this wasn't for my benefit, specifically; she just wanted the world to know how rough her lot in life was.

I made a point of avoiding Pudge. I couldn't imagine why she'd be calling me.

I got out of bed, padded into the living room, and dialed the number she'd left. It wasn't Fran's number, so apparently she'd moved—which wasn't surprising now that Fran had remarried.

A woman, not Pudge, answered the phone. "You want to speak to Miss Poge?" And then, suspiciously. "Who are you?"

"Is she home?" I don't like to leave my name when I don't know what the setup is at the other end of the line.

"She's home. She's always home. If you ask me, she should go out and get a job."

I hadn't asked her but I didn't say so. "May I speak to her, please?"

"Hold on." Footsteps retreated, and then I heard the woman calling, "Poge! Poge!" at the top of her lungs, as if shouting up a stairwell. "Telephone!"

Eventually, the voice that had left the message on my machine said, "Yes?"

"Ms. Poge? This is Victor Newman. I got your message."

"Oh," she said coldly. "You."

"You asked me to call."

"It took you long enough."

"I'm sorry, Ms. Poge, I've been out of town."

"This long?"

"This long." The woman was beginning to irk me.

"I called weeks ago. Weeks and weeks. After Fran died."

My hand tightened on the receiver. "What did you say?"

Her voice hardened. "I said, after Fran died. I didn't see you at the funeral."

I echoed, "Funeral? Fran's funeral? Fran's dead?" Memories started flooding in on me: of Fran washing the dishes while Billy and I sat blowing bubbles on the floor. Of Fran taking a freshly baked loaf of banana bread out of the oven—she always made banana bread when the bananas got so soft we wouldn't eat them. Then recollections of my father, blurry ungraspable memories of my mother . . . "How did she die?" I managed to say. "This is the first I've heard of it, I just flew in last night. What happened?"

There was a silence. "I can't talk here. I have no privacy whatsoever. I guess you could come over, if you like."

"Give me the address and I'll be right there."

I should call Sabina, I thought as I hung up. I should check in at the office.

But the woman who'd practically raised me was suddenly and inexplicably dead; a foundation stone of my life had crumbled away without warning, and everything else was going to have to wait. Besides, Sabina didn't know for sure that I was back yet.

I threw on my clothes and took a quick shave. I have kind of a heavy beard, and even though the color is on the light side I have to shave often. I've been thinking about growing a beard, because my face is, not bad looking exactly, but ordinary (which I have to admit can be an asset in my line of work); also because I'm not crazy about being told I look like a kid when I'm really twenty-seven.

This morning the face in the mirror looked neither ordinary nor particularly young, especially around the eyes. Jet lag and the death of friends can do that to you.

Outside, the air was steamy and already eighty degrees. If it was as hot as that at nine in the morning, we were definitely in for a Maryland scorcher. The leaves on the willow tree my father had planted when I was born were starting to turn yellow, always the first sign of fall; I had the feeling I'd missed the whole summer. The grass in the yard hadn't been cut for more than six weeks and was up to my knees. I supposed I'd have to do something about that.

Across the street in Fran's driveway, the Jaguar was still parked. By daylight I could see that it was bright red. Some snazzy car, I thought. Did it belong to Fran's husband? Aside from the car, there was no sign the house was occupied. All the shades were drawn.

My gaze shifted to the house next door, and at the sight of it I got my second shock of the morning. Old man Geissdorf's lawn, the lawn he always kept clipped to cemetery length, had grown raggedy and a foot high. Had the guy finally flipped out

8

completely? It was hard to imagine Geissdorf neglecting his lawn, no matter what the circumstances. Maybe he'd moved away.

What the hell was going on in the neighborhood?

I got in my car and headed for Laurel, where Pudge had said she was living. On the way I thought about the last time I'd seen Fran.

It had been six weeks ago. She'd knocked on my door at a couple of minutes past midnight, right after I'd gotten home.

"Vic? I saw your light. Is it too late to come in?"

"Never too late for you, Fran." I swung the door wide. Fran didn't go in for midnight visits as a rule, she was a believer in early to bed. I stepped aside to let her in, and caught a whiff of scotch as she passed by, a little unsteadily.

She headed for the living room and collapsed into the over-stuffed rocker where my dad used to sit. There was an anxious expression on her kind, homely face, but otherwise she was looking surprisingly good. She'd lost weight since the last time I'd seen her, and her hair was styled differently, and tinted. I'm no expert on women's clothes, but my guess would have been that the dress she was wearing hadn't come from a suburban shopping mall but one of the fancier downtown boutiques.

"Can I get you a beer?" I said.

"Make it something stronger."

"Scotch and soda?"

"Fine. Only leave out the soda." I fixed her a drink while she looked around. "My God," she said, "same furniture, same curtains, same rug—I almost expect your father to come strolling in from the kitchen. He was a helluva nice guy, you know that? Did I ever tell you I used to have a crush on him?"

"I'll be damned. Did I ever tell you I used to have this fantasy you were going to divorce Charlie and marry Dad?"

She sighed. "Poor Charlie, I miss him. Well, it's water over the dam. You know, this place needs a good cleaning, Vicky. I could give you the name of my cleaning lady—"

I laughed. "Same old Fran." She was the only person who still called me Vicky.

Fran O'Donnell had been my mother's best friend, and her son Billy had been mine. Many's the cookie Fran O'Donnell had given me, not to mention Band-aids, tickets to see the Redskins, and well-meaning advice. After my mother died, I spent more time in her house than my own.

Our lives didn't overlap much any more, except that we both still lived on Cinnamon Lane in Bowie, a sprawling Levittown on the outskirts of Washington, D.C. Her husband Charlie had died some years ago, and Fran had gotten a job working with teenage drug addicts. Once in a while she would invite me over for dinner, or I'd take her out to the local Chinese restaurant. Mostly we just waved at each other and smiled from our cars as she pulled into her driveway or I pulled out of mine. I always gave her car a wide berth because she was a terrible driver.

"It's good to see you," she said.

"You, too. How are things?"

"Wonderful," she said promptly, which surprised me. "Wonderful and terrible. I don't know if I can stand the strain, I'm used to a quiet life."

"Wonderful and terrible how?"

"Well, shall we start with terrible? Vic, honestly, can't something be done about Paul Geissdorf?" She gave me a serious, beseeching stare over the rim of her glass, as if I, being a detective, must be able to come up with a solution to the problem that had plagued the neighborhood for as long as I could remember.

Old man Geissdorf had feuded with most of the families on Cinnamon Lane at one time or another (the streets in the development have cutesy names, and in each section they start with the same letter—Candy Lane, Cardamom Lane, Caramel Lane—I guess to confuse people who might be trying to find your house). Geissdorf hated kids, especially, and the feeling was mutual; we used to play tricks on him at Halloween. By trade he was a hairdresser, and though I'd have hated to have him hovering around me with a pair of clippers, the occupation fitted him, in a way. I've never heard of a man who loved cutting more than he did. He mowed his lawn compulsively, he pruned his shrubs until it was a miracle they didn't bleed to death, and he committed instant infanticide on any weed that had the nerve to show its head in his beloved petunia bed. Other people's weeds infuriated him, too, and since my yard was rich in dandelions, we'd had words. His theory was that I was growing the dandelions on purpose so the seeds would fly across the street and contaminate his lawn. A hostile, paranoid kind of guy. I'd gone to school with Geissdorf's two kids, both of whom had left home at an early age.

Geissdorf's dim little wife Ida managed to keep a lid on him, barely, and when he wasn't around she'd knock on people's doors and make excuses for him, after he'd done something especially outrageous. Everyone felt sorry for her, which was one reason Geissdorf had never been prosecuted, though he'd been arrested on occasion for harassing people. Another was the kind of stuff he went in for—loud arguments followed by nasty, sneaky tricks that were hard to pin on him.

I said, "What's he done lately?"

"Well, I have this friend." Fran blushed. "A gentleman friend. He brings his dog when he comes over—it's a German shepherd. We keep it out back, where the yard is fenced. You remember."

"Sure do. Billy and I used to play in there where you could keep an eye on us."

She blinked a couple of times and shook her head. "Long ago, Vicky. It seems like another life." Billy had fallen out of a tree and died when he was fourteen years old. He'd been her only child. "Anyway, we keep Wolf out there, only this morning he jumped the fence and got into Geissdorf's petunias."

"Oh, no." I couldn't help laughing.

"Vicky, this is serious. Geissdorf and Keith got into an argument and I thought they were going to kill each other—I mean

I had to get in the middle and push, literally push the two of them apart."

"That doesn't sound like Geissdorf."

"I know. Everybody thinks he's going off his rocker now that his wife's gone."

"What, Ida finally left him?"

"Apparently. Nobody's seen her around for ages. Anyway, Geissdorf threatened to kill Keith's dog. And if *that* happens"— her eyes were frightened—"I don't know *what* Keith might do. Is there any more scotch in that bottle?" I refilled her glass. "Keith has a little bit of a temper, and he's crazy about Wolf, don't ask me why."

"You think Geissdorf would really hurt the dog?"

She bobbed her freshly tinted head up and down. "Oh, yes. I definitely do, he poisoned Pudge's cat, and Dot Reidy says she saw Geissdorf going through her garbage can one night. Her husband just got a notice he's being audited by the IRS, and he's positive Geissdorf put them up to it. He'd nudged Geissdorf's bumper, by accident. There wasn't even any *damage*—"

"Hey, wait. One thing at a time, okay? Let's start with Pudge."

"Okay." Fran made a face. "God, that woman's a pain."

"Why don't you ask her to move, then?"

She shrugged. "Oh—it's handy having her around, in a way. She does a few chores, and I can't keep up with that big house myself, now that I'm doing the job of two workers. They've cut the agency's funds again. Anyway, I feel sorry for her. Only trouble is, I can't stand her. Can I have another drink?"

I poured her one. I hoped she wasn't going to ask for another one after that, because if she did I was going to say no, and it's hard to tell your dead mother's best friend she's had too much. I wondered if Fran had developed a drinking problem since Charlie's death. "Tell me what happened to Pudge's cat."

She shook her head. "Poor old Snowball. He'd done his, you know, business on Geissdorf's lawn a couple of times. You just can't put a cat on a leash, it's their nature to roam. One day the poor thing came dragging himself up the driveway, and we could see he was really sick. He'd been fine before. We tried to get him to the vet, but he died on the way." She shook her head. "Oh my God, did Pudge carry on! I mean, not that you could blame her. She went to the police and they said there was nothing they could do." Fran pushed herself up from the chair and walked unsteadily to the window, where she stared out toward Geissdorf's house. "I'm just so sick of that creep! I've had it up to here! I'm getting paranoid myself, I feel like everybody's out to get me. Pudge keeps watching me. She's jealous of Keith, she thinks I'm going to throw her out so he can move in."

"Is she right?"

She gave me a quick grin. "Could be. I've dropped one or two hints." She leaned on the windowsill. Behind her I could see the glow of the street lamp. "Vicky—" She hesitated. "I'm thinking seriously about selling the house and moving away. Though why I should have to move . . ." She brightened. "At least it'd be a way of getting rid of Pudge." After a moment she added, "Nobody knows this yet, but Keith and I are talking about getting married."

"Married? Sounds serious."

She nodded, and a little extra color crept into her face. "I thought maybe—you know, in this day and age—he was going to ask me to live with him, and as a Catholic I just—" She shook her head. "But he says two people who love each other should make a commitment." Suddenly she smiled, and in spite of the spiffy clothes and the fancy hairdo, and even the alcoholic glow, she looked a lot more like the Fran I remembered from childhood. "I think that's really sweet, I can hardly believe my luck! Most of the men my age are looking for younger women." She beamed at me. "And you, Vicky? When are you going to find a nice girl? You're not such a kid anymore."

"I know, Fran, I know. Find me one and we'll see."

She shook her finger at me. "I just might do that."

"In the meantime, congratulations. You really like this guy?"

She nodded. "He's different, Vic. This man is exciting, he's a doer, he takes me to the theater, we travel, we go to the races—actually, he likes the races *too* much, but you can't have everything, can you? We have fun! God knows I could use some." She grinned. "It's all I can do to keep up with him—I'm no chicken, and actually he's a little younger than I am. I can't figure out why, but he wants to show me Europe—we're even talking about a trip around the world! In a way, I'd *like* to sell the house. And I wouldn't mind quitting my job—this work can really burn you out. As far as Keith's concerned, I could quit tomorrow. He's quite well off."

"What does he do?"

"He's retired. He used to be in business in Wisconsin, but he made a lot of money in the market and decided to take a few years off and enjoy life. He showed me a picture of his house on Lake Mendota. It's a mansion, Vic. Big white columns, long curving driveway going up a hill—I mean, a split-level in Bowie is not what this man is used to." She paused. "This stuff with Geissdorf—what does it matter in the long run? All I want is to be with Keith and be happy. Is that asking too much? I've paid my dues. You know."

"I know, Fran. Well, tell Keith to leave his dog home when he comes to see you. No point looking for trouble."

She shook her head, and the anxiety came back into her eyes. "He won't listen, he's stubborn. That's one other fault he has. I'm not saying he's perfect, Vicky. And he's got a thing about that damn dog." She sighed. "Oh, well, with Charlie I had a mother-in-law, with Keith I have Wolf. Could be worse. Could be a *lot* worse." She flashed me a mischievous smile. "It so happens he's also a very *handsome* man." Her hand dipped into the pocket of her skirt and came out holding her keys. "So what you're telling me is, there's nothing I can do about Geissdorf. Right?"

"Well—it's tough. Maybe Lester could help." Lester Yates and Billy and I used to pal around together as kids. Now Lester was a sergeant on the Bowie police force.

She sighed. "I doubt it. Lester never was too bright. You were the bright one."

"Maybe," I said. "I haven't come up with any bright ideas this time. You might try bringing charges—he did threaten your friend, assaulted him, I guess you might say—" I wished I could think of something more helpful. "Maybe you could get Lester to threaten him with arrest unless he agrees to see a shrink. Who knows, it might do Geissdorf some good."

Fran looked skeptical. "He'd never go. If he'd been willing to go, he'd have gone by now. Oh, well."

She gave me a kiss on the cheek and I took her to the door. Watching her weave her way down the path, I thought it was lucky she lived across the street. In her present condition she'd have been more of a menace on the roads than usual.

A good person, Fran O'Donnell. Someone who deserved a little happiness.

I figured I'd have a talk with Lester Yates the next day, not that I thought it would do much good, but in the morning the call came from cousin Eric's doctor. I have to admit that after that, Fran's problems slipped my mind.

Three

Elnora Poge was living in the old part of Laurel, in a sagging frame house with a rickety porch and a sign in the front window that said ROOM FOR RENT. It was one of those neighborhoods outside the Beltway where cheaply built apartments alternate with video arcades and junk-food restaurants, and the few old houses that are left are falling apart while their owners wait for the real estate deal at the end of the rainbow. I recognized Pudge's beat-up old Chevy, slouched in a muddy driveway it was sharing with half a dozen other cars.

She was waiting for me on the porch. She was about forty, ten years younger than Fran but without any of Fran's gusto; she gave the impression of a perpetual bystander, someone who lived on the edges of life, watching other people and resenting them. "I haven't seen you for a long time, Mr. Newman," she said in her high-pitched voice. Her light blue eyes bulged in my direction, and she gave a nervous sniff that wrinkled her fleshy, inquisitive nose. Breathlessly she added, "I guess we better go up to my room so we can talk." She reddened slightly, as if she'd made an indecent suggestion.

"Call me Vic," I said. "Did you know your car has a flat?"

She turned her back on me and headed for the front door. "A flat is the least of it, it needs a new transmission. Where the money's supposed to come from, I have no idea. Have you noticed it's impossible to get a job in the suburbs without a car, but you can't afford a car if you don't have a job?"

"I've noticed," I said, remembering the time I'd been laid off during an economy drive at Crownsville State Hospital, where I'd been working as a psychiatric aide. "I could change your tire. Do you have a spare?"

She turned, her face suspicious. "How come you're being so kind to poor little me? What have I done to deserve it, I wonder."

Fran had been right, the woman was a pain. "You don't have to deserve it, Pudge."

"Don't call me that!" She sniffed angrily.

We had gone through the front door and were standing in a dingy hall with a pay phone on the wall. Ahead of us, a narrow, worn staircase mounted steeply. Some old houses are gracious even in decay. Not this one. It was flimsy and the carpentry was bad, as if it had originally been built to house the poor.

"Sorry," I said. "It just slipped out." We began to mount the stairs.

"I always hated it when she called me that. Why didn't she call me Elnora? It's a perfectly good name."

"Miss Poge! Miss Poge!" Below us in the hall, a stout, red-faced woman in an apron was standing, her hands on her hips. "We don't allow men in the rooms! I thought I made that clear when you moved in."

Pudge rolled her eyes in my direction. "He's here on business, Mrs. O'Brien. He won't stay long."

"Business? I didn't realize you had *business*." The landlady's voice was sarcastic. She stared hard at me and then turned away. "Don't forget what I said about the rent, Miss Poge." She disappeared into a room off the hall.

Pudge flushed in dark blotches and bit her lip, but said nothing. We climbed up into the baking heat of the third floor. Her room was directly under the sloping roof. There was a large, scaly patch on the ceiling, and below it the floor was whitened, as if plaster dust had been sifting down and working its way into the floor boards for some time. In the corner, an ancient fan rattled feebly, barely disturbing the air. I could feel the sweat breaking out on me as I sat down on a metal folding chair. "Ms. Poge," I said. "Please tell me about Fran."

"Fran," she repeated, and her neck jerked as she darted a quick look around the room. "Oh, everything is in such an awful mess, I can imagine what you think of me!" She gave her nervous sniff. "And after our beautiful home on Cinnamon Lane, with all those lovely things . . ." She seated herself on the edge of the bed, giving me a demure glance. "I took wonderful care of Fran's things. *Loving* care, Mr. Newman," she added angrily. "The kind money can't buy! I used to polish the dining-room table—I'm positive that table is genuine Queen Anne—with lemon oil every two months. *He* has it now. He has everything. Before he came, we were so close!" That was hardly the impression I'd gotten from Fran, and I wondered if Pudge believed what she was saying and, if not, why she was trying to convince me they'd been great friends. "We went to church together every Sunday—did you know?" I shook my head, somewhat surprised. Fran had been religious, but she'd never told me that she and Pudge attended church together. "What she needed *him* for I'll never know, we were fine the way we were." Pudge folded her hands in her lap. "And barely a month after she threw me out in the street, she was—dead." She turned her head aside abruptly, gazing out the narrow dormer window.

"Fran threw you out in the street?"

"Well—I hadn't really found a place yet. Not one I liked. It comes to the same thing. You know what she said to me? 'That's *your* problem, stop dragging your feet!'" Resentment flared in her eyes.

I cleared my throat. "Would you—tell me how she died?"

"She was driving over the railroad tracks and her car got hit by a train."

"My God!"

She nodded emphatically. "I saved the article from the *Washington Post.*" She rummaged through the pile of papers strewn on a bridge table. "Here, you can read it." She handed it to me.

CAR STALLS ON TRACKS
BOWIE WOMAN IS KILLED

A woman was killed instantly last night when the car she was driving was hit by a freight train at 11:10 P.M. at an unguarded railroad crossing in Gorton, Maryland. The engineer, Henry Freulinger, stated that he saw the car on the tracks as he came around a curve, and blew his whistle repeatedly, but although he applied the emergency brakes, the train was unable to stop in time.

The dead woman was identified as Frances O'Donnell Browdy, 51, a Bowie resident for twenty-two years, who was well known in the community for her work on behalf of the Boys Club. Mrs. Browdy, a social worker, had remarried only last month.

The railroad crossing where the accident took place has been the scene of other fatalities in the past, including the death seven years ago of four teenagers, who were killed on their way home from a high school prom when the car in which they had been riding was hit by a train. A group calling itself Citizens for Safety has been campaigning for a state law that would require all railroad crossings in Maryland to be provided with gates . . .

I looked up. "Could I borrow this?"

She nodded. "I was in church when it happened, and if she'd been there—But she didn't show up. *His* influence, no doubt. Or maybe she was trying to avoid me. After the way she treated me, I wouldn't be surprised—not that I mean to speak ill of the dead." She leaned toward me and added, "I saw the *whole thing* the next day on TV, her car, what was left of it, everything." She gave a ladylike shudder, and leaned closer. "Fran drank, you know. She used to keep a bottle under the bed—she thought nobody knew about it."

"You're suggesting she was drunk at the time of the accident?"

"Oh, I don't know about *drunk*. But she was a terrible driver anyway. Dangerous, actually. I mean—it's possible she just wasn't paying attention. Or . . ."

"Or what?"

"Oh, nothing really."

"There must have been something. Why did you leave a message on my answering machine?"

She gave a couple of nervous sniffs, and an evasive look came into the pale blue eyes. "It just seemed odd, that's all."

"What did?"

"The coincidence. I mean, it was such a short time after Paul Geissdorf'—her lips twisted as she spoke the name, and her voice dropped to a whisper—"threatened to kill her."

"Geissdorf threatened to kill her?" It didn't sound like him, he'd never threatened anyone's life before. Animals, maybe—not people. I said, "How come?"

Her eyes met mine and slid away. "Mr. Newman, I called you in the shock of the moment. I couldn't think clearly, but now I can see that's all it was—coincidence."

"Maybe. Tell me anyway."

She hesitated. I got the feeling not many people came to see her in her depressing little room, and she didn't want me to leave. "Well—if you insist. A few weeks after Fran got married, I went back to Cinnamon Lane to pick up a trunk I'd left in the basement. I hadn't seen her since a few days before the wedding." She sniffed indignantly. "To which I was *not* invited, by the way. She said it was private—too private for me, apparently. We had words about it, and afterwards, frankly, I didn't care if I spoke to her again or not. But when I dropped in to get my things she was actually quite friendly. We had coffee in the kitchen—it was like old times."

"How did she seem?"

"Kind of nervous, I thought. I asked her how she liked married life and she said it had its ups and downs, but it would be fine once she talked Keith into getting rid of the dog. It had jumped the fence and gotten into Paul Geissdorf's yard again, and he'd come storming over when Fran was the only one home, and threatened to kill her if she didn't get rid of Wolf. What he actually said was"—her eyes gleamed—"'I'll kill you, I'll kill the dog, and I'll kill that guy you're screwing around with.'" She averted her eyes modestly. "Apparently he didn't know she'd gotten married."

I shook my head. "Sounds like Geissdorf finally went off the deep end. And you figured there was a connection, when you heard about the accident?"

"I don't know *what* I thought, whether maybe he did something to her car—" She waved her hands vaguely. "Can't people do things to cars to make them break down?"

"It's possible. Though he couldn't have known the car would break down on the railroad tracks."

"That's what Sergeant Yates said."

"Oh, you went to the police."

She gave an angry sniff. "I did, and they treated me like I was some kind of mental case. It was the same when poor Snowball died. My beautiful Persian—you remember him? Sergeant Yates acted as if *I* was the one who was crazy, not Geissdorf!" Suddenly, her faded blue eyes clouded over. "Poor Snowball! I'll never forget the way he suffered. The way he looked up at me so trustingly on the way to the vet. He died in my arms." She dabbed at her eyes with a tissue. After a moment she blurted out angrily, "Geissdorf killed *him*—maybe he killed

Fran, too. You know, I haven't had that easy a life, Mr. Newman, and I don't have a high opinion of human nature. People are out for what they can get, and they don't care one bit for anyone's feelings; if you're in their way they just—shove you aside. Like that!" Her mouth closed into a bitter line, and her arm flew out in a jerky, violent movement that swept a pile of papers off the bridge table.

I bent to retrieve them, and saw that one of them was a photograph of Fran, an eight-by-ten glossy. I picked it up. It showed her in the kitchen, flattening a slab of dough with a rolling pin. Flour had whitened her hands above the wrist as if she were wearing gloves. Sunlight streamed in through a window, and she was smiling to herself, apparently unaware that her picture was being taken. I felt tears prick my eyes. "What a great picture!" I said. "Who took it?"

"Keith. I'll say this for him, he's a good photographer." Pudge wiped her eyes again and then blew her nose. I wasn't sure whether the tears were for Fran, the cat, or herself.

Studying the photograph, I said, "I wish I had a copy."

She took it from my hand. "You could try asking Keith, I guess. He made me this enlargement. That was when he and Fran first started going together, while he was still trying to get on my good side." She gave a couple of angry sniffs.

"Do you know where I can reach him? Is he living in Fran's house?"

She shook her head. "I have no idea."

"Well—" I said, rising from the folding chair. I took out a handkerchief and wiped the sweat off my face. In the corner, the fan was still turning ineffectually. "Thanks for telling me about Fran. And for the loan of the clipping." Pudge stood up, and I left.

I got in the car wondering whether Fran had been happy with her new husband. The photograph seemed to have been taken by a man who appreciated her; I hoped he had, anyway. I wished I was sure. Ups and downs, Pudge had said—that sounded normal enough, but wasn't it a little early for downs? They'd only been married a few weeks.

I thought about stopping in at the Bowie police station for a chat with Lester Yates. It was almost eleven and I was starting to get antsy about Sabina, but I wanted to hear from Lester the details of how Fran had died.

The police station first, I decided. It wouldn't take long. Afterwards I could drive to Georgetown and show up at the office around lunchtime.

Four

 When I got to the station house, Lester Yates was on duty. I shoved aside some papers and sat down on the corner of his desk.

He said, "So you finally showed up."

"Whaddya mean? Am I on salary around here, that I'm supposed to show up?"

"I just thought I'd hear from you sooner, that's all." He threw me an unfriendly look.

"You mean about Fran? Listen, Lester, I just heard. I've been away for six weeks."

"Well, hurray for you. Some of us poor working stiffs don't get to see the world." I've noticed before that people get hostile when you go away.

Lester was looking like he'd just had a haircut, all that was left was a few short, blondish bristles on top and even less on the sides. His ears seemed to stick out more than usual. He was a tall, gangling guy, twenty-seven years old, like me, with a long, scoop-shaped chin and a big Adam's apple. "Great haircut," I said. "Old man Geissdorf give it to you?"

"Why don't you just fuck off? Us peons have to work, believe it or not."

"Peons, eh? Those mail-order Spanish lessons are really paying off."

"And you can get your ass off my desk."

"That's no way to speak to a taxpayer."

He sighed, and crossed his arms over his chest. He had long arms and long legs, used to be a hotshot basketball player when we were in high school, hotshot by local standards, that is. He said, "How'd you hear?"

"I found a message on my answering machine from Fran's old housemate. I just came from seeing her. She gave me this."

I took out the article and laid it on his desk. "The cat lady, yeah. What'd she tell you? She hire you? I doubt she has the money."

"She hasn't, and she didn't. But she thinks Geissdorf killed Fran."

"She's got a bee in her bonnet about Geissdorf. Thinks he killed her cat, too."

"Could she be right?"

"About the cat, maybe. About Fran, no. It was just one of those damn lousy things, Vic. She stalled her car on the tracks, and a train came along before she got out. These things happen."

There was a silence. "Yeah," I said slowly. "They happen. One thing bothers me, though. According to the article, the engineer blew his whistle a number of times. Fran must have heard it. Why didn't she jump out of the car?"

Lester's eyes slid away from mine. "I guess we'll never know the answer to that. Maybe she thought she could get the car started in time. Maybe the engine started to turn over and then conked out again. Who can say?" He shrugged. "Anyway, this I can tell you—Geissdorf had nothing to do with it."

"You sound positive."

"I am."

"How come?"

"He happens to have been in a locked ward at Crownsville at the time."

"What?"

"Flipped out a few days before Fran died, ran all over Bowie stark naked, shouting obscenities, and finally lay down in the middle of Caramel Lane and started yelling, 'Run over me! Run over me!'" Lester shook his head. "A couple of cars almost did. Boy, did we get calls that day, let me tell you."

"So that's why he hasn't been cutting his grass."

"That's why. Some of the neighbors are talking about getting together to do it. At first they figured, the hell with him, but— you know, property values . . ." He grinned. "Maybe while they're at it you could get them to take care of yours."

"I know," I said. "The grass slipped my mind when I was out of town."

"Better cut it soon," said Lester warningly, "I hear the natives are restless."

"Never mind about that. Tell me about Fran. What was she doing in Gorton?"

He leaned back in his desk chair. "I guess you heard she got married." I nodded. "Okay, according to her husband, they were home watching TV, and about ten, ten-thirty she left the house, took her car, and went for a drive."

"Seems kind of late."

"Apparently they'd been arguing. She got mad and left. He was pissed and didn't try and stop her. She'd had a few drinks." He hesitated, and his eyes slid away again and then swung back to meet mine. "Well, more than a few—and he was getting on her back about it. She didn't care for that."

"She wouldn't." I thought it over. "But why Gorton? I mean, what can you do in Gorton at eleven at night?"

"Not much. However, there's a tavern on Route 1. We checked it out and she was known there—used to show up from time to time, do some serious drinking. Alone. I guess it was far enough from Bowie so nobody would recognize her."

I shook my head. "I never knew that, Lester. Charlie's death

26

must have hit her harder than I realized. I wish—" What did I wish? That I'd known? That I'd been there for her the way she'd been there for me? Too late now. I said, "Was she seen there that night?"

"No. She hadn't been around for months—since she started going with this Keith Browdy, apparently. But she died only a few blocks away."

"So she was on her way to her old hangout to have a couple. That the way you figure it?"

"That's the way."

I thought it over. It was possible, but—I said, "Was there an autopsy?"

"Believe me, the cause of her death was obvious."

"Yeah, but was there one?"

"God damn it, Newman!" Lester leaned over his desk, trying to stare me down. "You ever hear the expression R. I. P.?" He swallowed, and his big Adam's apple bobbed up and down in his long, skinny neck. "It stands for Rest in Peace, in case you didn't know, so why don't you let her do just that? What's the point of all the questions?"

"No particular point," I said mildly.

"Then quit bugging me!"

"I just want to know how she died."

"I already told you! You want details? How about multiple injuries, massive hemorrhage, a crushed trunk, both legs severed at the hip—"

I held up my hand. "Okay, enough."

He glared at me, and I saw his lip quiver for a second. "You think I enjoyed it at the time? You think I like talking about it now? It was quick, Victor. That's the best I can say for it. The cause of death was obvious. I should know. I identified the remains."

"You?"

"Yeah. We got a call from the county police, after they found a Bowie address in her wallet. As soon as I heard the name, I went down to the scene. Between you and me, she reeked of alcohol. The autopsy—sure, there was one—showed she'd imbibed freely. She had a bottle of scotch in the car. Believe me, she had no business on the road in that condition, she could have killed somebody, easy. That's why she didn't get out of the car, if you want to know the truth. Too sloshed—it slowed her reflexes." He tapped the article I'd borrowed from Pudge, which was lying on his desk. "We kept that detail out of the papers." He folded his long, skinny arms. "A lot of people came to the funeral. Half of Bowie, the kids from the Boys Club . . . They didn't need to remember her that way."

"You talked to the husband?"

"Sure I talked to the husband. He was all broken up. He said he never should have let her take the car that night, which was one-hundred-percent correct, and I told him so. If he'd kept her home, she'd be alive today. But he said she was kind of headstrong. Which I have to admit was true. I mean, we both knew Fran, Vic. She was one terrific lady, but pigheaded."

"What's the husband like?"

"Okay, I guess. Very broken up, like I said." He paused. "I wasn't too crazy about him."

"Why?"

Lester scratched his head. "Couldn't really tell you. He's a big talker. Talks a little too much."

"Where is he now?"

"Still in the house as far as I know, but I don't expect he'll be there long. Says he wants to get rid of it. Unhappy memories."

"Well," I said, and stood up. "I think I'll pay him a call."

"What for? Don't stick your nose in, Newman."

"Nothing wrong with a condolence call, is there?" I could see Lester trying to think of an objection and failing. He's a conventional kind of guy, and how can you object to a condolence call?

My conscience was bothering me about Sabina. I knew she'd been expecting to see me, or at least to hear from me, all morning. Pushing Sabina too far, I'd learned long ago, was never a good idea; and besides, she'd been decent about letting me take time off, and hadn't hassled me while I'd been away.

Still, Cinnamon Lane was right around the corner and I was feeling a definite need to talk to the widower.

I got in the car and started it up. The car headed around the corner. Okay, that settled that.

But when I got to Fran's house there was nobody home—at least, nobody answered the door and the red Jaguar was gone from the driveway. Figuring I'd talk to Keith Browdy later, I turned around in the driveway and headed for the office.

Five

Sabina Swift's house in Georgetown is hidden behind a high brick wall. There's a wrought-iron gate she keeps locked at all times, with an intercom for visitors. I pressed the electronic gate opener under the dashboard of my car, and the gate swung open and then closed behind me as I drove up the gravel driveway. The house, Sabina explained once in an attempt to educate me, is in federal style, like many in Georgetown; it's made of weathered pink brick with black shutters, and has two projecting wings, one containing the office and the other the studio where she does her painting.

I parked the car, half expecting to see her waiting in the doorway to bawl me out for coming in late; but she wasn't there. I let myself in to the office wing with my key. She wasn't in the office, either. Wondering if she could be out on a case, I checked the answering machine and found it wasn't turned on. That meant she had to be around someplace. I left the office through the door that leads into the hall of the main house. The hall is a fair-sized room, almost bare of furniture except for

30

a Shaker chair Sabina brought back from a trip to Pennsylvania, don't ask me why; it's so hard I'd just as soon sit on a rock. She claims it has "refined simplicity," and I claim that's irrelevant because when you're sitting on a chair you can't see it anyway, and what counts is what it does for your rear end. Next to the chair stands a table with, as a rule, a vase of flowers on it; but there were no flowers today, although I did see a droplet of water on the tabletop. In the middle of the rear wall, an archway with sliding doors leads to the living room and the rest of the house; off to one side, a curving wooden staircase mounts to the second floor. Under the staircase is the door to the studio.

I found her in the studio, in the early stages of a tiny painting of a Rubrum lily in a Chinese vase I had a hunch had been on the hallway table earlier in the day. This was not a good sign. Usually when she starts a picture she makes a big deal out of selecting a special type of flower at the flower stall on Wisconsin Avenue. She looked up briefly as I walked in, and the cupid's-bow mouth in her heart-shaped face flattened into a slit. She leaned back over her canvas, deposited a dot of pink pigment with a tiny brush, and studied the effect for quite a while. Finally she swished her brush in a baby food jar of turpentine and placed a white dot next to the pink one. I circled around behind her and leaned over her shoulder.

"Hey, off to a good start," I said, but she didn't respond. "I mean it, I really like it." She cleaned her little brush again, and wiped the hairs on a twist of paper towel. I've been in the studios of quite a few artists, and all of them have one thing in common—mess—except Sabina's. Hers is as neat as a marine recruit's bed during inspection.

"You're breathing on my canvas. Don't."

"Oh. Sorry." A green blob landed where the stem was going to be.

Sabina claims she took up art for the exercise, though it's really because laying tiny dots on a tiny canvas—which would drive me nuts—is good for her mental health. I looked around the studio and tried to think of what to say next. Her paintings

31

hang on the wall at eye level (hers, which puts them at the height of my shoulders) in a straight line that starts next to the big north window, turns the corner and runs behind the table where she lays out her paints with scientific precision, and turns again to run along the south wall almost as far as the door to the main house. There's room on the wall for a lot of her pictures, since most of them are only four-by-six inches, although a few biggies range up to eight-by-ten. Some day the line is going to extend all the way to the far side of the north window, and then we are going to be in for a crisis of major proportions until she figures out where to start hanging her new productions. Fortunately that isn't going to happen for a while, because it takes her a month to do one painting.

"Business must be slow," I said. "You don't usually paint this early in the day."

She threw me a look over her shoulder. "I was agitated."

"Oh yeah? Sorry to hear it. How come?"

She washed her brush, dried it on the paper towel, laid it down and swiveled her chair around to face me, crossing her legs, which are outstanding for a woman of forty or so, especially when she's wearing the needle-thin high heels to which she's addicted. Sabina's not a bad-looking woman when she's in a decent mood. Her eyes are what you notice first—light blue, with a look of cool appraisal that gives you the feeling you'd better shape up. There's also something about the way she carries herself, maybe the way she holds her shoulders, that's kind of imposing—regal, even. She said, "You're a detective, Victor"—she only calls me Victor when she's upset; usually it's Vic—"so perhaps you can figure it out for yourself. Unless your skills are rusty from disuse."

"Look, I'm sorry I didn't come in earlier—"

"Or call."

"Or call, okay, but I only got back last night, and it's not that late."

"It's a quarter of one, and how was I supposed to know when you did get back?"

"I wrote you I was coming, didn't you get my letter?"

"Yes, but I expected to hear from you. I've been trying to reach you."

"Well, I'm here," I said. "You can relax. I didn't get swallowed by a glacier or anything." She distrusts glaciers, which she feels are inherently unstable, and before I'd left for Alaska she'd warned me to stay away from them.

"I left a message on your answering machine."

"I got it. Look, I'm sorry I didn't call, but something came up."

"Something of vital importance?"

"Yes, as a matter of fact." I was getting tired of being given the third degree. "A woman I know died while I was away."

She raised her eyebrows. "Woman? What woman?"

"Her name was Fran O'Donnell. Fran Browdy, I should say—she got married while I was out of town."

Sabina's eyebrows returned to their normal level. "Oh, then this was not one of your—" She hesitated.

"Flames?" I said. It was a term from the dark ages I'd once heard her use. "Inamorata? That's a classy one, I like it. No, Sabina, this was a woman I've known all my life, she was like a second mother to me after my own mother died."

She took in the information. A look of concern came into the blue eyes. "I'm sorry to hear it, Vic. Truly. How did it happen?"

"She was hit by a train. Apparently her car stalled on the tracks, somewhere in Gorton," I said. "Sabina, this was truly a wonderful woman. She hadn't had an easy life—she lost her only child and then her husband died—but you'd never have known it, she was always smiling, always cheerful, she cared about other people. And she just got married—to a guy she seemed to be crazy about. . . ." I couldn't go on.

"Well—" Sabina cleared her throat. Emotion makes her uncomfortable. "Where—ah, how did you find out?"

I told her. I repeated everything I'd learned about Fran's death, describing my conversation with Fran the night before

I'd left for Alaska, and my visit to Pudge and then to the police station. I showed her the clipping from the *Post*.

She read it twice and gave it back to me. "Citizens for Safety," she said thoughtfully. "I've heard of that group. It's supposed to be pretty much a one-man crusade, led by the father of one of the teenagers who died in that terrible accident when they were coming home from the prom. Arnold Spinks is his name, I believe. He's certainly got a point, these unguarded crossings are dangerous." She tapped the article with one long fingernail. "Are you dissatisfied with this account of your friend's death, do you feel it's inaccurate?"

I sighed. I'd been asking myself the same question. "No," I replied slowly. "Not really, I've no reason to. Fran was a lousy driver, and she had a drinking problem, apparently. Still, there seems something so—I don't know, unfinished about the whole thing. Unresolved. And the new husband—where does he fit in?" I sat down on a stool. "Lester Yates didn't care for the guy, and Browdy must have benefited financially from Fran's death—not that she was a wealthy woman, but Maryland's a community property state. I don't know. There's something about it that doesn't feel right."

"Is it possible you just haven't taken in the fact of her death yet?" Sabina's tone was sympathetic.

"Sure it's possible! You think I don't know that? The whole thing's so damn sudden. So unexpected! If I'd been here when it happened, gone to the funeral, it would be different. Maybe. As it is, I have this unreal feeling." I stood up and went to the window. Outside I could see a neatly trimmed bed of ivy at the foot of a pink brick wall with a stone urn on top. More ivy was growing out of the urn. I said, "I wish I knew why I keep thinking it's somehow my fault."

"Survivor guilt."

"Maybe. Or maybe if I'd been here I could have prevented it—don't ask me how."

"It seems unlikely, Vic. I think you're simply feeling the shock of losing a dear friend."

34

"Maybe. Probably." My right hand balled into a fist, and I socked the palm of my left with a force that took me by surprise. "I just want to know what was going on with her! I wish I knew she died happy! She was such a—"

"Vic. Falling apart won't change things."

"I'm not—"

"Do a little investigating, if it'll make you feel better. I can't say I'm eager for you to take any more time off, but if you need a few hours here and there I suppose I could spare you. Not too much, you understand. And feel free to discuss the matter with me at any time."

"Thanks. I thought I'd drop in at Fran's house tonight and talk to Browdy."

"That seems appropriate." She stood up. "And now if you're ready, perhaps we might do a little work?"

"Sure," I said. "I'm ready. I guess."

"Good." She took off her white lab coat and draped it over a hanger. There wasn't a speck of paint on it. Then she stretched a sheet of plastic wrap tightly over the enamel tray she uses as a palette, and led the way to the office.

Six

Someone was taking potshots at the animals in the National Zoo. Whoever it was had killed several tropical birds and a lemur, and the zoo people thought the police weren't giving the matter enough attention.

I spent a long, hot afternoon looking into the situation, once Sabina had explained to me what a lemur was, and by the time I got home the sun was low in the sky and it was starting to cool off a little.

The red Jaguar was parked in front of Fran's house. I pulled into my driveway, got out of the car, and walked across the street. As I rang Fran's doorbell I wondered how many times in my life I'd stood where I was standing and heard the familiar ding-dong of the chimes. Hundreds, maybe thousands. Nobody came to the door for a while, though I could hear a dog barking, and as I waited it occurred to me that maybe I was never going to stand on Fran's doorstep again—this could be the last time. It wasn't the easiest concept to take in. Finally I heard footsteps and a good-looking guy opened the door.

36

He was tall, about my height, with big shoulders and an athletic build, and he was wearing running shorts and nothing else. He was sweating lightly, although the air conditioner was blasting, as if he'd just been working out. Behind him in the living room I could see a bench press and a pair of barbells where the coffee table was supposed to be. Maybe the picture that came into my mind of the widower lifting weights in the middle of Fran's Oriental rug prejudiced me against him, but I can't say I took to him any more than Lester Yates had, though I reminded myself there could be a lot of different ways to handle grief.

"I wasn't sure I heard the doorbell," he said, sounding surprised and looking me over carefully.

"I'm Vic Newman, I live across the street," I said. "Fran was a good friend of mine. I just heard what happened—I've been away. Hope I haven't come at a bad time."

He continued inspecting me, his narrow eyes expressionless, and then the skin around them crinkled as he smiled. "Oh, sure. Vicky. Fran mentioned you—come in." At first I thought he was thirtyish, because his body was so good, his skin so smooth and fine-grained, his blond hair so abundant. He looked like a television heartthrob, the boyish kind, and I was surprised at what that told me about Fran. But the crinkles around his eyes said forty at least, and the pair of deep grooves that bracketed his mouth when he smiled had probably been engraving themselves longer than that, or else he'd spent a lot of his life smiling. His teeth were very white, even, and rather small. "Fran said you—" He broke off, and the upturned lips drooped into an expression of sorrow. "Poor Frannie." He shook his head. "Poor girl." He extended his hand and I took it. "I'm Keith Browdy. You knew Fran and I got married?" I nodded. Beside him, a black-and-brown German shepherd dog bared his teeth and growled at me threateningly. "Wolf! Behave yourself!" Browdy hooked his finger in the dog's collar. "Sit!" Wolf didn't sit, but he didn't leap at my throat either, which I appreciated.

I said, "I don't think he likes me."

Browdy gave a sharp tug on the collar, and the dog reluctantly sat. "Don't pay any attention to Wolf. He just takes his responsibilities seriously."

"His responsibilities being—"

"To protect me." He squatted down and patted the dog's flank. "Right, boy? He can't always tell who's my friend and who isn't, that's his problem. This is Vicky, boy. Friend!" Browdy looked up at me. "Right? Any friend of Fran's is a friend of mine. Goes without saying." Browdy straightened up and the dog got to his feet, growling again. "Friend!" Browdy repeated more sharply. Twisting Wolf's collar, he gave it a jerk. The dog whined softly. "Why don't you, ah, come in, Vicky?" Browdy's manner was polite, but there was a reluctance in his movements as he stood aside to let me step past him into the familiar living room that suggested he wasn't too pleased to see me. His eyes were darting around the room as if looking for something. They settled on the shirt lying in a heap on a small table. Above the table, a mirror hung on the wall. "Sit down," he said. "Make yourself at home. I don't have much company. It's lonely here, without Fran." He gave me a sincere-looking smile—definitely, he was a handsome guy—but I had the feeling there was something on his mind that had no connection with anything he was saying. He headed in the direction of the shirt, but in a funny way—sidling, as if he was afraid to turn his back on me. But why should he be?

On the blue striped armchair where I always used to sit when I visited Fran, there was a magazine, opened to a half-finished crossword puzzle. I shifted the magazine to a table and sat down. When I looked up he was stretching out his arm to grab the shirt. In the mirror I saw that his back was covered with old, healed scars from his shoulders down to the elastic waistband of his shorts. My guess was the scars didn't stop there. Some time in his life, and more than once, Keith Browdy had been beaten severely. I wondered under what circumstances.

He slipped the shirt on quickly and said, "Can I offer you a drink?"

"No, thanks."

At the sound of my voice, Wolf bounded to his feet and growled. "Wolf! I said, down!" said Browdy sharply. Wolf's lips twitched back from black gums; his yellowish fangs looked about three inches long. His head swiveled back and forth from me to his master, and finally he lay down on the floor next to the couch. Browdy came over and sat where his bare toes could burrow into the fur of the dog's flank. A couple of dead leaves fell off Fran's big rubber plant and landed with a dry rattle on the floor, where others had accumulated.

I said, "You ought to give that plant some water."

Browdy smiled again, disarmingly. "Afraid I just don't have a green thumb." He looked at his hands. They were long and tanned, with carefully manicured nails.

"About Fran," I said after a moment or two. "I just wanted to express my condolences." He nodded, watching me, wearing a melancholy smile. I said, "I don't really know exactly what happened, I've been away most of the summer. I mean, I heard there was an accident."

He nodded. "A terrible accident. You know her car was hit by a train?"

"I heard."

He leaned forward. "Unguarded railroad crossings are an invitation to tragedy. Why don't people realize that?" He'd raised his voice. He sounded sincere. He sounded indignant. Far back in the dark eyes a spark flickered dangerously. "Right?" I didn't answer, and he crossed one bare, muscular leg over the other, flexing his foot and studying it. "You know, I blame myself, actually." He waited, as if to see what my reaction would be.

"You do? Why?"

"Though probably I shouldn't." He gave me a frank, man-to-man look, straight in the eyes. The flicker I'd caught was gone, but I knew I hadn't imagined it. "It so happens Fran and I had a fight that night. Oh I don't mean a *fight*—nothing physical. A lovers' quarrel. I said some things I didn't really mean, and she got angry and left the house. I should never have let her go, because frankly she was in no condition to drive." He shook his head. "In the heat of anger . . ." With his toe, he prodded the dog lying at his feet. "We do things we regret, Vicky. Right?"

Keith Browdy was having a peculiar effect on me. The more he talked, the less real he seemed. Maybe the word I want is "empty." I could see the man, I could hear him, and I sensed he was watching me closely; yet I kept having the feeling there was nobody there. What had Fran seen in him that had attracted her? I said, "Most people call me Vic."

"Beg pardon. Vic. Positive you won't have a drink?"

"I don't think so."

"Well, I wouldn't mind a beer." He stood up and headed for the kitchen, and I followed him. He opened the refrigerator. There was a six-pack inside, a loaf of bread, and some eggs and tomatoes. "Sure you won't change your mind?"

"Oh—maybe a beer."

"That's more like it." He took out a couple of bottles and handed me one. I twisted the cap off. There was a stench of rotting garbage in the kitchen. The sink was piled high with dirty dishes, and on the table I could see the remains of what looked like several meals: a frying pan lined with congealed bacon grease and shreds of scrambled egg, a jar of instant coffee, an open can of condensed milk with flies buzzing around it, spilled sugar, a couple of partially eaten frozen dinners. The way Browdy was living didn't fit the wealthy cosmopolitan of Fran's description. We went back into the living room and sat down again.

Browdy took a swig from his bottle. "You know, it amazes me how much I miss Frannie," he said. "We only had a short time together in terms of days, weeks, and months, but I felt as if I'd known her forever." He smiled, the brackets on either side of his lips deepening. "I find that happens sometimes. When we met it felt as if it wasn't for the first time." The dog seemed to have gotten used to my presence and was asleep on the floor with its head on Browdy's bare foot.

"You mean déjà vu? Or did you really think you'd met her somewhere before?"

"More déjà vu." He glanced at his wristwatch.

"Fran said you were a businessman. What business were you in, if you don't mind my asking?"

"No, not at all." He didn't answer my question, though. "So you talked to her about me, did you? When was that, I wonder."

"Six, seven weeks ago, before I left town."

"Oh, tell me what she said." He had been sprawling back on the couch, his bare legs relaxed, but now he leaned forward, his large, well-manicured hands gripping the beer bottle. "I'm really eager to know, I wish I could know everything about her, especially her thoughts about me."

"She said you wanted to take her on a trip around the world."

He laughed. "Oh, that. She mentioned it, did she? Yes indeed, I was eager to show her Europe and the Far East—India, especially. I find India fascinating."

"Sounds like you've travelled a lot. Where are you from?"

He looked up. "Milwaukee. I guess that doesn't sound very exotic. I was in business there for many years, until I decided to retire. I was fortunate enough to find myself in a position to retire early."

"Your business involved travel?"

"At times," he said.

"Well . . ." I took a sip of my beer. Something Browdy had said was bothering me, only I didn't know what it was. Mentally, I reviewed his words since I'd rung the doorbell, and couldn't find anything wrong with them. He glanced at his watch again. I stood up, saying, "Well, I didn't mean to intrude. Please accept my condolences, it's a terrible loss." I added, I'm not sure why, "I'm sure you and Fran would have had many happy years together. She spoke very highly of you." The second part was true, at least. I moved toward the door and he followed me. "If there's anything I can do, I live right across the street. Drop in any time."

"I might take you up on that."

"Oh, by the way—"

"Yes?"

"I saw a great picture you took of Fran."

The dark eyes narrowed. "You did? Where?"

"Pudge showed it to me. Fran's housemate."

He laughed. "Ah, Pudge. At least I got rid of Pudge, that was one thing I did for Fran, of all the many, many I'd planned. You liked the picture, did you? Photography is my hobby."

"Very much. I wonder—do you have a copy you could spare?"

"Why—I think so. If you'll wait a minute—." He went to the maple secretary that stood in the corner, and opened a drawer. It seemed to be full of photographs. He rummaged through them and pulled one out. "Here," he said, handing me a smaller version of the picture Pudge had showed me of Fran standing in the sunlight at the kitchen table, flour on her hands. "If you like, I'll make you an enlargement. Give me something to do—I've made a darkroom upstairs. Five by seven? Eight by ten? Any size you want." He smiled, the brackets at the corners of his lips deepening.

"If you're sure it's not too much trouble."

"No trouble at all."

"Well—eight by ten would be great, if you really don't mind."

"Eight by ten it is. I'll drop it off when it's ready. Which house is yours?"

We were standing at the top of the steps. "That one over there. And, thanks." I shook his hand. His palm was wet.

"So long, Vic. Thanks for stopping by. No doubt we'll meet again, very soon."

Seven

After I left the widower I took a shower, as if the condolence call, like a tour through the Dust Bowl, had left a residue on my skin. I went through the mail that had accumulated while I'd been away, and paid some bills. Then, feeling hungry, I hopped in the car and headed for the local Chinese restaurant, arriving just as the kitchen was closing for the night. Mr. Lee, the manager, let me in anyway, and I slid into a booth that Fran and I had occupied on more than one occasion.

The Szechuan Garden happens to have terrific steamed dumplings, only tonight they didn't seem as tasty as usual. I kept thinking about my conversation with Keith Browdy. Something had struck a false note, but I couldn't pinpoint what it was. I didn't think it was his reluctance to let me into the house, or the coolness I'd sensed underneath his apparent cordiality, or even the odd lack of substance to the man himself. It was something he'd *said*. Not that he'd said a whole lot. According to Lester, Browdy talked too much. To the police, maybe he had; but not to me.

I worked my way through the dumplings and a dish of General Tso's chicken that was hot enough to hold my attention. The other customers went home and so did the waiters, until only Mr. Lee was left to bring my fortune cookie, once I'd polished off General Tso. I cracked the cookie open. The slip of paper inside said, "Do not trust too much in appearances or you will lose your way."

That was all right as far as it went, but I could have used something a little more specific. I put the fortune in my pocket. Then I paid the bill and left the Szechuan Garden. It was still hot and muggy. I got in my car and headed for Gorton.

It was quiet in the warehouse district at night. Quiet and dark. Thick shadows gathered in the loading bays and between the parked trucks. Here and there a street light made a small spot of brightness. When I saw the railroad tracks in my headlights, I pulled the car to the side of the road and turned off the motor. Taking a flashlight from the glove compartment, I studied the clipping I'd borrowed from Pudge. "*A woman was killed instantly last night when the car she was driving was hit by a freight train at 11:10 P.M. at an unguarded railroad crossing. . . .*"

The luminous dial of my watch said eleven o'clock. Ten minutes to wait.

I looked around. Unguarded the crossing certainly was, except for a metal box, mounted on a pole, that contained a signal light. I got out of the car, half expecting a night watchman to appear. There had to be one around, but where? In some air-conditioned office was my guess, watching TV instead of patrolling the gloomy alleys.

I walked out on the tracks. I couldn't see a whole lot, just the rails running north in a straight line, gleaming dully under lights spotted here and there, while to the south the tracks curved away toward a ragged row of trees silhouetted against a patch of sky that was paler than the rest, where there was a town with bright lights. According to the article in the *Post*, the train that killed Fran had just rounded a bend; it must have come from the south.

As it should be doing any minute.

I started walking down the tracks, picking my way over the oily gravel between the ties and wondering why I'd come. To feel closer to Fran? To make her death more real, to understand how it had happened, and why, so that I could begin to grieve? Maybe this *was* my way of grieving. Or maybe I was just trying to shake the vague, frustrating feeling I kept having that something wasn't right, wasn't the way it seemed. What was it the fortune had said? I took it out of my pocket but couldn't read it in the darkness.

Why didn't the train come?

I listened, but there was nothing to be heard but the thrumming of insects. I turned around and started walking back, sweat trickling between my shoulder blades under my clammy shirt. When I reached the car I got inside, rolled up the window, and turned on the air conditioner. I looked at my watch. By now it was twenty past eleven. Where was the train?

Late, obviously.

I switched on the radio, found a station that was playing jazz from the fifties, and settled down to wait.

Quarter of twelve. Still no train. Clearly there wasn't much traffic around here at night, I'd only seen three cars in forty-five minutes.

Maybe that particular train ran only on certain nights, not every night as I'd assumed. It was now Friday. What day of the week had it been when Fran had died?

I checked the dateline on the clipping, and figured it out. Saturday.

There seemed something wrong with that—but what?

Again I had the annoying feeling that things weren't right, didn't fit.

Saturday night was for partying, for celebrating, for going

downtown to the movies, not for dying—was that it? No, there was something more.

I looked up. The signal light was flashing red. Then a bell started to ring.

A light *and* a bell.

Fran had had warning, then. The bell seemed loud enough to cut through a pretty thick fog of alcohol.

But maybe not.

It was five minutes past midnight. Was this the same train that had killed Fran, the 11:10, fifty-five minutes late? Or was this a different train entirely? I got out of the car and stood beside the tracks, waiting. In the distance a long-drawn-out, mournful whistle echoed. It sounded again, louder, and then I saw twin beams of light, closer than I'd have expected, cutting a brilliant swath through the darkness and turning the trees from black to green for an instant. Around the curve came the train, its headlights illuminating the warehouses on the other side of the tracks. The whistle kept blowing.

Fifteen seconds later I felt the shockwave as the engine barreled down the track, compressing the heavy air, and I took an involuntary step backward as the train roared past me. It was a long, long train, and the images that came to mind as car after car rocketed by weren't pretty.

Finally the train was gone and the disturbed air settled down. I got back in my car. I fastened the seat belt and locked the door. Then I looked at my watch, and when the second hand touched twelve I quickly unbuckled the belt, tried to open the locked door, unlocked it, flung the door open, jumped out, and ran a few feet. My watch told me this had taken seven seconds.

Even allowing for reflexes slowed by alcohol, she'd still had fifteen seconds to get out of her car, twice as long as I'd needed to do it. Actually she'd had more time than that, figuring from when the bell had started ringing. It seemed likely she'd have heard the bell, even if she'd stalled on the tracks before the red light started flashing.

So what had I proved? That nobody in a stalled car could

possibly be hit by a train? Yet it happened, everyone knew that. Four kids coming home from a prom had died on this very spot.

Why hadn't Fran gotten out of the car?

Sometimes people panicked, froze. . . .

Not Fran.

What did I mean, "not Fran"? Hadn't she been human?

I got back in the car and drove over the tracks, heading for Route 1. I'd proved nothing. My visit to Gorton hadn't brought Fran back. Or rather it had, but not the way I might have wished. *"Multiple injuries, massive hemorrhage, a crushed trunk, both legs severed at the hip . . ."*

I turned on the radio.

Except for a hamburger joint, a doughnut shop, and a bar called the Moonlight Lounge that had a neon champagne glass blinking on and off outside, Route 1 as it passed through Gorton was totally dead. Deduction: the Moonlight Lounge was the place I was looking for.

I parked and went in the bar. Despite the fact that it was Friday night, the place was practically empty. A color TV mounted on the wall was playing an old gangster movie, which only the barmaid was watching. At the bar, three men sat on stools with plenty of space between them, ignoring each other and staring gloomily into their drinks. They looked up as I entered, and after giving me a cursory glance, ignored me, too. In a distant booth, a middle-aged man and woman clutched each other's hands across the table with the intensity of people married to somebody else.

The barmaid, who was young and serious-looking, came over and said, "Help you?"

"A draught."

She drew the beer, set it in front of me, and lingered. "Haven't seen you before—have I?" she said, inspecting me through large granny glasses.

I shook my head. "I doubt it."

"I didn't think so," she said. "You're not the type we usually get."

"What type is that? Or should I say, what type am I?"

She tipped her head to one side, unsmiling. "Well, you're not a drinker."

"You can tell at a glance?"

"Mmhm."

"How?"

"I gave you a beer and you still haven't touched it. Haven't even looked at it."

"Your serious drinker would look at it?"

"Hungrily."

"Thirstily, maybe?"

"No. Hungrily. Take my word for it." Idly, she gave the bar a wipe with a rag.

"I see you're a student of human nature."

"Should be. I'm getting my Ph.D. in psychology at the University of Maryland. Right down the road."

"I spent four years of my life at Maryland. I was a psych major."

"Mmhm." Probably she'd be a great shrink some day. She'd already perfected her "Mmhms." "Who'd you have?"

I mentioned the names of my old professors. She knew some of them, and we talked about Maryland for a while. Then I said, "It's a hot night and I'd like to drink my beer, if you promise not to jump to any conclusions."

She gave a little smirk. "Sorry if I made you self-conscious, I mean that's why you're here, isn't it? To drink beer?" Her eyes narrowed. "Or maybe it isn't."

I decided the caliber of Maryland's graduate students must be going up. "Actually, you're right."

Her eyebrows rose above the granny glasses. "Then why?"

"By the way, what's your name?"

"Lucia." She pronounced it the Italian way: Lu-chee-a. She folded her arms. "So, why?"

I took out the picture of Fran and placed it on the bar in front of her. "I was wondering if you knew this lady."

She studied the picture. "I recognize her, yes."

"A customer?"

"Used to be." Lucia placed her elbows on the bar and leaned forward, propping her chin in her hands and regarding me steadily. She had oily, unpowdered skin with large pores on either side of her nose. She was less attractive than the average barmaid, but smarter. "She died in an accident."

"True," I said. "How'd you know?"

"It was on the news. Everybody was talking about it in the bar for days—you know, because it happened in Gorton. A policeman came in with her picture and asked questions." She gave me a shrewd look. "You get your kicks from going around asking questions about dead people? Like, a compulsion or something?"

"I guess that's a matter of opinion."

"You don't look like a kook."

"Thanks, Lucia." She still had a few rough edges the psych department was going to have to smooth out.

"But you could be one anyway."

"Actually, I do ask questions about dead people pretty often, but that's because I'm a private detective."

She demanded suspiciously, "If you used to be a psych major, how come you didn't get a job in your field?"

"There's not much you can do with a bachelor's degree. I worked at a state hospital as a psychiatric aide, until I was laid off. But this job kind of *is* in my field, if you think about it."

She thought about it. "Human nature, motives, like that? I see what you mean."

"But I'm not working tonight. Not right now." I looked down at Fran's picture. "This lady was a neighbor of mine, a neighbor and a friend. I spent an awful lot of time in her house when I was a kid."

There was a pause. Lucia looked around and sighed. "God, it's slow for a Friday night, I only hope this place doesn't close before I get my degree." She eyed me. "Okay, so you're not a kook. What is it you want to know?"

"Whatever you can tell me."

Lucia pondered. "The lady said her name was Fran. Used to come in here two or three times a week, sometimes after work and sometimes at night. She'd chitchat with me a little, just casually, but she didn't talk much to the customers and she never went home with anybody. She was a heavy drinker, though in a way she didn't seem the type." Lucia hesitated, nibbling at her lower lip with large, strong teeth. "Well, she was and she wasn't. She was Irish Catholic, and kind of religious was the impression I got. She was ashamed of her drinking, but definitely hooked. They're highly prone to it." She added, "I'm writing my thesis on alcoholism."

"This must be a good place to do research."

"It's great." She gave the bar another wipe. "I hadn't seen her for quite a few months before the accident. One day she just stopped coming. I wondered what had happened to her."

"She met a man," I said. "They got married and then she died." Lucia hadn't told me anything new, aside from her sociological theories, and I felt vaguely let down, though I don't know what else I'd been expecting. "Well," I said. "Thanks." I finished my beer and took out my wallet.

Lucia leaned her elbows on the bar again. "You mean, you're going to leave without telling me the real reason you're here?"

"Real reason?"

"Look, maybe she was a friend of yours, but private detectives don't go around asking questions about people who die in accidents unless they suspect foul play." She gave me a penetrating look. "You think it wasn't an accident, don't you?"

Possibly Lucia had watched a few too many TV shows, but as soon as she'd spoken I knew she'd put into words what I'd been feeling all along. "There's no evidence of that," I said. "Not a shred."

"I've shared with you," she said reproachfully. "Why don't you share with me, I'd appreciate it."

"There's nothing to share. All I know is, yesterday I got back from out of town and found out Fran was dead. Tonight I paid a condolence call on her husband—I hadn't met him before—

and then drove over to the railroad crossing where she died, and waited till the train went by. After that I came here. Don't ask me why."

Her eyes gleamed. "That's interesting," she said, and leaned a little closer. "It's probably your way of working through the loss. After all, you're a detective." Like other shrinks-to-be I've met, she was eager to analyze me. I guess they need all the practice they can get.

"Working it through emotionally, you mean?" I said, and she nodded. "Maybe. Could I have another beer?"

"It's on the house." Lucia drew one at the tap and slid it in front of me.

"Thanks." I took a sip. "The thing is, I can't seem to believe Fran died that way. She was too quick, too much of a survivor. I keep thinking she'd have managed to get out of her car somehow, I don't care how much she'd been drinking."

"You haven't seen some of the drunks I have," Lucia said. "But you're right, she was never a falling-down drunk." She frowned. "You know, you said before, 'She got married and then she died,' as if the two things were connected. As if her husband was responsible for her death. Is that what you really think?"

I replied slowly, "Maybe I do. He—anyway, somebody— could have left her in her car on the railroad tracks, when she was already unconscious or dead. By the way, when do the night trains pass through Gorton?"

"There's a commuter train from Baltimore around 5:30 in the afternoon, and one from Washington an hour later."

"No, freight. And later."

She shook her head. "I haven't figured the freight trains out. I don't go through the warehouse district that often."

"I see. Well, thanks."

"You couldn't leave a car on the tracks for long; someone would see it."

"That's right. You'd have to be sure a train was coming."

She shuddered. "It's a horrible thought. I kind of liked Fran. She was nice."

"Yeah." I finished my drink. "Well, thanks a lot."

My glass had left a ring of wetness, and she mopped it away with a cloth. Then she said, like a doctor offering a prescription, "I think you should keep investigating. Don't stop until you're satisfied, one way or the other. Right now, you don't have closure."

Closure. Right. Was that what was bugging me? Lack of closure?

On the way back home I passed a beer truck with the word MILWAUKEE written on the side in big letters.

I kept on driving.

Milwaukee.

Keith Browdy had told me he used to live in Milwaukee.

But Fran had said he'd showed her a picture of his house on Lake Mendota, which wasn't in Milwaukee but in Madison.

Madison and Milwaukee are a hundred miles apart.

Eight

At four the next morning I was in Washington, lurking behind a bush at the National Zoo and waiting to see if the person who'd written an anonymous letter threatening Ling-Ling the giant panda was going to show up. Early weekend mornings seemed to be the times he favored.

I'd only had an hour of sleep, and I asked myself why I couldn't have found a more normal job, the kind that lets you spend Saturday mornings in bed. One of the worst things about the detective business is the hours.

Except for an occasional whoop, howl, or roar the zoo stayed quiet. I had plenty of time to wonder why Keith Browdy had lied to me about where he'd come from, and in fact I was becoming very curious about him, period. I wished I'd asked Fran more questions about him. It seemed unusual, to say the least, that this handsome, supposedly wealthy guy, ten years Fran's junior, had insisted on marrying her after he'd known her only a short time. Not that she hadn't been a fine person, but as she'd implied, wealthy, unmarried, middle-aged men are scarce and can take their pick of younger women, and usually do.

The morning passed, the zoo opened for the day, and the tourists started straggling in. I went back to Bowie and took a nap. The doorbell woke me up, and when I went to the door and looked out through the peephole, there was Keith Browdy.

"Hello, Vicky," he said as I opened the door. The sun flashed on his thick blond hair. He was dressed up in a beige linen leisure suit over an embroidered shirt, and he was carrying a manila envelope—beige, to match the rest of him. He smiled, the knifelike creases that bracketed his lips appearing for a moment, and his narrow eyes wandered over my shoulder and inspected the front hall and what could be seen of my living room from where we were standing.

"Well, well," I said, wondering what had brought him. "Come on in."

He followed me inside. "I can't stay," he said. "I just wanted to drop this off." He handed me the envelope.

I took it. "What is it, the picture? Already?" He nodded. "That was quick. Sit down."

"Only for a minute."

I opened the metal clasp of the manila envelope and drew out a very professional eight-by-ten glossy print of Fran's picture. "I appreciate this," I said, studying her face. Somehow the sunlight streaming through the window in the picture seemed to give every line and shadow a special significance. It really was a terrific photo, and I told him so.

Browdy crossed his legs and clasped his hands around one knee. He exuded confidence. "I always aim to catch the essence—of a person, an experience, whatever," he said. "I *seal* the essence into the photograph." He seemed in no hurry to leave, despite what he'd said earlier. "Probably you don't understand what I mean by 'sealing.'" There was a hint of condescension in his tone.

"I'm not sure I do."

He turned his head and looked out the window like an actor presenting his profile to the camera. I was sure that he was aware every moment of his good looks. "Sealing. You could call it capturing. You could call it preserving. You could even say, extracting the soul of." He smiled, showing his small, even teeth. "You see I'm a bit of a mystic. My pictures fascinated Fran, in fact she begged me to teach her the art of photography. I said I'd try, but of course it takes more than technique."

"She didn't tell me she was interested in photography."

He blinked, the long eyelashes concealing his eyes. "I'm sure there were things about her you didn't know. And there must have been things about her *I* didn't know; things I'd be happy to learn. For instance, yesterday as you were leaving you said she spoke highly of me. What exactly did she say, if you don't mind my asking?" His question hung in the air, and I had the feeling we'd come to the real reason for his visit.

"She said you took her to museums. And the races."

"True."

"In fact, that you liked the races a little too much."

"That was *her* opinion."

"She said you showed her a picture of your house on Lake Mendota."

"Did she."

"Lake Mendota's in Madison, isn't it?"

"Yes, it is. Madison's one of the most attractive small cities in America, if you'll forgive a prejudiced opinion. It was my home for many years." He smiled modestly. "Madison was very good to me, very, very good."

Casually I remarked, "I thought yesterday you said you came from Milwaukee."

There was the briefest of pauses. "No, you're mistaken, I said Madison."

"I'm pretty sure—"

"I said Madison," he repeated sharply, and stood up. "Well, I must go." He smiled, his eyes watchful. "Let's get together again, shall we? Now that we're neighbors."

"Yeah, let's do that."

I showed him to the door and watched him walk across the street. He got into his car and drove off. What was it my father used to say? "Always tell the truth, Vic, so you won't have to remember what you said."

Nine

It was late afternoon by the time I got to Georgetown. Already the well-dressed couples were strolling down M Street, studying the menus outside the restaurants, while college students—preppy, grungy, or punk—prowled hopefully in search of a good time and various illegal substances. A group of Hare Krishnas in orange robes were clashing cymbals and dancing on the corner of the narrow street that led to Sabina's house. I turned and drove uphill, past townhouses with flowers and gaslights in front and walled gardens in the rear. There were cobblestones under the wheels of my car and a canopy of leaves overhead. The noise of M Street faded.

When I got to Sabina's I announced myself on the intercom, since I wasn't expected, and drove up the driveway. The front door was open, and Bruno Herschel stood there waving and calling. "Vic! Vic! Welcome back!" It was the first time I'd seen him since my return from Alaska. Bruno is Sabina's second husband—all I know about her first is that he died and left her with two small children and a detective agency, which is how she got into the investigative line. As for Bruno, he's a theoretical physicist and a hell of a sweet guy.

He gave me a bear hug when I came within range, saying, "How's Eric?" It was like Bruno to remember the name of my cousin, although he'd never met him.

"He's doing a lot better." I followed Bruno into the house, past the entrance hall with the Shaker chair and through the double doors that led to the living room. I noticed that while I'd been away, Bruno had gained back the ten pounds he's always either putting on or trying to take off. "Where's Sabina?"

He looked around the living room. In the last year it had gradually been going Shaker over his protests, though so far he'd managed to hang on to the big leather sofa where he likes to take catnaps. "She was right here," he said. "I don't know where she went." We sat down on the sofa.

The door from the kitchen swung open, and Sabina appeared with a teacart. "Hello, Vic. You'll join us for tea?"

"Sure."

"Oh, we're having tea." Bruno got up and as Sabina began pouring hot water into the pale green porcelain pot she'd brought back from China, he faded from the room.

Sabina has a tea fetish. More to be polite than because I really cared to know, I asked her what the tea was this time.

"Pingsuey." She filled the pot, giving it her complete attention.

"Never heard of it. Any relation to chop suey?"

"None, Victor."

"This Pingsuey's something special, huh?"

She tucked the pot into a quilted tea cosy a grateful client had made her. "If I had to choose only one kind of tea to be served the rest of my life, I would choose Pingsuey."

"You don't say. It's that good?"

"This is a tea you can steep all day—not that I ever would, of course. It never gets bitter." Bruno returned carrying a white paper bag. There were cookie crumbs on his beard. "What's that?" Sabina said. "I thought we were going to lose ten pounds."

58

"This is nothing," he said. "It's from a health food store." He opened the bag and dumped the contents on the tea tray.

"At least use a plate." Sabina shoved one forward as a shower of crumbs and coarse brown objects descended.

"Too late. Sorry." Bruno brushed the crumbs into a pile and pressed his thumb down on it. Quite a few crumbs adhered, and he ate them. "There's nothing in them," he said. "No salt, no sugar, no flour—just granola, zucchini—stuff like that. Nothing good." He picked up the largest piece and popped it in his mouth.

"There's *something* in them," said Sabina. "Just because you bought them in a so-called health food store doesn't mean they aren't fattening; that's a common fallacy." She frowned. "I suppose I should at least try them." She transferred several to a plate, tasted one, and announced, "Just as I thought, they're loaded with honey." Shaking her head she said, "They're not very good," and started pouring the tea into three cups.

Helping himself to a handful, Bruno said, "I don't think they're that bad."

I figured I better take some before they were gone.

Bruno put a Brandenburg concerto on the stereo and we listened to it. I decided the cookies were only fair and the Pingsuey tasted like regular tea, but the music was outstanding. Bruno has been teaching me to appreciate Bach.

When the record was over, Sabina stood up. "Vic and I will go into the cloister now, if you'll excuse us, Bruno. Come along, Vic." I followed her out of the room and into the hall, and waited while she unlocked the door to the office wing. We crossed the narrow waiting room, passed the doors to my office and to the smaller room Abby Rademacher sometimes uses, and then Sabina opened the inner door and we entered the cloister.

The cloister is a big square room that looks like a Spanish courtyard, except it has a glass ceiling. It's the place where Sabina does her heavy thinking, pacing around the stone walkway that forms the outer section of the room. The inner section is paved, too, except for a circular herb garden in the middle. The inner and outer sections of the room are separated by arched columns and a low wall that can be used for seating, with or without the square Chinese pillows that are stacked in a corner. The herb garden is laid out like the spokes of a wheel, and the hub is a fountain where a bronze girl stands on tiptoe, holding a jar from which water flows into a basin. The sound of the water, Sabina explained to me when I first came to work for her, is more tranquilizing than ten milligrams of Valium, and has no side effects.

"Let's walk," she said. "Tell me what's on your mind about your friend's death." We started pacing, side by side, her stiletto heels clicking on the flagstones.

"How'd you know that's why I came?"

"It's obvious, Vic. If something urgent had come up in connection with the zoo case, you'd have telephoned. Clearly this is a personal matter. You look troubled."

"Yeah, well I guess I am." I shook my head. "Sabina, I'm getting more and more convinced Fran's death wasn't an accident."

"I see," she said, and her voice was serious. "I had a feeling that's what it was. What do you suspect? Suicide? Murder?"

"Not suicide. She was a devout Catholic."

She nodded. "Murder, then. What makes you think so?"

I told her about my visit to the railway tracks where Fran had died, and the Moonlight Lounge, and my sense that Fran should have been able to get out of the car before the train hit it. I told her about my condolence call, and Keith Browdy's return visit. "He wanted to pump me about what I knew," I said. "And he lied about where he used to live. Why should he, unless he had something to hide? I keep having this feeling he killed her, Sabina."

She didn't reply right away, but stepped over to the herb garden and pulled a leaf off one of the plants. Rolling it between her fingers she held it thoughtfully to her nose, and I caught a whiff of something pungent, like licorice. After a while she said, "You think he lied."

"He did lie. Yesterday he said he came from Milwaukee, today it's Madison."

"I don't dispute that. Still, it's possible yesterday he made a slip of the tongue, and today he refuses to admit it, merely because he's one of those irritating people who hate to admit they're ever wrong, even about trivial things."

"I didn't think of that," I muttered.

"One has to consider all the possibilities, Vic."

We paced in silence.

After a while she said, "I agree there's one thing that seems rather odd."

"What's that?"

"The fact that she died on a Saturday. Yesterday, when you told me about your visit to Pudge, you mentioned that she seems to have expected Fran to be in church. But why? It wasn't Sunday."

"That's it!" I said. "That's what was bothering me! Still—that doesn't prove anything either, does it?"

"No, but—" Sabina nibbled on the leaf she'd picked. "Was your friend a wealthy woman?"

"Not at all. She was a social worker, her husband had been a shoe salesman."

"Still, she had *some* money. She owned a house. Many murderers kill for sums that are not immense. Do you have any idea how much she inherited from her first husband—insurance, whatever?" I shook my head. "Did she have a will?"

"Yes. She told me once she'd left her money to the Boys Club; there were no close relatives. But she could have made a new will, and even if she didn't, in Maryland the spouse gets half the estate, I think. Maybe I should talk to her lawyer. We play tennis together occasionally."

"You could certainly do that. You might also ask Pudge why she expected to see Fran in church the night she died. For that matter, why was she there herself? And, get copies of the train schedules." She hesitated. "You know, Vic, perhaps you should go to the police. Lester Yates liked Fran. He might persuade his superiors to open an official investigation."

I shook my head. "Lester's convinced Fran had an accident while under the influence of alcohol and I can't prove otherwise, Sabina. He doesn't take kindly to suggestions from me, without evidence to back them up. I think I better look into these other things."

"It's up to you. But don't alarm Browdy."

"I won't, don't worry." We walked some more. There didn't seem to be anything left to say. "Well, thanks," I said. "Sorry to barge in on you and Bruno." We'd reached the door to the waiting room.

"Nonsense. Any time."

"See you Monday." I opened the door.

"Vic." I looked back at her. "Be careful."

I nodded and left the cloister. As I crossed the waiting room I heard her heels resume their clicking on the flagstones.

Ten

On the way home, I stopped at the boarding house where Pudge was living. The front door was unlocked, and I went inside without encountering the landlady, climbed the stairs to the third floor, and knocked on Pudge's door.

After a moment, she called, "Who is it?"

"Vic Newman."

She opened the door.

"Oh—Mr. Newman—" Flustered, she tightened the belt of the bathrobe she was wearing. The hem of a wrinkled cotton nightgown peeked out below. It was only seven-thirty, too early for bed; I had the feeling she hadn't bothered to get dressed all day.

I said, "I hope I'm not disturbing you."

"Well, I'm not dressed for company." She motioned me inside but didn't ask me to sit down. "To what do I owe the honor?"

"I had a question, Ms. Poge. About Fran's death."

She gave her nervous sniff and blinked at me. "I don't know any more about it than I've already told you."

"Just one small point. The night Fran died, you seemed to be expecting to see her in church. But why? It wasn't Sunday, it was Saturday."

She looked surprised and then replied, "Yes, but a very *special* Saturday. On the first Saturday of every month there happens to be an all-night Eucharistic vigil at St. Anthony's."

"I'm sorry," I said. "I'm afraid I don't know what that is."

"You're not a Catholic then, Mr. Newman? I thought you might be, like dear Cardinal Newman. Well, it's the exposition of the Blessed Sacrament. Worshippers come and keep vigil— pray, you know—until early next morning."

"They stay all night?"

"Oh yes, many of them do. Vigil begins at nine in the evening on Saturday and ends before morning mass on Sunday. Of course Fran didn't go every month the way *I* do, but she always came to the one in August. I've never known her to fail."

I remembered, then, that Fran had more than once mentioned a religious service she used to go to downtown, once a year. I said. "Was this on the anniversary of Billy's death?"

"That's right. Well, it wasn't exactly the anniversary, but it was close. The same month—he died in August, she said." Pudge pursed her lips disapprovingly. "And when that man came along, even the memory of her son flew right out of her head! Like everything else!"

"That's hard to believe."

"Oh, but it did," she insisted. "Or why wasn't she there?" She gave me a challenging stare.

That was a good question.

She wasn't there because somebody prevented her, I thought. And that somebody had to be her husband, who'd told the police the two of them had been home together, having an argument about her drinking. On any other night of the year that might have been true, I supposed, but not on the night of this Eucharistic vigil thing. She'd have been right there in church—

64

a few weeks of marriage wouldn't change a person *that* much. I said, "Where is St. Anthony's?"

"In Washington, near the National Shrine."

"Nowhere near Gorton, then? She couldn't have died on her way to the church?"

She shook her head. "Oh no, Mr. Newman. I know you were fond of her, and far be it of me to speak anything but good of the dead." She pressed her lips together. "But you're completely wrong if you think she was heading for St. Anthony's. It's quite in the opposite direction."

When I left Pudge, I got in the car and headed back to Bowie. Herb Weinstein, Fran's lawyer, who lives a few blocks from me, had told me to come over whenever I got home.

They say Herb graduated in the lower third of his class at George Washington University Law School. This could be true, yet he seems to be doing all right for himself. In the daytime he works for a small, suburban law firm that specializes in zoning cases, and evenings and weekends he moonlights out of an office in the basement of his seven-room Colonial on Caraway Court. A lot of the folks in Bowie bring him their legal problems, because even if he's no great brain, he listens when you talk to him and his fees are reasonable. He handled the probate of my father's estate, which consisted mostly of the house on Cinnamon Lane, and didn't charge me an arm and a leg. That's how I got to know him. Since then, we've played an occasional game of tennis together, not that Herb likes the game—actually, he detests all forms of physical exercise—but he's been told every professional man should have a lifetime sport, such as golf or tennis, and he hates golf worse than tennis because it takes longer to get through a game.

Herb met me at the side door that led downstairs to his office. "How ya doing, Vic!" he said, and clapped me a little too heartily on the back. He was only about four years older than me, a short, chubby, balding guy with a mustache, in a three-piece suit and a tie secured with a gold tie-bar. I could remember him from high school. I'd been a freshman and he'd been a shy, bespectacled, overweight senior who didn't fit into any of the cliques; he didn't smoke, drink, or use dope; he wasn't athletic; and he wasn't smart enough to be on the "It's Academic" team.

Since that time, Herb had started wearing contact lenses and he'd taken on a set of good ol' boy mannerisms, like the back-slap that he seemed to have learned by watching the lawyers who hung around the county courthouse in Upper Marlboro. The style didn't fit him, but maybe in time it would if he kept working at it. I'd heard he was getting interested in local politics. "Where you been all summer?" he said. "We gotta get out on that court." He slapped his midriff. "So! What can I do you for?"

We were heading downstairs. There was a smell of mildew, even though a dehumidifier was humming in the hall; Herb's house, like a lot of houses in Bowie, had a wet basement. He led me into his office, which was decorated with an American flag on the wall, a couple of framed diplomas, and a glass case filled with baseball memorabilia—autographed balls and gloves and so forth, which he'd collected just long enough to fill the case. I took a seat on a chair that looked like leather but wasn't. He slumped down in the chair behind his desk and yawned. "Sorry," he said. "It's been a long day. Marlene dragged me to Sears, they had a sale on microwaves. Okay, let's hear it."

"This is highly confidential, Herb, so don't mention it to Marlene." His wife is a compulsive talker—not an asset to a man in Herb's profession.

He sighed. "Between you and me, Vic, I stopped mentioning things to Marlene a long time ago." In a fake German accent he added, "De more ve get oldt, de more ve get schmardt."

"No, no. It's, 'De more ve get oldt, de *less* ve get schmardt.'"

"Are you sure?" I nodded. "Oh. Thanks for telling me." I could see he was making a mental note.

I said. "Herb, I'm investigating Fran's death. I don't think it was an accident. I think it was murder."

66

"Fran O'Donnell? Murdered?" He jerked forward in his chair. "Are you serious? What gives you that idea?"

I hesitated. What could I tell him, that she should have been in church? I still had no proof, only a suspicion that, by now, was close to a certainty although I might not be able to convince anyone else. I said, "At this point I'm not at liberty to say." Lawyers have no trouble accepting statements like that, because they make them all the time. He nodded, sitting up straighter and doing his best to look cagey. "Herb, you were Fran's lawyer. Did she make a new will when she got married?"

He stared at me, chewing his mustache and trying to make up his mind how much to say. Finally he said, "Listen, I've got no business telling you this, but what the hell. She made a new will when she got married. Tell you the truth, I was a little uncomfortable about it." He paused for reflection. "I guess you know she got married in July. And by the way, all Fran's girlfriends were pissed because they didn't get invited to the wedding, according to Marlene. Didn't even get to meet the bridegroom. Talk about frustration!" He shrugged. "I didn't think anything of it. They wanted a little privacy, in this town who could blame them? Couple of days after the wedding they showed up in my office, wanting to make new wills. Nothing wrong with that, lots of people make new wills when they get married, in fact it's a very good idea. I gave them some forms to fill out at home, listing their assets—that's my standard procedure. A few days later they came back and made their wills." He hesitated. "Hey, what have I got to lose, I'll tell you what was in them. They were simple wills. Each one left everything to the other, period. That was the part that was a little unusual."

"Why?"

"Well, in the first place, these were not kids, these were two mature people. In my humble experience, by the time people reach a certain age they want to leave a little something to this one, that one; maybe they have a favorite charity or a sick

67

nephew; maybe there are children by a previous marriage. Well, Fran of course lost her son, we know that."

"And Browdy didn't have any kids?"

Herb shook his head. "Didn't mention any." He leaned forward. "Now, even after Billy died, Fran remained an active member of the Board of the Boys Club, ran their annual fundraising dinner, and if you won't spread it around I can tell you the Boys Club was the principal legatee of her former will."

"I knew that."

"Oh, you knew that. Okay, so you know the Boys Club was near and dear to her heart. And she still wanted to leave them some money in the new will; only she couldn't make up her mind how much. I had the feeling she and the new husband had kind of disagreed about it. She needed a little more time to think about it, only the husband got kind of pushy in a subtle way—made it seem like it was proof she really loved him, that kind of crap. He wanted her to sign the will then and there. I told her there was no rush. Then the husband said she could always add a codicil, and she signed it. I mean, why the big rush, was he expecting her to drop dead?" We looked at each other. "My God. You saying he *was?* You think he—"

"Maybe. But keep it under your hat."

"Oh, come on." He reared back, holding up his hands like a wall between us, the palms facing me. "Who'm I gonna tell? Not Marlene. So who else is there? Don't worry." He shook his head again. "Son of a bitch. Fran was one helluva fine lady."

"Could I take a look at their financial statements?"

He stood up. "I guess you can see hers." He went to a file cabinet and took out a folder.

"Why not his?" I wanted to know how much Fran had been worth, true; but I was also interested in obtaining any information I could on Keith Browdy's background.

"Best reason in the world. I don't have it. He told me his accountant was preparing it and I'd be receiving it through the mail. I never did. Tell the truth, it slipped my mind until just now. It's not necessary, the financial statement, you understand—just something I recommend to my clients for their own good."

"So you don't have his. Too bad." I took the sheet on which Fran had listed her assets. I recognized her handwriting. The house was the main one—she'd estimated its value at $120,000, and there was a $32,000 mortgage. When the house was sold, Keith Browdy should net about $80,000, once the realtor's fee and the costs of settling the estate were deducted. She'd listed a savings account at Suburban Bank containing $48,000, most of it from her first husband's insurance policy, according to Herb. Also there was a small checking account. That was it.

I stood up. "Can I make a Xerox of her financial statement? And the wills?" There was a copying machine in a corner of the office.

"Well—I don't know about a Xerox . . ."

"Herb, you knew Fran O'Donnell pretty well. This guy comes along, he wines her and dines her for a couple of months, he marries her and they live together for a few weeks—now he's entitled to a hundred and thirty grand. How does that smell to you?"

He thought it over. "It stinks." He hesitated and then added, "Between you and me, Browdy's been bugging me to push the will through probate faster. You wouldn't expect a wealthy guy to be in that big of a hurry, would you? Listen, go ahead and Xerox the papers." He leaned toward me over his desk. "Just remember, if anybody ever asks, I was out of the room when you did it."

Eleven

What the hell had Fran seen in Keith Browdy, I asked myself as I drove home from Herb Weinstein's house. I did my best to be objective, but it wasn't easy considering that whenever I thought of Browdy I wanted to smash him.

Sure, he was handsome and had a good body, and an equally good line, judging from the bit about love and commitment Fran had quoted to me. Still, why hadn't she felt, as I had, that there was something about the man that hadn't rung true? She was a shrewd lady, and working with drug addicts she must have dealt with plenty of tricky customers. So how come she'd thought Keith Browdy was Mr. Wonderful? It was puzzling.

I asked myself how Mr. Wonderful had managed to get himself home after he'd killed her. If he'd driven to Gorton with Fran on the seat beside him, unconscious or dead, and left the car on the tracks to be destroyed, how had he returned to Bowie? He'd been home when the police came to the house to notify him, after Lester had identified the body. The Gorton industrial tract was a lonely spot at eleven at night, but on the other hand it wasn't far from Route 1, and Browdy could have walked there, found a phone, and called a cab. I didn't think there was a bus he could have caught; bus service in the county was notoriously bad. Everybody went everyplace by car.

Or maybe he'd set something up in advance, left the Jaguar parked nearby earlier in the day, and taken a cab home at *that* time. These were lines of investigation that could be pursued. The Jaguar might have been noticed; it wasn't the kind of car you'd see every day in that part of town. Or maybe someone would recall having seen Browdy on the night of the accident. I needed a picture of him, and where was I going to get it?

I turned the corner into Cinnamon Lane. Browdy's Jaguar was standing in Fran's driveway, and there was a light in the bedroom window. I remembered the drawer full of photographs. It would be good to rummage through it, there might be one of Browdy I could use. He must go out some time during the day, and when he did I could let myself in with the key Fran had once given me so I could water her rubber plant when she was out of town. I felt an impulse to drop in on Browdy right now, and ask him where he'd been at the time Fran had died; I wanted to hear what he'd say, what lie he'd come up with, but I knew it wasn't a good idea. Better not alarm him.

I parked in front of my house and got out of the car. Just before I turned to head up the path to my front door, I noticed the lights were on in Paul Geissdorf's house. Was he home from the hospital? I'd gotten the impression from Lester that Geissdorf was going to be there for some time to come. There was a rusted-out Dodge I didn't recognize in the driveway, and as I stood considering the situation, the shadow of a woman passed across a curtained window on the second floor. That explained it—Ida Geissdorf was back. Probably heard her husband was in the hospital. Too bad for her she hadn't stayed away, I thought as I let myself into my house. On the other hand, maybe she hadn't liked it any better where she was.

I opened a beer, sat down in the living room, and studied Fran's will and her financial statement. They were simple enough—she'd had a total of $130,000 in cash and property, and she'd left it all to Keith Browdy. People had been killed for a lot less.

At eleven-thirty, across the street, the light in Fran's bedroom—I still couldn't think of it as Browdy's, and I didn't particularly want to—went off. For some reason that bothered me. I didn't know why. I decided to go to bed. I was supposed to show up at the zoo again at four the next morning.

When I got to the zoo, I made myself comfortable behind the same old bush and settled down to wait. I had a little trouble staying awake, for nothing of any interest happened. The pandas were still alive and well by the time the gates of the zoo opened and the public started streaming in, and I left and found a drugstore on Connecticut Avenue, where I bought a candy bar and asked for a couple of dollars' worth of change. Then I went into a phone booth and closed the door. Even on Sunday, I figured, somebody would be answering the phone at MARC, the commuter railroad, and could tell me the names of the freight companies that shared the tracks that passed through Gorton.

Turned out there were several different companies. After using up my quarters, I was finally directed to the chief dispatcher of the Old Dominion System. It was one of their trains that had crashed into Fran's car.

Once I'd explained that I was writing a history of transportation and that, in my opinion, freight trains had been unfairly neglected in the literature, the dispatcher seemed ready and willing to tell me anything I wanted to know.

I started off by asking him to send me a copy of the train schedule.

"I'd send one if I had one," he replied apologetically. "Only thing is, we ain't got one."

"You're out of them?"

"No. Freight don't work like that." He didn't seem surprised I wasn't aware of this already. "Freight runs kind of irregular. Like, we got that one train runs north to Philly between 10 P.M. and 1 A.M., but as to when, it sorta depends on what we have to pick up."

This wasn't what I wanted to hear; it contradicted the theory I'd been forming about how Fran had died. "I see," I said, and added reluctantly, "So you're telling me there's no way of knowing ahead of time when a particular train is going to pass by a particular place?"

"I didn't say that."

"How could somebody know, then?"

"Ask the dispatcher that same day."

"Call you, you mean?"

"Yep, me if I happen to be the one on duty."

"And *do* people call?"

"Sure they do."

I thought over what he'd said. "You mean, all day people keep calling the dispatcher, asking when a certain train is due to arrive? That kind of thing?"

"Not all day, no. Not every day. But sometimes."

"I see. Not that often. You think you'd remember if you got a call like that on a certain day?"

"Probably would."

I thought about what he'd said. "Just out of curiosity, what kind of people call?"

"Varies. Shippers, of course. Sometimes people who want to buy real estate near the tracks, maybe build a house. Want to know when a train is coming so they can go listen to it, see if they can stand the racket." He paused. "Railroad buffs. Photographers. Most times the photographers *are* railroad buffs, want to get a shot of a particular train, maybe a certain time of day, certain kind of light, certain location, add it to their collection."

Photographers?

I said cautiously, "My publisher wants me to have a section in the book on transportation accidents. People like to read about that kind of stuff, don't ask me why. Let's see, I guess freight trains have their share of accidents, too, isn't that right?"

"Afraid so. Of course, Old Dominion wouldn't care to have that played up."

"No problem. I don't have to mention names of companies. In fact, wasn't there something in the paper about an accident in Gorton a few weeks back?"

"Yep, a fatality that one was. Sad thing. And the engineer was real shook up, I mean that man is in *bad* shape."

I took out the article from the *Post*. "Henry Freulinger, isn't that what the paper said his name is?"

"That's him. Known him for years, he lives right here in Richmond. One of our best drivers. Henry's a real stickler. Take my word for it, if anybody could have stopped that train in time, Henry Freulinger's the man. Hope he gets himself together."

I said, "I don't suppose you happen to remember whether anybody called you that day, about the train Henry Freulinger was driving?" It seemed a long shot.

There was a pause. Then he said slowly, "You know, come to think of it, somebody did call. Kind of a coincidence. A photographer wanted to know when the late train would be passing through Gorton, so he could get a shot as it came around the bend. I wondered if he could of been there when the accident happened, maybe even took a picture of it. Boy, *that'd* be some shot! But I guess not, or the picture would have been in the papers. Photographers don't always get there when they say they're gonna—then they call back a couple days later and ask me when that train is coming through again."

"Did this particular photographer call you back?"

There was a silence while the dispatcher thought about it. "No, I don't think so. I don't believe I heard from him again."

After I'd hung up, I walked down Connecticut Avenue mulling it over. I felt a sickening kind of elation. Sure, there was a one-in-a-million chance the call the dispatcher had received had been a coincidence, as he thought; but I was convinced the caller had been Keith Browdy—Browdy, who had planned to kill Fran by faking a railway accident; Browdy, who must have known, perhaps because he was a photographer, that it was possible to find out from the dispatcher when a train would be coming.

But there was still no *evidence*—nothing you could take into a courtroom, nothing that would prove it was Browdy who had called the dispatcher; nothing, in fact, to prove he'd done anything at all to cause Fran's death.

It was incredibly frustrating.

If only there'd been a witness.

But there had been, I realized. The engineer. What had he seen in the glare of the headlights, during those seconds after the train had rounded the bend?

I walked back to my car through the heated air that shimmered like a curtain above Connecticut Avenue. I had no plans in mind for the rest of the day, and though I'd have liked to talk things over with Sabina, I'd barged in on her and Bruno once already, and that was enough for one weekend.

There could be worse ways, I decided, to pass a hot Sunday afternoon than to drive down to Richmond in an air-conditioned car.

Henry Freulinger lived in an ugly, immaculate, blue-collar neighborhood on the edge of Richmond. Small, mostly frame houses were set close together, separated by chain-link fences that seemed to assert the pride of their owners in every hard-earned inch of property they possessed.

Henry Freulinger—or his wife, if he had one—grew tomatoes the size of small grapefruit in his front yard, on vines that had been tied to old broom handles with strips of rag. Aluminum foil pie plates, hung up on strings, flashed to scare away the birds. Freulinger's house was of cream-colored stucco. All the window shades had been drawn, even the ones on the shady side.

There was a wife. She came to the door, a birdlike, gray-haired, worried-looking lady who, when I asked if I could speak to her husband replied, "Well, I don't know. . . ." and stood staring helplessly at me, as if a trouble she was unprepared to cope with had come late and unexpectedly into her life.

"I just want to speak to him for a moment," I said. "I'm not trying to sell anything."

"No," she agreed vaguely. "I thought, maybe you were from the Disability. But I guess you couldn't be, on a Sunday."

"Can I come in?"

She took a step backward. "Well, I don't know. Maybe it would be good—"

I followed her into a small, crowded, painfully neat living room. The place wasn't air-conditioned, but a fan was turning at top speed, fluttering lace curtains and ruffled slipcovers that looked homemade. A man in his sixties sat in a flowered rocking chair, his calloused hands clasped together, staring straight ahead. As I entered the room his gaze took me in, but without interest.

"Henry, you have a visitor," Mrs. Freulinger said, speaking loudly and distinctly as if to someone deaf. He didn't respond. She threw me a helpless look that said, 'You see?' "Henry," she repeated. "This young man's come to call on you!" She turned to me. "What did you say your name was?"

"Vic Newman. Can I please sit down and talk to you, Mr. Freulinger?"

He didn't reply, but his eyes turned to rest on me with a look of profound hopelessness. He sighed—a big man, with powerful arms and shoulders as if he'd spent all his spare time doing physical work for the pleasure of it; when he sighed his shoulders sagged as if he was shrinking before our eyes.

76

"Sit down," Mrs. Freulinger said. I pulled a chair with a ruffled seat cushion close to her husband and sat down next to him. "I don't know if he'll talk to you," she said. "You can try."

"He seems pretty depressed," I said. "I used to work with depressed people at a hospital in Maryland, so I know."

"Depressed?" she said, and shook her head uncertainly. "No, he's just stubborn."

"Has he been like this since the accident?"

Henry Freulinger sighed again, deeply.

"Everybody *told* him it wasn't his fault," his wife said. "Well, it *wasn't* his fault. Henry," she said with exasperation. "Say something, we have company." He didn't respond, and she blinked at me. "That's how he's been."

"I understand. I wonder—could I have a cold drink, if it's not too much trouble? Water's fine."

"I'll make you some iced tea."

"That would be nice," I said. She left the room, and Mr. Freulinger sighed again. I leaned over and took his hand. It lay slackly in mine. "You're very depressed, Mr. Freulinger. You know that?"

He blinked once. The powerful shoulders shrugged slightly.

"Mr. Freulinger, I heard about the accident. That's why I came to see you. The woman who was killed was a friend of mine."

The big man said nothing but he flinched perceptibly, and the tip of his tongue licked his lips.

"I'd appreciate it very much if you'd tell me what you remember about it, even though it's hard for you to talk. Who knows, maybe you'll feel better afterwards. Mr. Freulinger, I don't blame you for what happened. You hear me? Like your wife said, it's not your fault. I mean, it's *really* not your fault. I think my friend was killed deliberately." A look of alarm came into his eyes. At least he was listening. "No, no, not by you. Somebody put her car on those tracks, just so your train would run into it. I'm sure he figured it all out—how far the car had to be from the curve, how long it would take the train to stop.

There was nothing anyone could do, you didn't have a chance." I waited. Still he said nothing. I said, "If I were you, I'd be mad as hell."

There was a long pause.

Henry Freulinger said, "I never had a spot on my record." His voice was creaky, rusty with disuse.

"I know. I spoke to the dispatcher. He said you're one of the best they have, he said if anyone could have stopped in time, *you* could have."

"Should've braked sooner."

"Mr. Freulinger, it wasn't your fault."

There was a long silence. "Sonny, what do you want?"

"Mr. Freulinger, please tell me exactly what it was you saw, when you came around the bend."

His eyes darkened. "There she was, right smack on the track. Too close! Lights kept flashing and I pulled the whistle and plowed right into her. Should've braked sooner." He shook his head and kept shaking it. "Should've braked sooner."

"Could you see anyone in the car?"

The headshaking stopped. His gaze went inward. "One person in the driver's seat."

"Did she try to get out? Did she open the door?"

"Didn't make a move. Didn't even try." The headshaking started again. "Supposed to retire next year, and now this," he muttered.

"Well, you can," I said. "There's no reason you can't go back to work, is there? Finish up the year?"

"I won't drive no more."

"Why not? You can." He didn't answer. "Mr. Freulinger, did you see anyone else, maybe off to the side of the tracks?"

"Made me piss in a paper cup, see if I was on that dope!" He started to cry, making no sound, the tears running down his broad, lined face.

His wife came in. "Here's your—Henry! What's the matter? What did you say to him? Get out, you! Get out!" she cried, with all the fury of a woman who's been looking for a good reason to get angry. I thought she was going to throw the iced tea in my face. "What did you say to him? That man never cried in his life!"

"Maybe he needs to, ma'am."

"Never mind, you! Get out! Get right out! Right now!"

I got out.

Twelve

I spent most of Monday morning making telephone calls from home in connection with the zoo case, keeping one eye on Fran's house through the picture window and waiting for Browdy to go out. It was time to take a little action, of what I'd call a semi-legal nature. Letting yourself into a house that doesn't belong to you isn't exactly breaking and entering if you've been given a key by the owner—although if the owner is deceased I admit the legality is borderline.

But Browdy's Jag remained standing in the driveway. Didn't the guy ever go out? Next door, Ida Geissdorf was pushing a lawnmower through the tall grass in her front yard. She was going to have a lot of raking to do.

It was around noon when I finished my phone calls. There'd been no sign of Browdy yet, so I got in my car and drove to the local branch of Suburban Bank. The first time I'd ever been there I'd been ten years old; making a big deal of it, my father had taken me to open an account where I could deposit my paper route money and any presents of cash that might come my way. The episode had made quite an impression on me. The cool, silent bank had seemed huge, with immensely high counters I'd had to stand on tiptoe to reach.

Since that time, nothing at the bank had changed except the design of the calendars they handed out at Christmas. Still the place had somehow dwindled into an insignificant little branch with imitation wood panelling on the walls and a fence made out of some kind of plastic around the desk of the manager, Mrs. Huffman. She'd known my father, and I'd chatted with her on occasion. I figured I wouldn't have too much trouble sweet-talking her into giving me a few droplets of information about Fran's account.

Wrong.

"I'm sorry, Mr. Newman," she said severely, frowning and shaking her short, iron-gray curls. They didn't bounce when her head moved, didn't even budge; they looked as if they'd been sprayed with cement. "It would be quite improper to divulge any such information." People who use words like "divulge" can be hard to deal with.

"But she's dead," I said for the second time, keeping my voice low. "It's not as if she's going to object."

"In the event of the decease of a customer of the bank, there are regular procedures that have to be followed to the letter. The contents of any accounts there might be—and I'm not saying whether she did or didn't have an account with us—would become part of the estate, and our normal rules of confidentiality would continue to apply. As you are no doubt aware." She gave me a disapproving stare through her rimless, octagonal glasses.

"Mrs. Huffman, I *know* she had an account here. And I'm a customer of the bank myself, it's not like I'm a stranger. It so happens I'm a private detective, and I'm investigating the circumstances of Fran's death. Mrs. Huffman, she must have banked here for twenty years. If there was something suspicious about her death, don't you feel some obligation to cooperate? To see that the truth comes out?"

"We would cooperate with the proper authorities, yes. Not," she said, "with you. I'm sorry, Mr. Newman, and I hope you won't take it personally. Suppose somebody walked in and made inquiries about *your* account. Would you want us to divulge your personal affairs?" That word again. I gave up hope. She rose. "Of course not! There was a saying during World War II— perhaps you're too young to remember—'Loose lips sink ships.' There's a lot of truth in that, Mr. Newman, if you think about it. A lot of wisdom." Gazing at me, she waited for me to sop it up. "Well, I see there are others waiting, so if you'll excuse me. . . ."

Feeling frustrated, I turned in a couple of rolls of pennies I'd been accumulating, cashed a check for a hundred dollars, picked up a brochure about certificate accounts, not that I have any spare cash lying around to invest, and left the bank.

I cruised down Cinnamon Lane. The Jaguar was still there, so I headed for the office.

I buzzed myself through the gate outside Sabina's house, and parked on the gravel driveway beside a gray limousine with diplomatic plates and a chauffeur asleep behind the wheel. Sabina had company, apparently. I went inside, peeked across the cloister in the direction of her office, and wasn't surprised to find her door closed. So I went into my room and started typing up my notes on the progress of the zoo case, which so far could be summed up in one word, zilch. At least I'd eliminated a few possibilities, and nobody had killed any animals since we'd been hired.

When I was finished, I left my notes in the box on Sabina's door and went out and ate sushi in a Japanese restaurant on Wisconsin Avenue.

The limousine had departed by the time I returned. Sabina was sitting in the Shaker chair behind her desk, reading my notes. She put them down as I entered, saying, "Nothing much so far, I see. Well, sometimes you just have to keep plugging."

I sat down. "Who was the diplomat?"

"The Zambaudi ambassador. He suspects one of his wives of having an affair."

"Why doesn't he send her home?"

"She's his favorite wife."

"Poor guy, a tough situation."

We discussed cases for a while.

Then Sabina said, "Vic, I've been thinking about your friend. Were you able to find out why Pudge expected to see her in church the night she died?"

"I did. And that's not all I found out."

I gave her a complete rundown: what Pudge had said about the Eucharistic vigil, my conversation with the chief dispatcher—including the fact that someone had called to find out when the train that killed Fran would be passing through Gorton—and finally my visits to Henry Freulinger and to the bank.

"I see," she said when I was finished. She had her elbow on her desk, her chin propped in her hand, and her pale blue eyes were focused on my face with total concentration. She leaned back in her chair and said decisively, "Vic, your hunch was right. Fran's death *wasn't* an accident, and I completely agree that her husband was the one who killed her—everything points in that direction. The call the dispatcher received was no coincidence, the odds are just too high." She stood up and went to the window and, folding her arms, gazed thoughtfully outside with her back to me. "That poor man," she said finally. "The engineer, I mean. Keith Browdy destroyed his life, too—as surely as he killed Fran!" Turning to face me, she said slowly, "Tell me again what Mr. Freulinger said."

"What he said?"

"Yes! Everything he said to you—word for word, if possible."

I tried. I'd say I got pretty close.

"Suggestive," she murmured when I was done, more to herself than me. "But is it possible—it seems terribly risky—"

"What?"

"Just a passing thought." She shook her head. "What are you planning to do now?"

"Search the house. I need a picture of Browdy, something I can use to try and place him in Gorton, the night she died or before."

Sabina looked worried. "Vic, don't you think it's time you went to the police? That call to the dispatcher—"

"Even if they pay attention, as far as they're concerned, it's just one more case. To me it's—"

She came over to me. "I understand, but that's not quite true. Lester Yates knew Fran too."

"Yeah, but Lester's—"

"Don't be stubborn, Vic," she said. "The police have all sorts of resources at their disposal."

"You mean, go there now? Don't you have any work for me to do?"

She pressed her lips together and her eyes strayed to the dictaphone machine. But all she said was, "There's nothing that can't wait. Go to the police."

"About the will, big deal," Lester said. He was on his feet, his long arms crossed, standing by the window of the station house. "Plenty of couples make new wills right after they get married. And as for lying about where he came from, maybe he did and maybe it was a slip of the tongue."

I said, "Where'd he tell *you* he came from?"

"I didn't ask him. Why should I? It was an accident." His neck reddened. "Also, and I don't want to hear any remarks, it so happens the whole force just had sensitivity training the week before, and I was trying not to harass the guy, I mean he'd had a bereavement." He glared at me. I made no remarks. "About her not going to church"—he shrugged. "Listen, Fran was that certain age when they get unpredictable. A good-looking guy comes along, gives her a tumble, suddenly it's not so important to go to church, I don't care *what* the reason was. She figures she just got married, it can wait till next year."

"Not Fran."

"Why not Fran?"

"Not where Billy was concerned. It would have been totally out of character."

"Come on, women are women."

"You're a sexist pig, you know that?"

"Watch your language, Newman."

"Watch yours. Listen, Lester, I haven't told you everything I found out." I repeated my conversation with the train dispatcher. When I told him that somebody had called to ask what time the train would be passing through Gorton the day Fran died, a thoughtful look came into his eyes. I said, "So? You gonna say the dispatcher had a bad case of hormones, too?"

He didn't answer, but stood there applying traction to his long, narrow chin, the way he does when he wants to stimulate his brain. Finally he said, "It might be coincidence and it might not, but let me talk to the captain. Could be we ought to ask Mr. Browdy some questions."

I went home. Browdy's Jaguar was still standing in Fran's driveway. Two doors down, Ida was raking the Geissdorf lawn.

I settled down in an easy chair beside the window of my living room to watch Fran's house. Next to me on a table stood a camera with a telephoto lens, a can of Mace, and my key to Fran's house. If Browdy came out I planned to snap a few shots of him—with any luck, at least one would be good enough to use for identification purposes. And if, as I was hoping, he went off somewhere, I would let myself into the house with the key. There was the dog, of course. That was what the Mace was for. If he tried to attack me I could zap him and shut him in the bathroom.

I ate a sandwich at the window, turned on the stereo, read the paper, played a game of solitaire, got out my checkbook and paid a few bills. Ida Geissdorf dragged a couple of big plastic bags to the curb and left them there. Probably grass clippings. Then she took off in the rusted-out Dodge. I wondered if she was going to the hospital to visit her husband. Time passed. Browdy never came out of the house. The school bus stopped at the corner and kids streamed out. After that the street was livelier, with kids passing on bikes or zipping around on skateboards.

Traffic picked up. Fathers were coming home from work. Quite a few mothers, too. Pretty soon the mothers started calling the kids in for supper. By seven the street was deserted. There was still no sign of Browdy. After a while, it started getting darker. If he came out now, I probably wouldn't be able to get a decent shot of him. But he didn't come out.

At eight-thirty, a light went on in his living room.

And at eight-thirty, I knew I'd been had. At eight-thirty, I knew why it had bothered me when the bedroom lights had gone out the night before at eleven-thirty sharp. Nobody was home. The automatic timer was turning the lights on and off— the timer I'd installed myself, a couple of years earlier, as a favor to Fran, after there'd been a series of burglaries in the neighborhood.

But what about the Jaguar? There it was, standing in the driveway. Dummy! I told myself. A car in the driveway was no guarantee of a driver in the house. Browdy was gone. I was sure of it.

I went outside. The street was deserted. Most of the neighbors must be watching TV by now. Quickly I crossed the street, keeping my footsteps light, and faded into the shrubbery. Slipping around behind Fran's house, I stood for a few moments with my ear pressed to the back door. Silence. The house had to be empty—if the dog had been there he'd have been barking up a storm by now. Quietly, I unlocked the door and stepped inside. I was in the kitchen. Enough light from the living room was coming through the open door for me to see that the room was empty. The pile of dishes in the sink was higher than the last time I'd seen it.

I tiptoed into the living room. Sure enough, the lamp in front of the picture window, the one I'd wired to the timer, was the only light on. I went through the whole house thoroughly. Nobody was there. Browdy had taken his clothes, cleaned out the photographs from the drawer in the living room, and removed his weightlifting equipment and his photography supplies. Fran's clothes were still in the bedroom, but all her papers were gone, her jewelry—not that she'd had much of it—and the silver. The TV set was missing.

"Son of a gun!" I kept thinking. "Son of a bitch!" My challenging him on the mistake he'd made by saying he'd lived in Milwaukee must have scared him away. What else could it have been? He could know I was a detective, it was the kind of thing Fran might have mentioned. Why hadn't I realized sooner how little it would take to send him running? I picked up the phone to call Lester, and just then the doorbell rang. Company? Who would be dropping in at nine-thirty in the evening—maybe somebody he knew? I went to the window and peeked around the corner of the shade. Outside I saw a couple of policemen. One of them was Lester.

I went to the door and let them in. "Hi there," I said. "Join the party. I hate to tell you this, but you're too late. Looks like our friend is gone."

Thirteen

"I should have foreseen it," said Sabina. We were walking in the garden outside her house in Georgetown.

"*You* should have foreseen!" I said. "What about me? I was living right across the street from him!"

"Yes, but you're impetuous."

"What does *that* mean?"

"Impulsive. Vehement. Passionate."

"I know what the word means, not that I admit it applies to me. What I meant was, I don't see the relevance."

Sabina's high heels clicked on the flagstone path that curved under the plane trees. The trees, lined up in rows, had been clipped until they looked like Tootsie Pops—a comparison I'd made only once, because it wasn't appreciated. Under each tree was a geometrically perfect circle of bare earth, with lawn around it. Sabina said, "All I meant is that you're prone to being carried away by a desire for action. I, being older, am supposed to be more capable of reflection."

"You mean you should have guessed he was going to take off?"

She sighed. "The irritating thing is that the thought did occur to me. I underestimated Mr. Browdy; he's shrewder than I'd realized. A brand-new Jaguar such as you've described is a cherished masculine toy; very few men would be capable of abandoning it, to give the impression that the owner of the car was still in the house. It was a stroke of genius."

"Okay, he's a genius. Where is he?"

She shrugged. "Could be anywhere—except Prince George's county, or for that matter the Washington area. We really know very little about the man. Except"—she pivoted on her stiletto heel and headed in the direction of the house—"that he happens to be a murderer."

I followed her inside. We went through the cloister and into her office, a room that contains only the necessities, except for a glass paperweight with swirls of color inside that she keeps on her desk. She sat down at the desk and picked up the paperweight, while I took a seat facing her. She said, "All right. Let's consider what we know about Keith Browdy."

I started counting on my fingers. "He looks to be in his early to mid-forties. He lifts weights. He's an amateur photographer, and a good one. He has a German shepherd named Wolf he seems to be very attached to. He likes fancy cars, in fact according to Fran he has expensive tastes generally—theater and travel were mentioned. Though when I dropped in on him he seemed to be living the simple life, to say the least."

"Perhaps he was waiting for the excitement caused by Fran's death to die down before moving on. He may have felt it was necessary to play the part of the grieving widower for a while, to forestall suspicion."

I went on with my enumeration. "He likes the races—too much, according to Fran."

"In other words, he gambles—that's what people usually mean when they say that."

"Could be. Let's see, what else? He's a retired businessman."

"Now we move into a more speculative realm."

"Supposedly from Wisconsin, either Milwaukee or Madison. Nature of business unknown." I paused. I still had some fingers left.

"And you saw scars on his back. Old, healed scars, you said. From your description, scars consistent with his having been savagely beaten with something like a belt, wouldn't you say? Possibly in childhood?"

"Possibly. But where does that get us?"

"At the moment—nowhere." Sabina set down the paperweight with a thud. "Nowhere at all." She swiveled impatiently in her chair.

"I can try and get a line on the car he used to take the stuff away in—obviously he had to have one. Though the police are looking for it, and that's something they're good at. They're taking the case seriously, they're putting out a general bulletin on him. They got a call from Mrs. Huffman at the bank—I guess my visit must have made her nervous, though when I talked to her she looked about as nervous as a Mack truck. Lester tells me she said that Browdy showed up at the bank around noon and tried to withdraw $20,000 from Fran's account, which had been changed to a joint account after the two of them got married. Twenty grand was all that was left in it, because he's been cleaning it out gradually since her death. Mrs. Huffman stalled, she told Browdy there was some kind of problem about withdrawing the money, and he left in a hurry. Lester didn't say in so many words that the sergeant she talked to when she called the station house isn't famed for his mental capacity, but that was the general idea. The report kind of lay around for a while."

"Really!" said Sabina, disgustedly. "What do we pay our taxes for, I'd like to know? Browdy must have been right in the middle of making his getaway when he stopped at the bank.

Clearly, he wouldn't have stayed on in Bowie any longer than necessary once he'd removed his things from the house."

"I must have just missed him. If only I'd started watching him earlier!"

Sabina shook her head. "I'm sure he's been watching you, too, ever since your visit. He'd never have tried to leave while you were home, Vic."

"I wonder if Ida Geissdorf saw anything. She was working in the yard most of the day."

"Well—I suppose you could ask her."

"You don't sound enthusiastic."

"Let's be realistic, Vic. No doubt the police have questioned her already. She may not have seen anything. And if she did, she's already given them a description of the vehicle Browdy used to take away his things. If it's to be found, they'll find it. But—" She shrugged. "I don't believe that trail will lead anywhere. It's too obvious, and Mr. Browdy is far from stupid. My guess would be that before he left, he arranged to have a second car waiting in some quiet spot outside the Beltway, went there and transferred his luggage, and abandoned the original vehicle." She placed her fingertips together, propping her pointed chin on them. "What we need is a line on his background prior to his turning up in Bowie. He appeared in your friend's life as if out of thin air, but he has to have come from somewhere. Who is this Keith Browdy?"

"For a start, I could go to the library and look him up in the Milwaukee and Madison telephone books," I said. "Call the local papers out there, try and get a line on a retired businessman named Browdy."

"Go ahead and try, certainly," she said. "But we have only his word that he comes from Wisconsin, or even that his name is Keith Browdy. You might talk to Pudge again, and other people Fran knew. Ask them how Fran and Browdy met. Did someone introduce them, someone who perhaps knows his background?"

I took out my pad and started making notes.

"You might try photographic societies and photographic supply houses. Camera stores. Gyms and spas. Veterinarians. Someone might have a previous address on file, or a forwarding address. Maybe you can trace him through the Jaguar."

"This would be a lot easier if I had a picture of the guy."

She sighed. "I know. It would also be easier if we had a client to pay for your time. This could stretch out into quite a lengthy business, and in the meantime the Swift Detective Agency isn't going to derive much benefit from your services."

"I can't help it, Sabina; you know how I felt about Fran. Put me on leave of absence, unpaid, if you want. That would be reasonable. Or I could hand in my resignation—"

"Spare me a repetition of this performance, Victor. Twice in two months is excessive. Of course you have to investigate your friend's death, I never implied the contrary. I was simply expressing my feelings. You're always telling me I should do so more frequently."

Fourteen

Sabina turned out to be right about the car. Ida Geissdorf had seen Browdy taking off in a blue Dodge station wagon the police learned had been rented to a man answering to Browdy's description, who had given his name as Dwight Raymond and showed a driver's license that turned out to be false. For a few days hopes were high that the fugitive might be found by tracing the station wagon; they died when it turned up, empty, in the parking lot of a brand-new development of garden apartments, still under construction in Gaithersburg, north of the Beltway. An article in the *Washington Post* stated that Keith Browdy had disappeared, and that the police were interested in asking him some questions about the death of his wife.

The police checked fingerprints that had been left, presumably by Browdy, on dirty dishes in the sink; the results were nil. According to Lester, the guy seemed to have no police record.

I paid a return visit to Pudge. The landlady wasn't around, and I climbed the narrow stairs to the top floor of the rooming house without encountering anyone. As I approached Pudge's door, I could hear the sound of typing.

I knocked. "Why, Mr. Newman," she said when she saw me. "To what do I owe this honor?"

"I don't know if it's an honor, but I wanted to give you back the article you loaned me. Thanks a lot."

"So nice," she said. "You actually returned it. Won't you come in?"

A battered typewriter and some boxes of envelopes stood on the bridge table next to the bed. She'd gotten a temporary job, she told me, addressing envelopes for a firm that had employed her before. Then she said she'd seen in the paper that the police were looking for Keith Browdy.

"So it wasn't an accident, was it?" she said, her washed-out blue eyes gleaming with satisfaction. "I was right after all, wasn't I?"

"You certainly were, Ms. Poge," I said. I didn't remind her it was Paul Geissdorf, not Browdy, she'd accused of killing Fran.

"If the police had paid more attention when I went to them in the first place, Keith Browdy would be behind bars today."

"They goofed," I agreed. "If only they'd listened to you."

She smiled. "Can I offer you a cup of tea?" There was a dented kettle steaming on a hotplate.

"Why not?"

She took out a cup and poured hot water over an A&P teabag. Sabina, who hates teabags, would have been pained. "I'm investigating Fran's death," I said. "I'm hoping you'll be able to help me. As far as I've been able to learn, you're the only one of Fran's friends who actually met Browdy."

She nodded emphatically. "He *refused* to meet her friends. He *said* he just wanted to be with *her*, but he acted like he was too good to associate with them." She gave her nervous sniff.

"Did he?" I said. "Well, that makes you an even more important witness." She looked gratified. "Do you happen to know how they met in the first place?"

"Actually, I don't," she said regretfully. "I asked Fran, but she was very evasive. Said something about meeting in a coffee shop." Her mouth turned down in disapproval. "I wouldn't have thought she was the type to pick up a man in a public place."

"Did she mention the name of the coffee shop?"

"No."

"Tell me, what do you remember about Browdy? Anything at all—maybe some little thing that might help us fill in his background."

"Well. He made it clear he didn't care for me—of course the feeling was mutual, I assure you—and he told Fran lies about me." She gave a couple of angry sniffs. "Soon she started dropping hints that I should look for another place." She paused. "I remember the very first time he came to pick her up in that flashy car of his. It was obvious she hadn't bothered to mention my existence, and when we were introduced I could see he didn't care for the idea she had a housemate." Pudge flushed. "I thought that was because he had—ideas. You know, for when he brought her home after the date. . . ." I nodded discreetly. "Actually, in that way he turned out to be a perfect gentleman, whenever he brought Fran home he would see her to the door and give her a little peck on the cheek. He never came in." She gave a sly little smile. "I think Fran was disappointed! But he believed in marriage, or so he said. He thought people should get to know each other well before—before—"

"Rather unusual, in this day and age, didn't you think?"

"Nobody cared what *I* thought, Mr. Newman. As soon as a pair of pants appeared on the horizon, *my* presence was no longer required."

I shook my head sympathetically and said, "Tell me more about Browdy."

"Really, I only met the man a few times. He was conceited. Oh my, yes. Thought he was so smart, so good-looking, so—" She flushed. "You know, well built. He strutted around in these tight body shirts, I think they call them. Fran couldn't keep her eyes off him. He used to brag about how strong he was, but once when she made a barbecue he ran in the house and wouldn't come out because there was a bee! That made me laugh—men are so childish. What else, let's see. Oh, he pretended to be fascinated by Fran's work and asked her questions about the children she worked with. Juvenile delinquents, most of them, *not* nice children at all." She shook her head. "Oh, and he was always taking pictures, he even took some of me. But he couldn't *stand* for anyone to take *his* picture, he got very upset when I snapped him with my Instamatic."

I leaned forward. "You took a picture of him?"

She nodded. "He tore it up, he said it was terrible. Can you imagine? I mean, it was my film. He could at least have asked permission."

"That's really a shame, Ms. Poge. We could use a picture of Browdy."

She gave her sly smile. "Oh? Now I wonder—how much would you give for one?"

"Why? You don't happen to have one, do you?"

She laughed girlishly. "Oh—just for fun, how much would you give for it, if I did?"

She had one! "I thought Fran was a friend of yours. I thought you'd want to help find her murderer."

Her expression hardened. "I'm a working girl, Mr. Newman. I'd love to be a philanthropist, but I simply can't afford it. It so happens I do have a picture—I snapped it one day when I was out in the garden with my camera. Keith drove up to the house, and I caught him just as he was getting out of the car. Oh, he'd have been wild if he knew!" She gave an abrupt giggle.

"I'll give you twenty dollars for it."

She shook her head, narrowing her eyes. "I'm sure it's worth more than that."

"What's your price?"

"How about one hundred?"

I paid it. It was a lot to pay for a lousy shot; Browdy's head was lowered and his face was half in shadow. Still, you could see his hair and his general build—not to mention his dog, standing next to the car.

*   *   *

But the picture didn't do us any good. All the trails I tried to follow quickly petered out: the photographic supply stores, the car rental agencies, the inquiries in the neighborhood. I even flew out to Wisconsin and spent a couple of days trying to find someone, anyone, who recognized the man in the photograph, or the name, "Keith Browdy," or the dog. Nothing doing. The Maryland police looked actively for Browdy for a while, but they didn't get anywhere either.

Finally—by this time it was October—I had to face the fact that there was nothing more to be done. He'd been too slick for us. He'd killed Fran, helped himself to the money in her savings account, and her jewelry and silver, and disappeared. And I hadn't the faintest idea of where to start looking for him. My old friend had been the victim of a perfect crime, and I'd piddled around and let her murderer escape.

Two

RUTHANN

Fifteen

 It was three months later on New Year's Day that Sabina's answering service got a call from a Donna MacNiece.

I returned the call—it was a number out on the Eastern Shore near the Chesapeake Bay—and the phone was picked up by a woman with a throaty voice.

I said, "Is this Miss Donna MacNiece?"

"Ms."

"Sorry. Actually, I usually say 'Ms.'"

"Oh, do you."

I could tell she didn't believe me. "This is Victor Newman, calling for Sabina Swift."

There was a pause. "Why didn't she call me herself?"

"Two reasons. First, that's one of the things she pays me for; and second, she's in Jamaica."

"Jamaica, Long Island?"

"No, Jamaica, West Indies."

"If you meant Jamaica, West Indies, why didn't you say so?"

"I just did." I had the feeling the conversation wasn't going well. "You called to make an appointment?"

"Yes, but since she's in Jamaica, obviously I can't. Unless I fly down there. . . ."

She sounded as if she was considering it seriously. I said, "No, don't do that, she's on vacation. She'll be back Thursday and you could see her Friday." This conversation was taking place on a Tuesday.

"Why not Thursday, if she'll be back?"

Reminding myself I wasn't being paid to antagonize potential clients, I answered mildly, "Probably she'll be tired from the trip."

"Why? The flight is less than three hours. I just got back from Italy this morning, and I'm perfectly prepared to see Sabina Swift today. Or I would be, if she were available."

"Would you care to tell me what it's about?"

"I'd rather not."

It figured. "I'm her confidential assistant."

"Sorry, I prefer to deal with her directly."

Donna MacNiece was obviously used to having her own way no matter what; still, she did have a sexy voice and I was getting curious to meet her. Since the coffers were low and she sounded as if she had money, I let her talk me into making her an appointment on Thursday night at eight o'clock. Sabina wouldn't really mind, being a confirmed workaholic. Bruno hates cold weather, and every winter he begs her to spend a few days with him in the sun until she finally gives in. Otherwise she'd never have gone to an island in the Caribbean where she'd be forced to confront the problem of what to do with herself in an idyllic spot. God only knew what she'd been going through—it was pathetic, when you thought about it.

Donna MacNiece arrived at the office a few minutes before eight on Thursday. She was a tall, willowy woman in jeans and boots and one of those bulky, oversize sweaters that make you wonder what kind of a body is underneath. It was a casual out-fit, but on her it looked terrific. She gave me a handshake that seemed a little too emphatic, as if she wanted to convey the idea that she wasn't somebody you could mess with; and yet I got the impression she was one of those vulnerable people who decide, somewhere in the course of growing up, that the best defense is a good offense. She was about thirty-five. "You're Victor New-man?" she said, inspecting me a little longer than was strictly necessary. In person, the voice was just as sexy. Kind of a purr.

I was surprised she remembered my name, because I'd had the feeling she'd dismissed me as an underling. As I led her through the cloister to Sabina's office she paused to look around and said, "Hm. This isn't the atmosphere I expected. I like the sound of that fountain, it reminds me of Italy. Of course the statue's on the sentimental side."

I studied the bronze girl on the fountain. She seemed to be holding onto her jug in a pretty businesslike way, I thought. I said, "I may be dumb, but I'm never sure what that means."

"Too pretty. A cliché."

"I kind of like it."

"I'm not saying you shouldn't like it. If you like it, fine." She added after a moment, "I'm a sculptor."

"What kind of sculpture do you do?"

"Big welded forms."

"Oh." I didn't know what else to say on the subject, so I led her into Sabina's office. She settled herself in a chair, crossing one long leg over the other and pushing back her streaky blond hair, which was shoulder length and had a tendency to fall in her eyes. Her skin glowed golden brown, as if she'd spent a lot of time on the beach when she was in Italy. She looked as if she'd been living the dolce vita, but probably she'd been too busy welding.

Sabina came into the room and greeted her, seating herself at the desk while the client rooted around in one of those brown leather shoulder bags that look like saddle bags. Eventually she found what she was looking for, a newspaper clipping; placing it on her thigh, she smoothed out the creases.

"What can I do for you?" said Sabina. Donna handed her the clipping. Sabina glanced at it, and her eyebrows rose. Without a word, she passed it to me.

The client frowned. "You haven't read it."

"It so happens I've seen it before."

As I looked at the headline, my interest in Donna MacNiece mushroomed, for the article she'd brought in was the one from the *Washington Post* about Fran's death. The words, "she had remarried only last month" were circled in red ink.

I was about to say something when Sabina held up her hand. "One moment, Vic." She turned to the client. "Ms. Mac-Niece, this article appeared in the *Washington Post* last summer. Suppose you tell us why you're bringing it to me now, in January?"

The client pushed the hair out of her eyes. I noticed they were green and set deeply into the sockets, and that she'd brushed a greenish shadow on her eyelids that had a hint of irridescence, like the inside of a seashell. "As I mentioned to your assistant on the phone, I returned two days ago from Italy. I'd been away eighteen months, and during that time I'd rented out my house on the Chesapeake Bay. When I got back, the first thing I did was make a fire in the fireplace, using some old newspapers the tenants had left. I happened to see this article. It attracted my attention immediately."

"And why was that?"

"Because I have—had an older sister, Ruthann. She was my closest relative—my only relative, really." The throaty voice wavered and she folded her arms, wrapping herself more tightly in the bulky sweater. "A year and a half ago, she died. Her car was hit by a train." Sabina and I exchanged a glance. Sabina picked up the paperweight from her desk and revolved it gently between her fingers as Donna MacNiece continued. "She'd been driving late at night, and her car had stalled on the tracks. Supposedly. I found that hard to believe."

"Why?"

"She hated to drive—it was a phobia, really."

"She didn't drive at all?"

"No, she drove; but she avoided it as much as possible. She lived on Long Island, but she wouldn't drive into New York City or on the Long Island Expressway—that kind of thing. And she avoided driving at night. So what was her car doing on a railroad track at one in the morning?"

"What did *you* think had happened?"

Donna MacNiece gave a long sigh and the irridescent eyelids drooped. "I wish I could say I was capable of *thinking*, at that particular time; but I'm afraid I wasn't, to be perfectly honest. My marriage had just fallen apart, and with Ruthann's death, I was really a wreck. I got this idea in my head that her husband had killed her. All my friends told me I was crazy."

"Did you go to the police?"

"Yes." Impatiently, she pushed back her hair. "And they were impossible. They said there was no evidence of foul play and politely told me to get lost. Semipolitely. They seemed to think I was trying to get my hands on my sister's money, which she'd left to her husband. That was ridiculous. I have money of my own. Ruthann and I come from an old Eastern Shore family, tobacco farmers originally, that became—fairly prosperous." She tossed back her hair and raised her chin. "My father," she added with pride, "was in his fourth term in the state legislature when he died; and he was only forty-six. He and my mother were drowned out on the bay. They'd gone sailing." She said it matter-of-factly, as if she'd had a long time to get used to the idea; but I wondered if she ever really had. She pulled a pack of cigarettes out of the saddle bag. "I was nine years old, and Ruthann was twenty. She raised me—tried to, anyway. I didn't make it particularly easy. I insisted on studying art, and she didn't approve of what she thought of as my bohemian life-style." She struck a match.

Sabina said, "I'm sorry, I don't allow smoking in the office."

Donna looked annoyed. "You run a tight ship, don't you?"

"No tighter than necessary." That was a lie. "Smoking is bad for the smoker and everyone in the vicinity. I see no reason to condone slow suicide, or to join in it myself."

Donna put the cigarettes away. Then, suddenly and surprisingly, she smiled. It was a great smile—the green eyes flashed with the wry amusement of someone who can laugh when the joke is on her. "Remember, I'm from the Eastern Shore. Out in tobacco country we don't appreciate that kind of talk." She studied Sabina. "I've heard of you from several people," she said finally. "You're supposed to be very good. I liked the idea of consulting a woman; women are more reliable than men, in my experience." Her eyes flickered briefly in my direction. "I suppose I'll have to put up with your little quirks."

Sabina ignored the remark. "Tell me about your sister."

"Ruthann was a social worker. Probably only became one because she loved telling other people how to run their lives. God knows it wasn't because she needed the money—though actually I respected her for working when she didn't have to. She was—oh, a stiff sort of person. Conventional. Judgmental. The two of us were very different."

"Tell me about your brother-in-law. His name?"

"Malcolm Ellis."

I wrote it down.

"How long had he been married to your sister?"

"Less than two months." Sabina and I exchanged a glance. "That's what it was about this article that made me decide to come to you—the fact that this other woman had just been married. Like Ruthann. I know coincidences happen, but I'm leery of them. I want to know more about the death of this woman last summer, and I want you to look into Ruthann's death." She groped automatically for her cigarettes; then she remembered, and withdrew her hand from her bag. "It's almost two years since Ruthann died, and I've never been able to shake the feeling that there was more to her death than appeared on the surface. I should have hired a private investigator at the time, but as I said, I wasn't at my best and, well—I just didn't. And then I went abroad."

Sabina nodded. "What do you know about Malcolm Ellis?"

Donna MacNiece pushed her blond hair back out of her eyes. "Virtually nothing. I only met him once, and that was after Ruthann's death. She and I weren't on speaking terms at the time she got married."

"I thought you said you were close."

"We were, but it was one of those love-hate relationships. We'd had one of our fights, but we'd have made up eventually, we always did. I didn't care for something she'd said when I separated from my husband—she'd never approved of him— and I made a few comments about her own track record, which wasn't great. She'd divorced her first husband. So she never did tell me about meeting Malcolm, I guess because she was angry. And when she finally called to say she'd gotten married, I was in no hurry to go running up to Stony Brook to toast the happy couple. Actually, she didn't sound that happy, and in the mood I was in at the time I thought it served her right. God, what a bitch I was, how I wish now I'd gone to see her. . . ." She broke off, and the green eyes filled with tears. "A few weeks later she was dead."

After a moment Sabina said gently, "About Malcolm Ellis—"

"Ruthann hadn't known him long. She said he was a lawyer. I met him for the first time at the funeral. I asked him how come Ruthann had been out driving at night, when it was something she'd always avoided. He was very smooth, said she'd been 'trying to make a whole new life and turn her back on the past'—he made it clear that I was part of the past—and he claimed he'd been helping her to overcome her driving phobia. According to him, she'd been driving at night for some time."

"Did you believe him?"

"No—I told him that was bullshit. I made a terrible scene. Fortunately or unfortunately, there was hardly anyone at the funeral besides the two of us and the minister. Oh, there was a man from the agency where she worked—I guess they figured they should send someone. I'd had a few drinks, enough so I could get through the funeral, and I came right out and accused

Malcolm of having caused Ruthann's death. He handled it beautifully, I must say; and I could see the man from the agency thought I was drunk, deranged, or in very bad taste, whichever is worst. But I still think I was right—and now there's this other woman." She hesitated. "This may sound fantastic." She tossed her head. "The fact is, I can't stop thinking that Malcolm Ellis could be one of these Bluebeards you read about, who go around marrying women and then murdering them."

Sabina studied Donna without replying, absentmindedly revolving the glass paperweight in her fingers. Finally she said, "I see you've given the matter quite a bit of thought."

"Well, it's two days since I saw the article. It's all I've been able to think of since. I have an active imagination, maybe too active." She shrugged. "I admit artists have a tendency in that direction."

"I wasn't implying your imagination was overactive, Ms. MacNiece. Not at all. Tell me, what became of Malcolm Ellis, after your sister's death?"

"Call me Donna." She shook her head. "I never saw the man again, once the funeral was over. I'd won a prize that took me to Rome to study with a well-known sculptor, and I left the country. Eventually Ellis inherited Ruthann's estate—it wasn't enormous, her first husband had taken a good bite out of it, but there was still a fair amount left—and he sold the house and moved away. Where he went I have no idea."

"Did Ellis own a German shepherd?"

Donna MacNiece's eyes widened in astonishment. "Yes, as a matter of fact he did. How on earth did you know? Ruthann absolutely detested the animal."

Sabina turned to me. "Vic, would you show Ms. MacNiece the photograph?"

I went to the filing cabinet and took out the picture of Keith Browdy, which I handed to the client.

She studied it. Finally she said, "It's not a very good shot, is it? But I think—I'm almost sure—it's Malcolm. The dog looks just like his. He brought it to the funeral, which I thought was outrageous. Where did you get this picture?"

Sabina said, "Vic, please tell Ms. MacNiece about your friend Fran."

I proceeded to do so.

Donna MacNiece was a good listener. She kept her green eyes fastened on me intently, and didn't speak until I was finished. Then she said, "It's the same man. It must be. My God!" She sat back in her chair and wrapped her arms around her slender body as if she felt a chill. "You know how you can think something and at the same time you don't really believe it, it seems too bizarre? Now I believe it!" She leaned forward. "And I want you to find him! Suppose I give you three thousand dollars to begin with?" She took out a checkbook and began to write a check without waiting for a reply.

"That would be fine," said Sabina. "But Ms. MacNiece, although I'd like nothing better than to catch the man who killed your sister—and I must say I agree with your suspicions—I should warn you that it may be a prolonged and expensive investigation." She tapped the picture. "Malcolm Ellis, or whatever his real name is, is totally unscrupulous and quite clever. The method he used to murder your sister and Fran O'Donnell was very ingenious. Accidents like this, genuine ones, unfortunately do occur." Her face grew grave. "I suspect we're just looking at the tip of the iceberg. How large and lethal that iceberg may prove to be . . ." She shook her head. "It's too soon to tell."

There was a silence.

I thought over the implications of what had just been said. Before, I'd been trying to find a friend's killer; now it looked like the man I'd been searching for could be a mass murderer, and Fran only one of a series of victims.

Donna laid the check on the desk and Sabina picked it up, saying, "I'll accept your retainer, but without any guarantees."

"I understand."

"Now let me ask you a few more questions."

But the client had little additional information to offer, and as I listened a feeling of pessimism came over me. I already knew how elusive this man could be, how sensitive he was to danger and how well he covered his traces.

I wrote down the name of the social service agency on Long Island where Ruthann Duncan Ellis had worked, and the name of the colleague who had attended the funeral, a Dr. Nordholm. There were names of a few old school friends, though Donna thought Ruthann had probably been out of touch with them.

The lead that sounded most promising was Ruthann's psychiatrist, with whom the dead woman had apparently been in therapy for years. "Not that I ever noticed any great improvement," Donna said. "I think she was just dependent on him. Maybe she liked talking to him because she had so few friends—it was hard for her to make conversation with people, though I guess she could do it professionally. I think she was basically a very insecure person who covered it up with this mask of being totally together, because she hated anyone to see her weaknesses. It's too bad, because if she'd let them show she'd have been more likable—and they showed anyway, whether she thought so or not. Anyway, she'd been going for years to this Dr. Levesque, and I'd be surprised if she wasn't still seeing him at the time of her death. Dr. Oswald Levesque in Patchogue," she said for my benefit, and spelled it. She pronounced it 'Leveck.'

"That may be helpful," said Sabina. It was late, and I could tell she was tired—after all, only this morning she'd still been suffering on a beach in Jamaica. "When your sister told you she'd gotten married, did she happen to say how she'd met her husband?"

Donna hesitated. "Yes," she said finally. "I asked her, and she said they'd struck up a conversation while he'd been out walking his dog. But I didn't believe her."

"Why not?"

"Well—I knew her. I could always tell when she was lying. I don't mean she was a liar, not really; but she would fudge things she wasn't too proud of. As I said, she was always trying to keep up her image. I couldn't see her falling into conversation with some guy walking a dog, she wasn't the type, so I figured she didn't want me to know how she'd met Malcolm. But I had a hunch."

"Oh? What was it?"

"I thought she'd met him through the Personals."

Sabina picked up the paperweight again, and rotated it gently in her fingers. "Now that's intriguing. What gave you that particular idea?"

"While we were still on speaking terms, before we had our fight, she mentioned some woman who'd put an ad in *New York Magazine* because she wanted to meet men. She went on and on about it. And I knew Ruthann wanted to get married again—God knows why, you'd think once would cure anybody, it's certainly cured *me*—only she never seemed to meet men, or so she said." She tossed back her hair. "I don't know, it's just a thought; but I remember when she told me about Malcolm I suddenly wondered if she'd met him through the Personals. I may be completely wrong."

Sabina leaned forward. "Do you happen to know the name of the woman she mentioned who'd put in the ad?"

Regretfully, Donna shook her head. "I'm sorry. I'm afraid I have no idea."

Sixteen

The following day, Sabina and I flew up to New York City. There were still Christmas decorations in the airport, and the panhandlers were greeting travelers with "Happy New Year!" although it was already January fourth. We rented a car and drove through lightly falling snow out to Stony Brook, where Ruthann Ellis had lived and died. En route, I began to suspect that her refusal to drive on the Long Island Expressway hadn't been a phobia, just common sense.

I was to scout around at the agency where the dead woman had worked, while Sabina concentrated on trying to find a lead to the present whereabouts of Keith Browdy, or Malcolm Ellis, or whatever his real name was. I dropped her at the law firm that had handled the estate, and drove off to find the agency.

I located it near the hospital, in a rundown white frame building that had started life as somebody's home. In the back yard, a three-story brick extension had been clumsily added, dwarfing the original house. A sign beside the front door said

YOUTH ACTION ALLIANCE, A UNITED GIVERS FUND ORGANIZATION. I tried the door. It was locked.

I rang, but nobody answered. I rang again, turning up my collar against the biting wind. I kept my finger on the bell and eventually heard the sound of footsteps approaching. A hefty, middle-aged black woman opened the door a crack and peered out. "Oh," she said when she saw me. "Well, come in." The door swung wider. "I thought it was those darn kids again. They ring the doorbell and—like that!—they scoot away." Her hand made a lightning-like movement that just missed my nose, to demonstrate how fast they scooted. "Can't nobody catch them." She shook her head. "Wish that was all they did, ring the door. They bad, those kids." I followed her into a hall that was in need of a paint job. The Christmas decorations on the wall had been made by children. A Christmas tree was shedding its needles on the linoleum.

She led me into an office. Most of the floor space was occupied by plastic milk crates stuffed with files, which were piled up almost to the ceiling. What little floor space remained was taken up by a desk, a couple of chairs, and a portable electric heater.

"I'm Mrs. Atkins," the woman said, squeezing herself between the piles of milk crates and seating herself at the desk. "I'm the receptionist. Receptionist, typist, baby-sitter, you name it. What can I do for you?" She was fortyish and heavy, with a large bust and a round, dark face wearing an expression that seemed to say she'd seen it all and wasn't going to let any of it get to her, not if she could help it.

"I'm Vic Newman," I said. "I'm a private investigator." Her expression didn't change. She'd seen investigators, too. "I'm inquiring about an employee named Ruthann Ellis."

"Don't know her."

"Ruthann Duncan Ellis?"

"Oh, Mrs. Duncan." She shook her head. "She don't work here no more. She died."

"I know."

"Run over by a train," she said. "Flattened like a pancake."

"I'm looking into her death," I said.

"Died two years ago, just about." A faint spark of interest came into her eyes. "How come you asking questions? It was an accident."

"Maybe yes and maybe no. All kinds of things can happen in this day and age."

"Don't I know it."

"Possibly it only looked like an accident."

She folded her arms. "You don't say. Well, nobody liked Mrs. Duncan much. But wouldn't nobody around here have *killed* her." She thought for a moment. "One of her clients, maybe. Some of those boys are bad." She drew the word out: "ba-a-ad."

"I don't think her clients are involved."

"That's good, because I couldn't tell you anything if they were." She waved at the milk crates. "We keep our records strictly confidential."

I said, "How long had Mrs. Duncan been with the agency?"

"Longer than anybody. Longer than me, so I'm not exactly sure. Long enough so they couldn't get rid of her."

"Did they want to?"

Mrs. Atkins shrugged. "Some did. Thought she was old-fashioned. Too—what's that word they use? Controlling. These things come and go, in a place like this. People come and go. Director gets all fired up, comes in one day with a list this long, gonna reform the agency. Next thing you know he's moved out of state, gone into private practice, I don't know what-all." She shrugged. "I don't pay too much mind, just do my work. Got plenty of it, lord knows. Mrs. Duncan, she was kind of a tight-ass lady, went by the book, wasn't too popular with the kids—that kind. But—" She shrugged again. "I say take the good with the bad. She put in her time, didn't come in late like some of them. Didn't complain that much. Knew all the rules and regulations, it came in handy sometimes."

"Was there anyone on the staff she was close to?"

"You mean, like a friend?" She shook her head. "I wouldn't say so. Dr. Nordholm was her supervisor, you could talk to him."

"I'd like to," I said. Dr. Nordholm was the man who'd attended Ruthann's funeral. I took out the photograph and showed it to Mrs. Atkins. "Did you ever meet Mrs. Duncan's husband?"

"The one she married, you mean? The new one?" She squinted at the picture, holding it at arm's length, and then put on a pair of reading glasses and studied it up closer. "Sorta looks like him. He the one you're after? Came to pick her up one time, brought his dog. Same dog like in the picture. I said, 'You can't bring that animal in here.' You let one do it, first thing you know this place be a zoo. You don't think our kids have pets? He gave me a look, but I didn't pay him no mind. No mind atall."

"Do you remember what he did? What he said?"

She reflected. "Tied up that dog to the fire hydrant, asked could he leave the door open so he could see the dog was okay. I said sure, if it wasn't for long. Man was crazy about his dog, you could tell. What else . . ." She reflected some more. "He seemed kind of interested in the agency, walked around, read the diplomas on the walls, looked at the map of our catchment area, stuff like that, wanted to know what we did with the kids. Like, did we put them in foster care or what. Oh, one thing I remember."

"What was that?"

"He said one time he was in foster care hisself."

"Is that so? Did he tell you anything more about it?"

The doorbell rang. Mrs. Atkins hauled herself out of the chair and ambled down the hall to the front door. She opened it, leaned outside, and craned her neck left and right. After a moment she came back. "Drat those kids," she said as she sat down again and rolled a piece of paper into her typewriter. "Want me to buzz Dr. Nordholm for you?"

"Yes, but before you do, did Mrs. Duncan's husband say anything else?"

She shook her head. "Not that I recall. Seemed kind of antsy, like he was in a hurry to get out of here. She came down, they left, that's it." She pushed a buzzer. "Only time I ever saw him, like I said." There was an answering buzz. She picked up the telephone and spoke into the receiver. "Someone here to see you, Dr. Nordholm. A detective, he said." After a moment she added, "No, something about Mrs. Duncan. Mrs. Duncan, that's right." When she hung up the phone she told me, "Up those stairs, second door on your left. Just go straight in."

Dr. Nordholm was younger than I'd expected, maybe thirty at most. Behind the blond Vandyke beard and the horn-rimmed glasses was a chubby-cheeked, pink-and-white face and a look of permanent harassment. "Come in, Mr.—er—I'm very busy, but take a seat." His desk was an overflowing mass of papers, some of which had drifted down onto the floor. In this office, too, stacks of milk crates were bulging with files. Couldn't the agency afford filing cabinets? Maybe not. I sat down. On the wall behind Dr. Nordholm, a poster that had been mended with Scotch tape proclaimed. THIS IS THE FIRST DAY OF THE REST OF YOUR LIFE. Presumably the sentiment didn't extend to the two potted plants on the windowsill, which had died, from the look of them, long ago.

"I'm Vic Newman," I said. "I'm a private investigator, inquiring into the death of Ruthann Duncan Ellis. Thanks for seeing me, Dr. Nordholm. I'm hoping you can help me."

His face took on an expression of disapproval. I got the feeling it often did. "Matters relating to personnel are confidential," he said. "Confidentiality is the heart and soul of our profession. You may not know that, of course. But I have an obligation to uphold . . ."

The guy was hardly older than me, and already incredibly pompous. What would he be like when he was fifty? I said, aiming for equal pomposity, "Dr. Nordholm. I appreciate your position, I truly do. Under normal circumstances I would never dream of trying to worm out of you any information about an employee. But since she's dead . . . and there's a strong possibility she was murdered—"

"Murdered? What do you mean?" He examined me closely for telltale signs of being a weirdo. "Do you have any identification, Mr. Newman?" I took out my license and gave it to him. He looked it over carefully and when he handed it back, a trace of humanity showed through in the form of an apologetic dip of the head. "You really think Mrs. Duncan was murdered? Everybody said it was just an unfortunate accident. I'm shocked, really shocked." A thought struck him. "Come to think of it, there was a woman at the funeral—a sister, I believe—who was flinging around some rather wild accusations. She seemed a hysterical type, and I didn't take what she said seriously." He hesitated. "Should I have?"

"Maybe. It looks like she was right. What I've been hired to do, Dr. Nordholm, is to trace the man Mrs. Duncan married not long before her death. It appears he subsequently remarried, under a different name, and *that* wife later died in an accident exactly like Mrs. Duncan's."

He wasn't dumb. After a moment, he said. "I see." Behind the horn-rimmed glasses, his eyelashes fluttered. "Do you"—it came out in a squeak and he cleared his throat and tried again—"do you suspect there may be others?"

"Possibly. So far, there's no evidence of that."

He thought it over. "It seems a bit farfetched. Yet not impossible, of course. Serial killers do exist. I've never met one, professionally I mean, though I've treated a few murderers, people with impulse control disorders. But this is something different— almost the opposite, you might say."

"Carefully planned, you mean?"

He nodded. "Exactly. I did a bit of reading about serial killers when I was a resident."

"Anything you can tell me that might help? Is it known how they get that way?"

"Well, there are theories." He shook his head. "There are always theories, but as for facts . . ." He tried to come up with some, and failed. "One thing, they seem to be people with an overweening sense of their own importance, and utterly convinced of their own cleverness. They often *are* quite intelligent, as a matter of fact. Yet they seem to lack the ability to grasp the fact that others have an interior life, with feelings and needs, just as they themselves do. To them, other people are puppets, empty shells to manipulate for their own gratification. Generally, they believe they're too clever to be caught—and of course some never are. Look at Jack the Ripper. Well, I don't suppose that helps you much." He stroked his whitish-blond beard.

"It might, you never know," I said. "Dr. Nordholm, what can you tell me about Mrs. Duncan's second husband, the man she knew as Malcolm Ellis? I'd be interested in anything she may have said about him, or anything you noticed about him yourself, if you ever met him. I don't think I really need to ask you that much about her."

"That's good, because I don't know much. We worked together for only three months, and our relationship was strictly professional. I had accepted a position here after finishing my residency, and it was my duty to supervise the social workers, as well as to prescribe medication, and so forth. Ruthann Duncan had been here a long time, which I of course had not. She liked to stress that point, to a degree I considered somewhat inappropriate." He cleared his throat. "She didn't confide in me about her personal life. In fact, I didn't learn about her marriage from her directly, but only through office gossip." He shrugged. "So you see, I can be of little help to you. I never met her husband."

I asked him a few more questions, but got nothing useful. I stood up to go, and he stood up too.

"Poor Mrs. Duncan," he said, and shook his head. "I'm afraid I didn't much like her. Still, no one had the right to deprive her of her life. It's terrible, what you're suggesting." He shuddered. "Terrible!"

Seventeen

Sabina and I had agreed to meet for lunch at a restaurant we'd noticed while driving around Stony Brook that morning. I got there before she did, and while I was waiting for her to show up I called Dr. Oswald Levesque, Ruthann's shrink.

He picked up the phone after one ring. "Hello?"

"Dr. Levesque?"

"Yes, can I help you?"

"Dr. Levesque, my name is Vic Newman. I wonder if I could make an appointment with you. Today, if possible."

"Why—perhaps so, Mr. Newman. I think I might be able to fit you in. Might I ask what the problem seems to be?" His voice oozed professional sympathy.

"I'm a private detective, Dr. Levesque. I'd appreciate an opportunity to talk to you about a former patient who—"

"I don't discuss my patients," he said abruptly, the sympathy oozing right out of his voice.

"But she's dead," I said.

"Dead or alive." After a moment he added cautiously, "How did this person die?"

"Her car was hit by a train. I've been engaged to investigate her death. Supposedly it was an accident, but—"

He said sharply, "What are you implying?"

"I'm not implying anything."

"You're not suggesting this was suicide?"

As an experienced detective, I had no trouble deducing that the good doctor was afraid of a malpractice suit. "No, no. We think she was murdered," I said soothingly.

"Oh." He sounded relieved.

"It would really be helpful if you could spare me some time, doctor. You probably knew her better than anyone." A little soft soap never hurt, and in this case it might even be true. "Could I make an appointment to see you?"

He hesitated, and then said decisively. "No. Anything a patient tells me is confidential. Dead, alive, there's no statute of limitations as far as I'm concerned. What is the name of this alleged patient of mine?"

"Ruthann Duncan Ellis." He didn't say anything. "She was a patient of yours, wasn't she? For a long time?"

"I have no comment. Goodbye, Mr.—"

"Wait! I've been hired by her sister to find Ruthann's murderer. If somebody killed one of your patients, don't you feel an obligation to help bring the murderer to justice?" A little guilt trip never hurt either.

Slowly and reluctantly he replied, "I might possibly consider talking to a member of the family."

"But Dr. Levesque, the sister hired me. I'm her agent—"

He hung up.

I went back to my table and picked up the menu, hoping the lunch would be an improvement over the conversation.

The door of the restaurant swung open, admitting a blast of cold air. I looked up and saw Sabina, blue with cold in a fur-lined coat with the collar turned up. She headed for my table. "I'm freezing," she complained as she slid into the booth.

"Aren't you going to take off your coat?"

"I just said I'm freezing! Are you deaf?" She gets childish when she's cold. Childish and mean.

"But you're indoors now. It's warmer here."

"Thank you for pointing that out." She huddled deeper into her coat. "Can you give me one good reason why that wind is so penetrating? Is it the proximity of the ocean, or what?"

"Large bodies of water influence the weather, I've been told."

"Don't talk to me as if I were a half-wit, Victor." Cautiously, she opened the top button and loosened her collar. "I'm your employer, in case it's slipped your mind."

"Yes, *ma'am*! You know, maybe you should have stayed in the sunny Caribbean a while longer."

She shuddered and picked up the menu. "There are worse things in the world than a little cold weather."

We studied our menus. I said, "Any luck?"

She shook her head. The wind had whipped the hair out of the bun at the back of her neck. She tucked the strands back in place, pulling out the tortoiseshell hairpins and jabbing them in again. Then she took a lace-edged handkerchief from her pocketbook and blew her nose. Finally she replied, "Not really. It's exactly the same story as with Fran. I spoke to Ruthann Duncan's lawyer, and he told me that Keith Browdy—I suppose we might as well continue to call him that—talked her into making a will in his favor as soon as they were married. After her death he inherited everything, sold her house, and transferred the money to a bank in New York City. At least I learned that much—the lawyer was cooperative, and he happens to have a brother who's a banker, which was helpful. Browdy seems to have withdrawn the funds from the New York bank over a period of several months. After that, he closed the account"—she shrugged—"and disappeared. Again."

"You found out a lot."

"Unfortunately, none of it tells us where he is now. I suppose New York's a possibility—but New York's a huge place. And he may not even be there." She took out a chapstick, pursed her cupid's bow lips and applied it liberally, and thrust one last hairpin into her bun. There was a glint of anger in her eyes. "Let me tell you something, Vic. I'm starting to take this case personally. And I resent it, because personal feelings cloud one's reasoning powers. Still—this man! This Browdy person! The way he preys on women of a certain age, it's outrageous!" She added, "Women of *my* age!"

"The thing I don't get," I said, "is what they see in him. I mean, I met the guy, and I knew right away you couldn't trust him. Why didn't either of these women sense that?"

She shook her head. "You don't understand. A great many women in our society feel they *must* have a man in their lives, because otherwise they're nothing. Nothing! Do you realize what it's like to feel you're *nothing*? Certainly loneliness plays a part and so does sex, but it's more than that. Many women just don't feel like whole human beings unless they have a man." She added somberly, "That's what makes them vulnerable. That's why they can't use their brains or their judgment. It upsets me! I mean, it could happen to—anyone, almost." Did she mean it could happen to her? "Take your friend Fran. Was she a stupid woman? Obviously not. She knew a great deal about life and death, and she worked in a difficult profession. Yet she was at this man's mercy. And he showed no mercy—not to her, not to Ruthann Duncan. He cultivated them like a—a"—she groped for the word—"a *cash crop*! And as soon as he was ready, he cut them down. They weren't people to him."

"They were empty shells to manipulate for his own gratification?" I said, quoting Dr. Nordholm.

"Exactly!" She looked at me in surprise, and I could see she was impressed. "Though I suspect there's another aspect, something more complex, twisted . . ." Her voice trailed off. After a while she muttered, as if to herself, "I'm going to catch this man. Only, where is he?" She rapped her knuckles on the table impatiently. The waitress came over. Sabina ignored her. "Where is he, he must be somewhere!"

"You're waiting for another party?" the waitress inquired. "You want me to come back?"

"No, we'll order," I said. "I'll have a hamburger, medium rare, and coffee."

"You should never order a hamburger in a public place," Sabina said to me. "You can't tell what they put in it."

The waitress looked offended. "We use only Grade-A beef," she said.

"Of course, you're an adult," Sabina went on, "and you have to make these decisions yourself. There are things we learn only through experience. I'll have a bowl of the vegetable soup. An omelet. Coffee. Make sure the soup is hot, please."

"Our soup is always hot, madam." The waitress departed, with a look that said, One of those.

Tentatively, Sabina opened her coat. No icy blast zapped her, and after a minute she decided to live dangerously and pulled her arms out of the sleeves. "So," she said. "Did you learn anything useful at the agency?" She draped the coat around her shoulders.

I shook my head. "Not much." I described my visit to the clinic and my conversations with Mrs. Atkins and Dr. Nordholm. She listened intently and made no comment. The waitress brought our food. The hamburger was decent—not overdone, and served with lettuce and tomato and a slice of raw onion. We ate for a while in silence. I told her about my unsatisfactory call to Ruthann's shrink. To my surprise, that seemed to cheer her up a little.

"Good!" she said when I'd finished. "We'll ask Donna MacNiece to telephone him, since it sounds as if he'd be willing to speak to a member of the family. Why don't you give her a ring right now?" She pondered for a moment. "Tell her to try and make an appointment for tomorrow. If she succeeds, she could fly up tonight and meet us in New York, and tomorrow I'll accompany her to the doctor's office." We'd been planning to spend the night at Bruno's apartment on Riverside Drive (he commutes from Georgetown to New York once a week, because he's a professor at Columbia), since the Alvin Ailey dance troupe was in town and Sabina was determined to see them.

I said, "Listen, Sabina. It doesn't make sense for us to spend the night in New York. They're predicting a lot of snow. We'd have to drive all the way to the city this afternoon, and then back here tomorrow morning, with the roads in God knows what kind of shape. What we should do is stay in Stony Brook and find a motel."

"But we have tickets!"

"I know. It's rough. Tell you what—*you* go back to New York, I'll stay here." Nobly I added, "I'll pass up the ballet. Why should you miss all the tutus?"

"Not tutus, Victor. Not with Alvin Ailey."

"Tights, whatever. *I'll* meet the client, and go with her to the shrink." I didn't say I wouldn't mind spending some time alone with Donna MacNiece, but the thought crossed my mind.

I could see Sabina was torn. "If it wasn't the end of the run . . ." she muttered. "But how will I get to New York, if you stay here?"

"No problem. I'll take you to the train."

She hesitated. "Well—telephone the client first, and then I'll decide."

"What should I tell her?"

"Use your judgment."

I was back at the table in a flash, having used my judgment. Sabina said, "Well?"

I slid into the booth. "She'll try and reach Levesque and call me back."

"Fine."

While we waited, we went over what we knew about Browdy. "It's hard to generalize from two cases," said Sabina. "Apparently he moves from place to place, that seems clear, and looks for a certain kind of woman: middle-aged, financially secure though not necessarily wealthy, lonely, and without close relatives who might ask awkward questions."

"Ruthann had a sister," I objected.

"True, but at the time Ruthann met Browdy, the two women weren't on speaking terms. Browdy had no way of knowing that their relationship, although ambivalent, was actually quite

124

close." She stirred her coffee thoughtfully. "In a way, the most suggestive thing so far is that both Fran and Ruthann were social workers. It's possible these murders weren't committed solely for gain, although gain must have been a factor. I find it intriguing that he was in foster care at one time."

"That's what he told Mrs. Atkins, but how do we know it's true?"

"Why should he lie about something like that? He had nothing to gain." She shook her head decisively. "No, it's the sort of remark he could have made without thinking, because the agency reminded him of somewhere he'd been before. I think our Mr. Browdy made a slip when he said that—it's given us our first hint of his past, even if only a glimmer. Until now it's seemed as if he had no past, as if his life consisted solely of his associations with his two victims." Stirring her coffee, she gazed out the window at the steel-gray sky. Snow had begun to fall heavily.

The telephone rang in the booth at the back of the restaurant. "The client," I said. "I'll get it." I stood up and went to answer the phone.

"Mr. Newman?" It was the throaty voice of Donna Mac-Niece.

"Call me Vic."

"I have an appointment with Dr. Levesque tomorrow at seven in the morning."

"Seven in the morning! You've got to be kidding."

"Not at all," she said crisply. "I see you're not a morning person." There was a hint of laughter in her voice. "But I am. My father taught me that the first part of the day is the best part of the day, and he was right. Anyway, seven in the morning was the only time Dr. Levesque had available. I've arranged to fly to LaGuardia this afternoon and then take the Long Island Railroad out to Stony Brook. The train should be arriving at six-forty-five tonight."

"Terrific," I said. "I see you don't fool around."

There was a pause. "That," she said, "depends." This time there was actual laughter. "You'll be meeting me?"

"Oh yes," I said. "Yes, indeed."

"Good." She paused again. "By the way, Vic, I'm glad you called. I want you to know that. I've never liked sitting around waiting for other people to do things for me. I'd rather take action myself. If there's anything I can do to help find Ruthann's murderer, I'm more than willing—and I don't just mean pay the bill. That's—impersonal. Do you understand what I mean?"

"Yes," I said, thinking of Fran. "I guess I do. Well, tomorrow morning you can help."

"Fine," she said, and hung up.

I went back to the table. "The client wants to play detective," I said. "She says just paying the bill is impersonal."

"The client," said Sabina, "is the client. We are the detectives. You'll have to make that clear to her."

"It may not be easy."

"It doesn't have to be easy. Do it. I've never cared to work with clients who want to get personally involved in a case, as you very well know. Either they muddy up the investigation or they get themselves into dangerous situations. Remember Lawrence Schwartz?"

"Definitely."

"Then you see. Now—did Ms. MacNiece succeed in making an appointment with Dr. Levesque, or not?"

"She did, for seven o'clock tomorrow morning. She'll be arriving in Stony Brook tonight."

"Good." She signalled the waitress to bring us the check. "Take me to the railroad station. There might still be time for me to visit Browdy's New York bank this afternoon, if I hurry. You can go with Ms. MacNiece to see the psychiatrist." The waitress appeared and tore our check off her pad. She started to hand it to me, but Sabina intercepted it. "Why do you automatically give the check to *him*?" she asked the waitress. "Just because he's the man? Young lady, your assumptions are outdated." She took out her credit card.

"I didn't know you were paying," the waitress said. "You want to pay, that's fine with me." She rolled her eyes and sailed off with Sabina's VISA card in her hand.

Sabina sighed. "Sometimes I think there's no progress, none at all. It's discouraging."

"Sure there's progress," I said.

She slipped her arms into the sleeves of her fur-lined coat, ignoring me. After a while, she said in a businesslike voice, "You know, Vic, Browdy must have a home base. A place where he lives, where he keeps his belongings, perhaps even where he's known to his neighbors as a perfectly decent, normal man who just happens to be away much of the time. We have to locate that home base. The trouble is"—her blue eyes stared somberly out the window at the falling snow—"it could be any-where."

Eighteen

I waited in the station for Donna MacNiece's train to arrive. The station was beginning to feel like home— I'd put Sabina on a train for New York earlier in the afternoon, and since Donna's train was delayed because of the weather I'd been hanging around for quite some time. Snow was falling so heavily the snowplows couldn't keep up with the accumulation, according to the news on the transistor radios the people in the waiting room were carrying around. The storm was officially a blizzard.

Every now and then an announcement came over the loud-speaker. The train was half an hour behind schedule . . . then forty-five minutes . . . then an hour and twenty minutes. Finally, "the train has left New York and will be arriving late." As this last announcement was made, everyone in the station began to laugh.

Outside, the wind was blowing in forty-mile gusts. Inside, the coffee machine had run dry. I started feeling, for some reason, as if I were waiting for someone near and dear, someone whose arrival was going to make a big difference in my life; not just a client.

Finally the train pulled in, and I caught sight of Donna at the end of the platform. She was trying to tow one of those suitcases that have a long strap and those little wheels that never work right. I hurried down to meet her. By the time I got there, the wheels of the suitcase were stuck in the snow that had drifted onto the platform. "You made it," I said.

She gave me a big smile. The wind was blowing her blond hair into her eyes. "Of course!" She seemed energetic, unfazed by the delay. Ready and eager, I guessed, to start detecting. She pushed back her hair. In her narrow black pants and thick black sweater, under a red nylon parka she hadn't yet zipped up, she looked as good as I remembered her. Better.

"No problem," I said, and took the strap from her hand.

"They closed the airport after my flight took off!" She sounded delighted. "Isn't this glorious? I haven't seen a blizzard in years! It rarely even snows in southern Italy."

"If you think *this* is glorious, wait till you see the roads. We better get moving." I pulled at the suitcase and it keeled over into a snowdrift. I picked it up. "What have you got in here, the *Encyclopedia Brittanica?*"

"I have a tendency to overpack." We started walking toward the parking lot. "Anyway, I thought I might stay longer and help with the investigation, so I brought extra clothes." She was definitely gung ho; Sabina wasn't going to like it. "I hope you've been thinking of things I can do." The green eyes gazed deeply into mine and she took my arm.

I knew it had to be my imagination—that I couldn't possibly be feeling the warmth of her hand on my arm through the thickness of my down jacket. Donna MacNiece was starting to make me nervous. True, she was maybe eight years older than I, but that wasn't enough to make her totally safe. Abby Rademacher accuses me of having a fear of commitment, and maybe she's right but I suspect it's more complicated than that. I said, "Yeah, well we'll have to talk about it, Donna. It may not be such a good idea. Let's discuss it later."

She stopped short and tossed back her hair. "Why isn't it a

good idea? There must be all kinds of leads I could follow up!" I thought, Don't I wish there were all kinds of leads. She said, "I'm perfectly willing to do whatever you or Sabina suggest. Why not? It'd save money. *My* money."

Rich people, I've noticed, love to save a buck just like the rest of us. I said, "Later, Donna. Hm, snow seems a little thinner here, let's see if I can get this thing to roll." I set the bag down and pulled on the strap. The suitcase followed us for twenty feet, but when I tried picking up speed it flopped over on its side. Donna laughed. I said, "I don't see what's so funny. Lugging this thing could give a person tennis elbow."

She laughed again, flashing her green eyes at me. "If it's too heavy for you, I'll carry it," she said, bending over to pick it up.

"Did I say it was too heavy?" I wouldn't call myself macho, but there are limits. I wrestled her for the bag and won. That made me feel better.

We found the car and she helped me clean off the snow, though she'd have been within her rights if she'd sat inside like a client and let the hired help do all the work. I liked her for that. In fact, I liked her. It was kind of scary.

I'd reserved us a couple of rooms at a motel downtown. We got there eventually, skidding into the parking lot and swinging gracefully to a stop, fortunately without colliding with another car. I lugged Donna's suitcase into the lobby, allowing her to carry my overnight bag since she insisted.

The lobby was a mob scene of wall-to-wall people draped over the chairs—on the seats, on the arms—sprawled on the floor, or crowded around the counter yelling at the desk clerk, who obviously would have liked to be somewhere else. He was a cadaverous middle-aged man in a toupee that had slipped sideways, and you could tell he was the kind of guy who really suffered when he couldn't make people happy.

"Put me anywhere!" a red-faced man was shouting, banging his fist on the counter in case the desk clerk had missed the message. "Give me a maid's room, whatever, for God's sake! I'll double up with somebody else."

"Sir, I have nothing," the desk clerk replied, chewing on his underlip. "Not a *thing*." He did his best to produce an ingratiating smile. "I *wish* I could accommodate you, *believe* me. You're *more* than welcome to stay in the lobby—stay as long as you like!"

The angry man opened his wallet and waved a fifty-dollar bill. He said, "I have to get some sleep, I have an important meeting tomorrow."

"Probably be cancelled!" a woman in the crowd sang out.

The angry man turned around. "Madam, did I ask your opinion? When I want your opinion, I'll ask for it."

"Touchy, touchy."

The man's face became a shade redder. The desk clerk swallowed nervously.

I said, "Excuse me, we have a reservation."

The crowd stirred alertly. The clerk moved down the counter in my direction, relief on his face. "Good evening, sir, and may I ask your name?" I gave it to him. He turned to his computer and punched a few buttons. "Yes sir, I have your room."

Donna said, "Our *rooms*, you mean."

I told the clerk, "I reserved two rooms."

"Sir, I'm terribly sorry. I only see one."

Donna laughed. "You'd better look again."

He punched more buttons. "One," he said, and his eyes flickered back and forth between us as if appraising our relationship. "It's all we have available. I wish there was something I could do, but . . . He waved his hand around the lobby. "It's the blizzard. People simply can't get home, our facilities are stretched to the utmost." He gave us an apologetic smile. "The room is quite large, and contains two beds—two *large* beds."

Donna and I looked at each other. She tossed the hair back out of her eyes. "We reserved two rooms," she said. "We *want* two rooms."

The desk clerk shook his head.

"Well—" Donna's lips twitched and she threw me a glance

out of the corner of her eyes. She began to laugh. "Do you snore?"

"Not usually."

"Not usually." She turned to the clerk. "Okay, we'll share the room."

"Oh, thank you, madam." He handed us our keys.

The room had two double beds, as promised; also two lamps, a dresser, and a color TV. We went in and Donna closed the door behind us. Then she said, "Okay, Vic Newman. I want to know how many rooms you reserved."

I looked at her. There was a flush in her cheeks and a sparkle in her eyes that might have been anger or something else. I said, "Two."

The green eyes looked me up and down. "The truth, now!"

"Two!"

I was standing by the dresser. She came up next to me, a little smile on her lips. "You sure?"

"Sure I'm sure! That wouldn't be very professional. They're overbooked, it's the weather."

"Well, don't be so indignant. It's unflattering." We looked at each other in the mirror. "You're tall," she said. "I don't meet many men who are taller than I am." She grabbed my arm to steady herself and rose on tiptoe. "Now we're the same height," she said, laughing. She was wearing some kind of complicated perfume, and it was having an effect on me. My arm slipped around her waist before I stopped to think, and she said, "Well," and leaned back to study my face. "So you reserved two rooms. So this is just fate, right? I mean, here we are"—she laughed and declared dramatically—"a man . . . a woman . . . a hotel room." She kept laughing and watching me. "So . . . what should we do about it?"

"We could turn on TV, watch the news—"

She shook her head. "Dull, dull." She came a step closer. "We already know what's on the news."

"We do?" She placed her hands on my shoulders. It would have seemed impolite not to put my arms around her, so I did.

She leaned forward and whispered in my ear, "Yes. It's snowing." Her arms slipped around my neck.

I woke up to the smell of cigarette smoke and the sound of the TV.

Groggily, I opened my eyes. Donna was in the other bed, a cigarette in her hand, watching as an announcer in a down jacket warned people to stay off the roads. Airports were closed, he said. Cars were stranded on the Long Island Expressway.

I mumbled, "Is it morning?" Donna didn't answer. She was leaning back against the pillows with a blanket drawn over her. I studied her profile. I liked the way her nose sprang forward with a delicate arch, under the streaky blond hair that grazed her eyebrows. I said again, "Is it morning?" She ignored me. The announcer started reading a list of school closings. I got up and crossed the space between our beds, saying, "I guess it's just a fascinating program," and tried to slide in next to her under the blanket but she pulled away, taking it with her. "Hey, I'm freezing," I said. I reached for her, and again she managed not to be there. I said, "What's wrong?"

"St. Malachi's," the announcer said. "St. Anne's parochial school, St. Michael's middle school . . ."

Donna took a drag from her cigarette and stubbed it out in the ashtray on the night table. She folded her arms and stared straight ahead. "What's wrong?" I repeated, and got no answer. "Look, Donna, don't give me the silent treatment, it's childish. What's bugging you?" I looked over at the windows, but they were shrouded in heavy drapes. "Is it morning, or what?"

"It's morning."

"Good, we've established that. Progress." I moved over and reached for her.

"Don't."

"Why not? I thought we were on hugging terms. At least."

"Just don't."

I rolled back. After a while I said, "Shit." We lay side by side. The announcer finished the list of school closings and picked up a list of meetings that had been cancelled. I said, "Donna, this is extremely aggravating. Not to mention puzzling and confusing."

She reached for another cigarette. "Sorry to be confusing," she said coldly.

"Do you have to smoke? It's like a fog in here already."

"Yes, I do." She lit the cigarette, flicking her green eyes in my direction.

What the hell was the matter with her? Had something gone wrong for her, the night before? I'd have sworn the opposite was true. I went to the window and drew the curtains apart. There was a faint grayness outside. I wrestled with the catch of the window and managed to open it. The air was cold but clean, and a few snowflakes drifted in and melted on the rug. Snow was still coming down, but lightly.

"Must you open that window?"

"Yes, if you're going to smoke. What time is it?"

"Quarter of six. Our appointment with Dr. Levesque is at seven, in case you've forgotten."

"Is that's what's bugging you, that I just got up? There's plenty of time."

She didn't answer. I reminded myself we had a job to do, and whatever was bothering her, we still had to do it. "Fine, I'll shave. If you decide you want to talk, let me know." I went in the bathroom. I couldn't understand the way she was acting, but I wasn't going to get down on my knees and beg her to explain.

As I lathered my face, I went over the events of the night before, remembering the soft contours of her body and her responsiveness as I'd made love to her.

"We fit together perfectly," she'd laughed and then her body had arched under mine and her laughter had become a gasp. Of satisfaction, I'd thought. But can you ever be sure?

Soon afterwards, I'd fallen asleep.

Something had upset her, and I had no idea what.

I began to shave my chin.

The bathroom door opened. Donna appeared in a bathrobe, her green eyes half hidden under her fringe of hair. "Vic," she said. "Maybe I owe you an explanation." She didn't meet my eyes in the mirror.

"It would be nice." I didn't turn around.

"Something's bothering me."

"So it seems." I drew the razor through the lather on my left cheek.

"I don't think you'll understand."

I put down the razor and turned around. "Try me. I'm an understanding kind of guy, or so I've been told."

"It's about last night." She hesitated. "Vic, it's almost two and a half years since my divorce. And—since that time—"

If she was going to tell me she hadn't been to bed with a man, I wasn't going to believe it. The way she'd come on to me hadn't had the feeling of a first time, she'd been very much at her ease. "Well?" I said.

"I haven't had an orgasm."

Not what I'd expected.

I said, "Oh. You certainly had me fooled."

"No. That's not what I'm saying. Last night I had one. It was the first time." Her expression, which I could see in the mirror as I shaved, was tense and withdrawn.

I turned to face her. "Well, great!" I hadn't been wrong, then. "Congratulations! So how come you're mad at me?"

"I knew you wouldn't understand."

"But you should be glad! I mean, sure, it's rough you weren't able to, but now—"

"That's so typical." She turned away.

"Hey, wait! Typical of what?"

"Typical of a man. Forget it." She fished for a cigarette.

"I don't want to forget it."

"It's a great big ego trip for you, isn't it? You couldn't care less what it means to *me*!"

That shook me. Was she right? Sure I was pleased I'd pushed

the right buttons, I mean isn't that natural? But— She struck a match and I said, "I'd really prefer it if you didn't smoke."

"Well, I'd prefer it if I did." She let the match go out, though, as she said, "I guess you picked that up from your boss."

"Picked what up? It so happens I've been breathing longer than I've been working for Sabina. I like clean air."

She pushed her hair back. "You know, one of these days I may have to stop smoking, I can see it coming."

"Good. Now about last night—"

"Look. Let's forget about last night. I want to forget about it, and I want *you* to forget about it." She tossed back her hair. "It never happened, okay?"

I took a step toward her. "Donna, it happened. It was great, we both enjoyed it. I don't want to forget about it."

"Well, you'll have to!" she snapped. "I didn't intend to come last night, and I didn't want to."

"Didn't want to?"

"No! I don't want anybody having that kind of power over me, ever again!"

"For God's sake, that's ridiculous."

"Thanks a lot." Defiantly, she lit the cigarette. "I've said all I'm going to say on the subject. Last night never happened. You'd better finish shaving. I'll get dressed, we don't have forever." She turned and left the bathroom, closing the door behind her.

I finished shaving. I could understand a woman being upset if she *didn't* come, but this was a new twist.

I had a feeling that getting involved with Donna had been a big mistake. She had complicated problems, and I only hoped they weren't going to mess up the investigation in some way I couldn't foresee. Last night had been nice, in fact more than nice, but I definitely hadn't planned it and, no matter how attractive I found her, I should have remembered she was a client and kept things from getting out of hand.

Now Donna wanted us to forget that anything had happened.

The idea gave me a letdown feeling, but I could see it might be best, if we could manage it.

I came out of the bathroom. She was already dressed, in a conservative navy blue suit and a white blouse, a businesslike outfit that, I thought as I surveyed her, should have a favorable effect on Dr. Levesque. "Dressed for success, I see," I said in a neutral voice. "Very nice."

"Thank you." Her eyes avoided mine. "Now why don't we make a plan."

We made a plan.

She telephoned the psychiatrist's office to make sure he wasn't marooned somewhere because of the snow—after all, he had no way of getting in touch with her.

Dr. Levesque answered the phone himself. All his other appointments had been cancelled because of the snow, he told her, and if she wanted to cancel, too, he wouldn't charge her. She replied that she'd flown up all the way from Maryland to see him, and she intended to keep the appointment. She added that she was surprised he expected to be paid. They discussed this for a while. When she finally hung up she said, "Do you realize he's going to charge me for talking to him about Ruthann, as if it was a therapy session? He claims his time is valuable and I'm consulting him in his professional capacity. Is that reasonable?" She pushed her hair back out of her eyes, which connected with mine briefly and then slid away.

"My personal opinion? No, it's not reasonable. But you wanted to try your hand at detecting, and one of the first things a detective learns is that sometimes you have to lay out a few bucks for information. A twenty usually does the trick, though fifty isn't unusual. I have a hunch this'll cost you more."

"It's outrageous. I mean, the man's a doctor, he should *want* to talk to the relatives of a patient who dies. He should feel an *obligation!*"

"Maybe." I've never been that sure about what people should want and what obligations they should feel, but apparently Donna thought she knew. I said, "Try and look on the bright side. Maybe Blue Cross will cover it."

Nineteen

We walked to the psychiatrist's office, which was in a townhouse not far from the motel. It was easier to walk than drive, because of the snow. On the way over I said, "I have a feeling Levesque won't talk, if he knows I'm a detective. I'd better be a brother."

"He'll know Ruthann didn't have a brother."

"Brother-in-law, then. I'll be your husband—kind of a bossy, take-charge guy, protecting the little woman from the harsh realities. How's that sound?"

"Just peachy," she said. "Too sweet for words. But I guess it'll do." She gave a short laugh. "Nobody's ever protected me from the harsh realities, certainly not my husband. Not that I'd want it." I didn't say anything, and after a while she added, "Though Ruthann tried. I wouldn't let her, but she tried."

Dr. Oswald Levesque answered the door himself. He was a small, sallow man of about sixty, wearing a well-cut, dark suit that was a little too large for him, as if he'd shrunk since he'd bought it. There was a burned-out look in the eyes set deeply under his dark, bushy eyebrows. The mustache that bisected his face matched the eyebrows perfectly; they made a three-piece set, like a pair of earrings and a brooch.

He took Donna's hand, murmuring, "Mrs. MacNiece," and then glanced at me questioningly. "And this is—"

"My husband. Er—Hubert."

The doctor withdrew his hand and said, "You didn't mention you were bringing someone." His tone was reproachful.

I took a step forward and said, "I wasn't going to let my wife travel alone in this weather, Doctor. Do you have any objection?" I was half a head taller than he.

He said to Donna, ignoring me, "Why didn't you inform me?"

"Well—I never thought of it—I mean, my husband—" She was playing her part nicely.

I took her arm. "Naturally I came with my wife. This whole thing has been a terrible shock to her."

"I was sorry to hear about your sister, of course," the doctor said. "But I'd have preferred to discuss it one on one." He looked at me directly for the first time, taking his time about it as if formulating a diagnosis. "However, as long as you're here, Mr. MacNiece, let's all three of us have a chat. My office is this way."

He led us down the hall and into a spacious consulting room furnished with antiques. Despite the thick Oriental rugs, the fire burning in the fireplace, and the heavy drapes framing the windows, the room seemed cold. Motioning us toward a pair of red brocade armchairs, he went to the window and looked outside. "Ah, it's stopped snowing," he said. "Good! I happen to be a devotee of cross-country skiing, but I don't get much of a chance to indulge. However, since all my patients have cancelled . . ." He seemed more human, staring out at the snow as if he couldn't wait to get a pair of skis on his feet. The window where he was standing was actually a pair of old-fashioned

French doors that met in the middle, and there were so many layers of paint on the frames that they didn't close tightly—hence the chill in the air. The doctor must have had his concerns about security, for I noticed the narrow silver wire of a burglar alarm running down one of the panes.

After a moment he turned and sat down at the desk. Fingering his mustache, he said to Donna, "Well. As I explained to you on the phone, I don't see how I can be of assistance."

"I'm hoping there might be things you know about my sister that she didn't tell me."

He frowned. "No doubt there are. But you have to understand the doctor-patient relationship, Mrs. MacNiece. With all due respect, if there were things your sister didn't tell you, perhaps she didn't want you to know. Don't I have an obligation to consider her wishes?"

"But she's dead! She was murdered! She'd want the man who killed her to be punished."

He cleared his throat. "I know you believe that. What makes you so sure it was murder?"

I took Donna's hand. "Doctor. We've come a long way to see you. We also happen to have returned from Europe only a few days ago, and the first thing we learn is that Ruthann's death wasn't an accident." I described how Donna had found the article about Fran in the newspaper left by the tenant, and explained the similarities between the deaths of the two women, adding that we suspected the same man had killed both of them. He listened, frowning intently. I said, "Naturally, my wife is extremely upset about this. I don't want her grilled and interrogated. She's distraught." There was a box of Kleenex on the table next to Donna's chair, and she pulled one out and touched it to her eyes. "As a psychiatrist, you can understand that. What she needs from you is help—something that might enable us to trace her sister's killer."

"I doubt I can give you that kind of assistance."

Donna said, "Well—can't you tell us what was going on in the last few months of her life? I don't really know, because we'd had an argument."

"So she told me."

"It was nothing, really. We'd have made up eventually."

"Ruthann was very upset about it." There was a judgmental look in the burned-out eyes. Weren't shrinks supposed to be nonjudgmental? "She was devoted to you, you were the most important person in her life."

Donna looked stricken.

"The girls just had a spat," I said. "A tempest in a teapot. That's not what we're here to discuss, we want to know about this creep she married."

He looked at me, his nostrils flaring. "I know nothing about him."

Donna said, "But she must have mentioned him, discussed him with you."

"Your sister dropped out of therapy some time before her death," he said severely. "Prematurely, I felt. It was a great mistake, she'd been making real progress."

"What kind of progress?" said Donna. "I never saw much change in her."

"Quite possibly she didn't wish to tell you the full extent of her problems. Ruthann"—he swiveled his chair so he was facing the window—"was my patient for seven years. When she first came she had many phobias, and her condition was worsening. Planes, escalators, elevators, automobiles—any and all of them could precipitate a panic attack. This started after her divorce from her first husband. It was becoming hard for her even to leave the house, and she was terrified of becoming agoraphobic—with good reason."

Donna said in a subdued voice, "She never told me that."

"No. She wouldn't." He smoothed his mustache. "In my opinion her basic fear was of falling—of sexuality, really, becoming a 'fallen woman,' so to speak—but we needn't go into that." He paused, as if deciding how much to tell us. "She was a lonely person. It was hard for her to approach people, to initiate a conversation, that sort of thing. She isolated herself, she pushed people away."

"Including me."

"Possibly."

I said, "When you spoke to my wife on the telephone yesterday, you said you hadn't known Ruthann was dead."

"That is correct."

"But didn't you see it in the papers?"

"According to you, she remarried. I had no way of knowing her married name."

"It was Ellis. Her husband called himself Malcolm Ellis. So you say she dropped out of treatment before she remarried."

"Yes."

Too bad, I thought. What *was* it about this case, that all the most promising leads came to nothing? "Did she drop out before they started dating?"

There was a pause. Levesque nodded. His eyes were cagey.

"You're sure? She never even *mentioned* Malcolm Ellis?"

He seemed to relax a little. "I've never heard that name before today."

Donna said, "Maybe we could go through her records. There might be some little thing you've forgotten—"

Levesque's eyes flickered in the direction of a filing cabinet in the corner. "I'm sorry, Mrs. MacNiece. My records are strictly confidential, I never show them to anyone except at the direct request of a patient." He pushed back his chair as if preparing to rise.

I said; "Medical records can be subpoenaed."

"I'm aware of that, Mr. MacNiece." There was dislike in the glance he gave me, and some other emotion as well. Was it fear? I thought so—but of what? The one thing guaranteed to give the good doctor nightmares, I was pretty sure, was the idea of a malpractice claim. Could he be afraid something in his handling of the case made him vulnerable to a lawsuit? I said, "We could go to court and get her records, if necessary."

Donna said, "Wasn't there *anybody* she'd dated that you knew of?"

He smoothed his mustache with his index finger, while his heavy lids drooped to conceal his eyes. The skin beneath them was puffy and grayish. He sighed. "Well—there was a man. He's the only one I know of." He paused. "As I said before, Ruthann had made progress in overcoming her phobias—so much so, that she went to a meeting of the National Association of Social Workers in Toronto, which she'd have been quite unable to do prior to treatment. While she was there she had a few dates with a man she met at the conference. However, since he lived in—Detroit, I believe it was—it never developed into anything serious. On the whole it was a positive experience, however, and she became quite eager to meet men."

I said, "Are you sure she stopped seeing the man she met in Toronto?"

"That was my impression."

"What do you know about him?"

"He'd presented a paper at the meeting. A widower, I believe she said. He was about her own age." Dr. Levesque was suddenly bubbling over with information.

Donna said, "Ruthann told me she met Malcolm Ellis by striking up a conversation while he was out walking his dog. Do you think that's likely?"

The doctor shook his head. "Oh no, I would doubt it very much. That was just the sort of thing she found most difficult." He pushed back his chair and added, "Poor thing." He rose, and came around from behind his desk. "I'm afraid I really have no more information to give you."

We stood up. I said, "Did she tell you the name of the man she dated in Toronto?"

"You're very persistent, Mr. MacNiece. The answer is no." He opened the door and we followed him out of the office and down the hall.

"You're positive? It couldn't have been Malcolm Ellis?"

He didn't bother to keep the annoyance out of his voice. "As for 'positive,' I can't say. But I doubt it." To Donna he remarked, "Your sister didn't mention you were married, in fact I seem to recall her telling me you were divorced."

"Oh, I was." Donna slipped her hand through my arm.

143

"Hubert and I are newlyweds. We met in Rome." She gave me an adoring smile.

"Darling," I murmured, patting her hand.

She tossed back her hair. "Uh, Dr. Levesque."

"Yes." We'd reached the door. He placed his hand on the knob.

"Ruthann told me she was going to put an ad in the Personals."

Good for Donna, I thought.

He looked startled, and then the gray lids came down and hooded his eyes. "I know nothing whatsoever about that."

"But she said she discussed it with you."

"She did no such thing, and if she said so she was lying." We had reached the front door and he opened it. "Good-bye, Mrs. MacNiece. And Mr. MacNiece. I'm afraid I can't spare any more time."

Twenty

 We walked back to the motel. It had stopped snowing, and the sun was struggling to break through the clouds. I said, "You did great."

"Thanks." She tossed the hair back out of her eyes. "You see? I have natural talent. I must say I didn't care much for Ruthann's doctor—he's a cold fish. And he knows more than he's telling. Don't you think so?"

"Most people do, Donna. By the way, that was a nice try about the Personals, too bad it didn't pan out. Still, we might be able to trace the guy she met at the meeting in Toronto."

She shook her head. "*He* wasn't Malcolm Ellis, Dr. Levesque said she only went out with him a few times. *I* still think she met Ellis through the Personals, and I bet Levesque knows all about it."

"He denied it, Donna. In no uncertain terms."

She gave me a disgusted look. "And you *believed* him?"

"You believed him when he said Ruthann only went out a few times with the guy in Toronto."

We walked for a while in silence. Finally she said, "Okay, Hubert, I have an idea. What we need to do is find out what's in Ruthann's file."

"Subpoena it, you mean?"

"Of course not. If there's something in the file Levesque doesn't want us to see, he'd simply remove it."

"That's against the law. Supposedly, he's an ethical practitioner."

"But who would know, if he took something out of the file?" She gave me a sidelong look with those green eyes. "We have to find another way."

"We could hire a psychic."

"Very funny." She wasn't amused but she smiled anyway, winningly. "You'll just have to break in and get it, Vic. Levesque's going skiing. Once he's gone—"

"Now wait a minute."

"It won't be hard, you can—"

We were about to cross the street. I put my hand on her arm and said, "Donna. Ms. MacNiece. The answer is no. Forget it."

She took a step backward and looked up at me. "What do you mean, no? Are you working for me or aren't you?"

"Actually, I'm working for Sabina. The answer is no, because I don't care to lose my license."

She shrugged as if that were a technicality, and started across the street. I followed her. She said, "It shouldn't be hard to open those French doors. You'll be in and out in five minutes." She laughed. "Like having a wart removed."

"N. O. No."

"Then I'll do it."

"You will not do it."

"I told you I wanted to help with the investigation. This can be my next assignment."

"Donna, there is no next assignment."

She stopped. "What do you mean?"

"Sabina says no." I shook my head. "For you to talk to Levesque made sense. We couldn't have gotten to him otherwise. But that was an exception. Please forget the idea."

She scooped up a handful of snow and began packing it into a ball. "No. That's not acceptable."

"I'm sorry, that's how it is. We're dealing with a killer, Donna. We don't know where he is, or what it would take to stir him up—suppose you start poking around and he gets wind of it? I'm serious. This is an ironclad rule of Sabina's."

She tossed her head. "It's my money. Doesn't that give me a say in the matter?"

"Listen, we had a client once named Lawrence Schwartz. Owned a chain of auto body shops in northern Virginia. Suspected that someone in his employ was using the facilities to process stolen cars. He hired us, but he also decided to do a little investigating on his own. He ended up in the trunk of a Pontiac with his throat cut. Sabina was very upset."

She swallowed. "Still—this isn't a comparable situation. There must be loose ends I could follow up, little odds and ends—"

I was losing my patience. "Odds and ends? What odds and ends? This case doesn't have any—everything fizzles out. This is a tough case, Donna. The guy we're looking for is a psychopath. He moves around. He's here and then he disappears. This isn't like investigating a crime where you know who the suspects are, and pretty much *where* they are, and they're gonna stay put while you decide which one's the guilty party because they've got jobs, they've got families, they've got roots." I shook my head. "If you want to know the truth, I'm beginning to doubt we'll *ever* find this guy." Was that true, was I really that pessimistic about the case?

"But there must be something—"

"Sure. There's something. There's a guy from Detroit, a social worker who said he was a widower—maybe he was and maybe he wasn't, guys have been known to say all kinds of things when they're away from home—who attended a convention of the National Association of Social Workers in

Toronto a few years ago. I might be able to trace him and I intend to try, because that's my job. But it's not yours. You're the client, Donna. That's a fact of life, so face it."

She raised the hand with the snowball in it, and I thought she was going to smash it in my face. "Damn you!" she said, and threw it hard at a stop sign. She turned and stalked away.

"Where are you going?"

"None of your business. Back to the motel. I'm going to talk to Sabina directly."

"Fine. Lots of luck." I hurried after her. "You can tell her what a rotten spoilsport I am."

"I don't know why you're being so nasty." I didn't answer. What was the matter with me, why had I said all that stuff about how hopeless the case looked? You don't say that to a client. I caught up with her and took her arm. She jerked away saying, "Actually, I do know. It's because we made it—once! Now I'm supposed to do whatever you tell me. I'm supposed to say, 'Yes, dear.' Well, you can forget that." I tried to help her over a snowbank, and she snapped, "I can manage."

"Since you bring up last night," I said. "Did you or didn't you enjoy it?"

"So what if I did? That's not the point. You don't really care if I enjoyed it, not how *I* felt; what you care about is how you *performed*. Whether you were *great*." She glared at me. What she said wasn't true, but there was just enough truth in it so I didn't know how to answer. She said, "Look, I didn't *like* that I enjoyed it. That never occurred to you, did it? Well, I didn't. It—scared me."

"Why should it scare you, Donna? I mean, I can understand if you feel vulnerable but—hell, I wouldn't hurt you."

She turned to face me. "Please. Don't be nice. Don't be understanding. Okay? I'm not ready to get involved with a man, not *involved*, and I don't know if I ever will be. So nothing happened. *Nothing!* Get that through your head." We had reached the motel. As we walked through the door she muttered. "Maybe I should just go to the police."

148

*　　*　　*

I called Sabina from the motel and gave her a full description
of our session with Dr. Levesque. She agreed it made sense to
try and trace the guy Ruthann had dated at the meeting, though
she didn't sound excited about the idea. She agreed with me
that breaking into the doctor's office wasn't a good idea. Then
she instructed me to send the client back to the Eastern Shore,
and to come to Bruno's apartment near Columbia.

Next Donna got on the line and tried to talk Sabina into
letting her help with the investigation. She tried wheedling and
when that didn't work she started hinting around about firing
us, though she didn't come right out and say it; by the time she
hung up she was looking grim.

I'd already thrown my toothbrush and pajamas into my bag,
so I went down to the lobby to take care of the checkout, warning Donna to hurry with her packing so we could catch the next
train.

But when I came back to the room there was no sign of her,
except for a note on the table that said, "So long, Vic, maybe
I'll see you in Washington. I prefer to arrange my own transportation, Donna."

Twenty-one

I took the subway uptown to 116th Street, feeling sick to my stomach. Was I coming down with the flu, or was this a reaction to losing Sabina a client? Donna, I felt sure, would go home to the family mansion on the Eastern Shore, build a fire in the fireplace, think things over, give the police a call, and then tell us to send her a bill and get lost. And I knew whose fault that was. I'd behaved unprofessionally. I'd lost my cool. And the reason was—there was no getting around it—that I'd had sex with a very attractive but mixed-up lady who just happened to be our client. A mistake I'd never made before—the client part, at least. I could imagine Sabina's reaction when she found out, as she probably would; maybe I even had some kind of obligation to tell her. I should have remembered that Rule One of the detective business is: Never get emotionally involved with the client.

The train reached 116th Street. I got out and headed down the hill toward Riverside Drive. Less snow had fallen here than out on the Island, but it felt as if the wind knifing up from the river was trying to cut my throat.

Was that what I'd been, emotionally involved?

Maybe I wasn't cut out to be a detective. I wasn't hard-boiled enough. No matter how hard I tried, I still seemed to have this soft, runny center.

Could I find another way to make a living, though? Sure, I'd had a fantasy for a long time of going to graduate school and studying psychology, becoming a shrink. But did I really want to be one (even if I could afford the tuition, which at the moment was out of the question)? I thought of the pink, harassed face of Dr. Nordholm at Ruthann's agency, of the guarded, burned-out eyes of Dr. Levesque. Was that for me?

And I thought of Sabina, who'd been good to me in her own weird way, and who—though she didn't know it yet—was most likely about to fire me. Why shouldn't she? I deserved it.

I took the ancient elevator up to the twelfth floor of Bruno's building, and rang the doorbell. I dreaded the moment when I would have to confront Sabina, who could usually read my face. But it was Bruno who came to the door.

"Vic, you made it! Come in!" He clapped me on the back and led me into the living room, with its spectacular view of the Hudson River and the Palisades. In his hand he was holding a chess column he'd torn out of the *New York Times*. He sat down in front of a chessboard by the window, and I could see he'd been playing over a game by himself. The apartment, as usual, was a mass of papers, crumbs, piled books, old newspapers, and odds and ends of clothing. It always amazes me that Sabina can't seem to get Bruno to shape up in the housekeeping department. Bruno knows how to take evasive action.

"Where's Sabina?" I said.

"Zabar's."

"Yum-yum."

"She'll be back any minute. Then we'll have lunch." He

studied me and his eyes grew concerned. "Vic," he said, "You don't look good."

"I'm fine."

"You're not fine."

"No, no, I'm fine. I'm about to get fired, otherwise I'm fine."

"You? Don't talk nonsense." He looked alarmed. "Sabina could never fire you, without you she'd be impossible to live with."

"You think so? You really think she wouldn't fire me?" He nodded. "But you don't know what I did. I lost her a client."

"Is this the case with the terrible man who killed your friend? Yes? I'll tell you the truth, I don't like that case. It upsets her. She was up all night, couldn't sleep."

"Well, I lost the client, I'm pretty sure of it. And I did it in a really stupid way. I—well, I got too involved with her."

"Oh yes, the client is a woman." He hitched himself a couple of inches closer. "Young? Attractive?"

"Very attractive. Not that young."

"Still—attractive. A blonde, a brunette? Nice figure?" His hands made a curvy shape in the air, and he winked at me. "Were you . . . you know," he glanced quickly over his shoulder as if to make sure Sabina really wasn't around, and lowered his voice, "*intimate*?"

Bruno is the only man I know who uses the word "intimate" when he means sex.

"Yes." I shook my head. "I could kick myself. Talk about dumb things to do!"

"We all make mistakes, Vic."

"I'll have to tell Sabina."

"No, no."

"I think she has a right to know."

"No, whatever you do, don't tell her."

"I may have lost her a lot of money."

"So? She'll have other cases. She's well known. Easy come, easy go."

I had to laugh. "She won't see it that way."

152

He shrugged. "She'll get over it. I wouldn't tell her."

"She'll guess anyway."

"Guessing isn't the same as knowing. Listen to me, Vic." He hitched himself still closer. "First"—he tapped his index finger on the chessboard—"you're not sure you lost the client."

"I feel it."

"Feeling isn't the same as knowing. Second"—middle finger—"even if she *does* fire Sabina, you don't know it's because you were"—he lowered his voice again—"intimate. There could be other reasons."

"It's true she was pissed because she wanted to play detective and Sabina wouldn't let her."

"See? She could have a thousand reasons. Things you know nothing about. So keep your mouth shut. Wait and see what happens. Learn a lesson from this experience and, ah"—he hesitated and added regretfully—"don't do it again."

I could see he had a point, in fact several. "Well—okay, I'll keep quiet. But she'll know."

He picked up the chess clipping. "Never mind. Sabina's a very smart woman, but"—he tapped his forehead—"I'm no dummy either. Most of the things people worry about don't happen. That's my philosophy and I've heard worse. Oh, and before I forget, don't ask her about that visit she made to the bank. She said they gave her a royal runaround. No, I definitely wouldn't mention it."

"Okay."

Sabina turned up twenty minutes later, carrying two enormous shopping bags and wearing an expression of satisfaction. "They claimed the onion rye had been baked this morning," she announced as she walked through the door. "But I finally got them to admit it was really last night. It was so obvious it was pathetic. The crust had dimples. Hello Bruno, hello Vic, I hope you're hungry."

"If you went to Zabar's, we're hungry by definition." Actually—to my surprise after the queasiness I'd felt earlier—I did have an appetite.

"Fine. Vic, come with me in the kitchen in case you have anything further to report. Bruno, you set the table. Did you take out the garbage?"

"I forgot."

"Well, do it now. No—first, I brought you a present."

Hauling a box out of one of the shopping bags, she handed it to him. Pleased, he opened it and took out a plastic cylinder with a slot through which a brush protruded. His brow furrowed. "What is it?"

"It's called a silent butler."

"And it has some function?" Intrigued, he turned the object around in his hands.

"You run it over the table after you eat and it collects the crumbs."

"This little thing? Amazing. Let me try it. But wait, there are no crumbs."

"There will be. I guarantee it."

He looked contrite. "I know I'm not a neat eater. I've never understood how you eat so neatly, Sabina."

"That doesn't matter," she said. "Don't worry about it, you have a silent butler now." She turned and went into the kitchen and I followed.

"I take it that troublesome young woman went home," she said as she unloaded her bags on the kitchen table. "Home is the best place for her. Did you see what happened when I made an exception to my rule and let her help with the case? Did you hear her on the phone? She took advantage right away. It only proves my policy is correct." She took out a baking dish and set it down with a bang on the sink. "I don't need another Schwartz, I prefer my clients alive."

"What are those?" I said.

"Squabs stuffed with chestnuts. We'll heat them up."

"About the client—"

"What about her? As long as you're standing around doing nothing, clean those endives."

"Sure." I took the endives over to the sink.

"Well? What about the client?"

I remembered Bruno's advice. "Nothing. Forget it."

She gave me a suspicious glance as I rinsed the grit out of the endives. Then she shrugged and dumped what looked like pasta primavera into a red casserole. The telephone rang. She called, "Bruno, would you answer that?" and slid the casserole into the oven.

I said, "Do you want the endives sliced as well as washed?"

From the living room Bruno called, "Sabina, it's for you."

She went into the living room and I heard her say, "Hello?" A silence followed. Then she squawked, *"What?* You're *where?"* There was another silence, a longer one, and then, *"Victor!* Get in here!"

I dropped the endives and headed out the kitchen door. She was standing by the telephone with the receiver glued to her ear, listening intently and scribbling notes on a pad while Bruno hovered worriedly behind her. The look she drilled me with let me know I was in big trouble. She said into the receiver, "You remember what I told you on the phone? You didn't want to listen, you thought you knew better. Now you see why." She listened some more. Every now and then she screeched, "Calm down!" Once she said, "You did? No, don't say anything more over the phone." After a while she said in a calmer voice, "Ms. MacNiece, I have grasped the situation. Just stay put and don't make any further statements. Yes, yes, I know you have to stay put, that was a figure of speech. Say nothing except that you want to talk to your lawyer. Do you have a lawyer?" She listened to the reply, shaking her head. "That won't do, you're in New York and you need a New York lawyer." By now I had a good idea of what the problem was, so when Sabina laid her hand over the receiver and hissed at me, "The client is in jail!" I wasn't surprised. "What's the name of that lawyer out on the Island we once used?"

Bruno said, "I'll find it." He went in his study and came back in a moment carrying a piece of paper; even though his study is a mess, he manages to lay his hand on anything he needs.

"Good." Sabina took the paper and gave the client the

name of the lawyer, saying, "Don't worry, I'm sure he'll be there shortly. And Vic will pick you up." She hung up and said to Bruno, "Call the lawyer, please. Tell him our client Donna MacNiece is in jail in Stony Brook, accused of breaking into the office of Dr. Oswald Levesque. Here are the particulars." She handed him the notes she'd been making, and he started to dial. "Tell him to arrange for bail, but not to let her leave the jail until Vic gets there." Then she turned to me.

I said, "You mean I have to go to Stony Brook *again*? I just came from there."

She gave me a stern look. "Victor. I thought you said the client went home."

"Sabina, I—"

"Here I am cooking, and our client is languishing in jail! Do you think that's going to look good when it gets out? How could you let a client of mine go to jail?"

"I didn't *let* her! I knew nothing about it."

"Why not? You should have! Can't you control a client? This one was troublesome, we knew she wanted to play detective— you should have kept your eyes on her and made *sure* she went home, instead of leaving her in Stony Brook to burgle doctors' offices. This is sheer incompetence."

Bruno, who was talking to the lawyer on the phone, covered the receiver and said, "Sabina, don't get excited."

I protested, "That's unfair! How could I know what she had in mind? She didn't confide in me. I went down to check out of the motel, and when I got back upstairs she was gone. She left a note saying she'd decided to make her own arrangements about transportation. I mean, she had a right to, if she wanted. There was nothing in the note about burgling Levesque's office."

Bruno covered the receiver again and said, "Did the client find anything?"

"Actually, yes."

"Oh, yeah? What?" I said.

"I don't know. Something in her sister's records, I gather; she mentioned a filing cabinet. I told her not to go into details on the phone." She sighed deeply. "Presumably she broke into the cabinet as well as the office. Clients!" She shook her head. "Get your coat on, Vic. You're to accompany her here from the police station, as soon as bail is arranged. Remember, I don't want this woman running loose on Long Island."

"But what about the lunch from Zabar's?" By now I could smell the chestnuts the squabs were stuffed with.

She snapped, "I have nothing from Zabar's for you, Victor. Nothing!"

Twenty-two

"Do you at least admit it wasn't a good idea?"

Donna and I were leaving the police station, and the Long Island lawyer was retrieving his car from the parking lot so he could drop us off at the train.

"Oh, all right, so it had its down side."

"You call being caught red-handed on the premises of a prominent citizen, dragged into a police car with cuffs around your wrists, charged with breaking and entering, thrown in a freezing cell, and obliged to post two thousand dollars' bail—not to mention getting me bawled out by Sabina and practically starving me to death—the *down side*?"

"You're hungry? You want to stop for lunch?"

"Definitely not, I'm taking you straight back to New York." I repeated, "You call that the down side?"

"I'd call that the down side, yes."

"The up side better be good."

"It is."

"Well?"

The lawyer's car pulled up and we got in. On the way to the railroad station we discussed whether Dr. Levesque could be persuaded to drop the charges.

There was barely time to buy tickets before the train pulled in, but I managed it without losing sight of Donna; then I shepherded her to the club car where we ordered cocktails. I was becoming a connoisseur of Long Island Railroad trains—this was my third in one day—and, drinks in hand, I found us a comfortable, well-heated car, and two end seats where we could put our feet up.

"Okay," I said. "Let's hear the whole story. Don't forget the up side."

"You shouldn't drink if you haven't eaten."

"Never mind. The story."

She sighed. "Oh, all right. I suppose I did miscalculate a bit. What happened was this. After I left the motel room I waited a while and then walked back to Dr. Levesque's office. I figured by then he'd have gone skiing. I was right. At least, he wasn't home." She paused, and crossed her long legs. She'd changed back into the sweater and the narrow black pants she'd worn the day before. For a woman who'd just been through a harrowing ordeal she seemed remarkably perky—in fact she looked as if she was enjoying herself. Sabina wasn't going to like that. Donna took a pack of Marlboros from her handbag and shook out a cigarette.

I said, "This is a nonsmoking car."

"Oh shit. Let's move."

"No, these are choice seats. Go on with what happened."

She put the cigarette away. "I sneaked around to the back of the house."

"Because you'd noticed the French doors didn't close too well? And did you also happen to notice a thin wire running across one of the panes?"

She frowned. "Thin wire?"

"The burglar alarm."

"Oh." The green eyes widened. "So that's how the police knew I was there."

"That's how. I'm afraid you don't have a real aptitude for detective work, Donna. How'd you get the French doors open?"

"I just kept prying away at the lock with my VISA card."

"And while you were prying away, the vibrations were setting off an alarm at the police station. Okay, so finally you got in."

She nodded, started to take out her cigarettes again, remembered, and left them in her bag. It occurred to me that if I spent enough time with her I could break her of the habit. "I figured Ruthann's records were in the filing cabinet, but it was locked. I couldn't get it open with the credit card, so I used the poker from the fireplace. I found Ruthann's file and was looking through it when the police burst in. With drawn guns, Vic! That was a bit excessive, don't you think? Though I have to admit they were fairly decent once we started talking—not that they were *nice*, exactly, but they didn't beat me up or anything. They were polite. I pretended I was one of Dr. Levesque's patients and I had this obsession about the notes he made in our sessions. You know, I *had* to find out what he was writing down about me—I figured if the police thought I was kind of nutsy they might let me go. But they didn't. Maybe I shouldn't have lied to them."

"Honesty is the best policy, Donna. And crime does not pay. Now that we've got that out of the way, what's the up side?"

She looked out the window. "I don't know if I should tell you," she said musingly. "Maybe I should wait and tell Sabina."

"Why not tell me now, and tell her when we get to New York?"

She shook her head. "I don't like what you said about my not having an aptitude for detective work. I think I did very well on my first try."

"Your first and last try. And wait till you hear what *Sabina* says." She shrugged and stood up. "I'm going to find a smoking car."

"Must you? Because I'll have to come along, and I'd rather breathe clean air."

"Then stay here. I don't remember asking you to come with me."

"I can't stay here. Orders."

The green eyes flashed. "Oh, that's ridiculous! I'm your client, not your prisoner."

"Orders are orders."

She turned and flounced away, or at least it was as close to a flounce as you can get on a Long Island Railroad train in motion. Sighing, I got up and followed.

Once we got to the apartment, Sabina let her have it. "Those policemen had guns, Ms. MacNiece. Guns can go off." We were in the living room; across the river a blood-red sun was sinking behind the Palisades. Sabina was standing with her back to the windows, her hands on her hips. "I want you to realize this is not a game, it's a business that can turn deadly serious, *tragically* serious, from one moment to the next. I feel a responsibility to you as my client, but if you put me in a position where I can't fulfill my responsibility I'll have to resign from the case. Is that what you want?" Donna, her cheeks flushed, was perched on a stool, looking guilty. "Well? *Do* you want that? Because I'm perfectly prepared to return your retainer." She took a check from her pocket and held it out.

"No, don't do that."

Sabina took a step closer. "Please be absolutely clear in your own mind about your priorities, Ms. MacNiece. Do you want to find the murderer of your sister, or do you want to become a detective? If it's the latter, I can give you a reading list of books on criminology."

They stared at each other. Then Donna looked away, saying, "Find Ruthann's murderer. That's my top priority. Believe me, Sabina, all I wanted to do was help."

"You meant well, I realize that. Still, I must have your promise that you won't do this sort of thing again. Without that I won't proceed."

Reluctantly, Donna said, "I promise. Put the check away."

Sabina studied Donna's face and then nodded. "All right." She returned the check to her pocket. "Now, if you please, tell me what you found when you broke into Dr. Levesque's office."

Donna straightened her back. "You remember I had a feeling Ruthann met her husband through the Personals? Well, I was right. At least, she did run an ad. I skimmed through the notes toward the end of the chart, and she and Dr. Levesque discussed it in several sessions. I'm not sure whose idea it was in the first place. His, maybe. Anyway"—she paused, then said with a note of triumph in her voice—"I found a draft of the ad."

"*Did* you." Sabina nodded in my direction, and I began making notes. "Do you have it in your possession, by any chance?"

Donna shook her head. "Not anymore. I did remove it from the chart, but when the police came, they took it away from me."

"Do you remember what it said?"

Donna gazed thoughtfully into space. "Maybe not word for word. I could get pretty close."

"Vic, give Ms. MacNiece a pencil and paper. Ms. MacNiece, I'd like you to try and write down exactly what you saw. What I want you to do is close your eyes and see if you can recall it. Don't *think*, exactly; just try and *visualize* the page, as if you were looking at a picture."

Donna closed her eyes. We waited. "Okay," she said finally. "I can see it." She opened her eyes and began writing. When she was done, she handed the page to Sabina. "That's it, I think."

Sabina took it and I looked over her shoulder as she read it.

DWF—40ish, slim, social worker, no dependents, seeking to share quiet times with successful professional S/W/DM with varied interests. Goal: companionship, permanent possibilities.

Sabina said, "DWF—that's 'divorced white female,' I suppose. And 'S/W/DM' is 'single, widowed, or divorced man.' How accurate do you think this is?"

"I'd say close to a hundred percent. I was surprised I could visualize it that clearly."

"The ad included the words, 'social worker?'"

"Oh yes, I'm positive."

"And 'permanent possibilities'?"

Donna nodded. "That was there." She added with a catch in her voice, "Poor Ruthann. She didn't know *how* permanent."

"This may be helpful, Ms. MacNiece. Nevertheless—no more games, remember."

"I promised, and I keep my promises. You know, I don't see why Dr. Levesque didn't tell us she'd run an ad, when I asked him specifically."

"We can't be sure. I gather from Vic that he worries about malpractice suits—not altogether unrealistically, since lawsuits against doctors have gotten completely out of hand. Or perhaps he's been sued in the past. We don't know. He may have felt that if he advised a patient to advertise, and by that means she met a man who subsequently killed her, it might be actionable. I doubt that it would be—after all, your sister was an adult, capable of using her own judgment—but he may have been unsure and therefore denied it when you asked him point-blank."

"But where does this take us?" I said. "So what if she met him through the Personals."

"At the moment, nowhere. Eventually it may prove helpful. Ms. MacNiece, was there anything in the chart, anything at all, about any of the men your sister might have met through the ad?"

"Not really. The notes on her last session said, 'replies to ad,' but without going into details."

"In other words, responses had started to come in. Was that the last notation in her chart?"

"Yes, except that she made three more appointments with Dr. Levesque and cancelled all of them."

"So Ruthann placed the ad, received replies, and then dropped out of treatment. It seems likely that she met a man she felt attracted to, started going out with him, and then decided she didn't need therapy any more."

I said, "What about the guy she dated in Toronto? I still feel he might have been the one."

"I haven't forgotten him, Vic. I plan to make inquiries at the headquarters of the National Association of Social Workers, as soon as we get back to Washington." She turned to face the window and stood gazing out toward the Palisades. "As for you, I have a different assignment in mind." A barge with twinkling lights floated past, heading downriver. Beyond it, darkness was settling over New Jersey. "There are more than two," she muttered, sounding more as if she were talking to herself than to me. "There must be. We have to find them."

Twenty-three

It felt good to be back in Bowie, in my own house and my own bed. I slept soundly—overslept, in fact, and when I opened my eyes it was half past ten and I was in danger of being late for my appointment with a guy named Arnold Spinks. I didn't figure it really mattered. "I'm here most of the time," he'd said when I'd telephoned him.

That was the assignment Sabina had given me—to get in touch with Spinks and find out whether he happened to know of any other middle-aged women who'd died the same way as Fran and Ruthann. Spinks was the president of Citizens for Safety, the group that was lobbying for railway crossing gates in Maryland.

I dressed, downed a cup of instant coffee, and left the house. Across the road, Paul Geissdorf was shoveling every last flake of snow off the sidewalk in front of his house. He'd been released from the state hospital a couple of months earlier. As I headed for my car, he waved and called, "Morning, Victor!"

I was stunned. It was the first time I'd ever received a civil greeting from the man. What had gotten into him? Something they'd prescribed at Crownsville, most likely.

Waving back, I called, "Morning, Mr. Geissdorf!" and slid behind the wheel. I revved up and drove down Cinnamon Lane, trying to remember whether I'd ever addressed the man by name before; maybe long ago when I used to play with his kids? I didn't think so. I'd spoken to his wife. *Him*, I'd always avoided.

Once I left Bowie, all the roads were free of snow and I drove to Riverdale, where Spinks lived, without needing to pay much attention. My thoughts drifted off to Donna MacNiece. She'd hurt my feelings, I decided with a sudden brilliant flash of insight. Yep, that was it. She was supposed to have been so overwhelmed by my lovemaking that she would—well, what? Fall madly in love with me, something like that?

And I'd worried about *her* expectations?

It was just as well we hadn't gotten further entangled, I decided. I felt attracted to her, there was no denying it, but that didn't change the fact she wasn't ready to get involved with anyone right now—that's what she'd said, and it might be smart to take her word for it. The emptiness I felt at this thought was mixed with relief. Maybe some day things would work out with Donna. Maybe not. Either way, I had a hunch I was going to survive.

The house where Arnold Spinks lived wasn't what a realtor would call a desirable residence. It sat right on Route 1 near a big, messy, commercial intersection, and had a decrepit, neglected look. It seemed to have been subdivided into several separate apartments at some time in the past. The entrance to Spinks's apartment was in the back.

I rang and he came to the door. He was a stooped, skinny, mild-looking man with long white hair, the kind of long hair that doesn't make any kind of a statement but just happens to be there because its owner hasn't remembered to get it cut. He was

166

wearing clean, worn, wrinkled chinos, an embroidered cotton shirt from India, leather sandals, and spotless white socks. Blinking at me weakly through pink-rimmed eyes, as if he hadn't been outside the house in a long time, he said, "You're Mr. Newman?" His weak, mild voice matched the rest of him. "Come in."

I followed him into a living room that looked like an office: bookshelves and filing cabinets; a computer and a couple of printers; even a Xerox machine. There was no sign that a woman lived anywhere on the premises. Anyway, Spinks didn't look like a man who had a wife.

He motioned me to a plastic office chair, and sat down himself in another one just like it. They were the only chairs in the room.

"So" he said. "You're interested in railway crossing safety."

"In a way, Mr. Spinks. And I gather you're the local authority on the subject."

"I gather I am," he said, sounding kind of surprised to be an authority on anything. "But you know, anybody who devotes all his time to one subject is pretty much bound to become an expert."

"And that's what you do?"

He nodded. "Since my boy Lenny was killed, that's right." His eyes drifted to a longbow and a quiver of arrows mounted on the wall above a bookcase. On top of the bookcase there was a row of archery trophies I hadn't noticed before. "That's what I do day and night, you might say. I seldom go out. Except when the legislature is in session. You like to give us a hand?" The pink-rimmed eyes blinked hopefully. "We can always use people in Annapolis to buttonhole legislators. Just give what time you can spare. One morning a week? One morning a month?"

"I'm really sorry, Mr. Spinks. I can't. That isn't why I came."

He sighed. "Oh, well. People are so busy." I wondered how many active members there were in his organization. "I guess you want *me* to help *you*. Well, how? I'm willing. Helping you might help me—know what I mean?"

167

"That's possible, come to think of it," I said.

"It's called enlightened self-interest. What would you like to know?"

"Do you keep records of railway crossing accidents?"

"Certainly. The Federal Railroad Administration puts out statistics. And we have what you might call an informal network. Friends. Friends of friends. The word gets around that I'm interested. People from all over the country send me items from their local paper, if they think of it. I keep the clippings on file."

That sounded promising. I said, "This may sound like a funny question, but do you remember hearing of any middle-aged women who happened to have been alone in their cars on the railroad tracks when a train came along and killed them?"

He fastened his mild, pink-rimmed gaze on me, and I got the feeling that not much escaped his notice once his interest was aroused. After a while he remarked, "There was one last summer. Bowie woman."

"Fran Browdy," I said. "I knew her." He looked interested. "Know of any others?"

Arnold Spinks blinked a couple of times. The Adam's apple in his scrawny neck rose and fell. "Sondra Turette. July 1981."

"That's a while ago. I'm surprised you remember the name without looking it up."

"I should." His eyes wandered to the archery trophies. "Sondra Turette died only a month after my son and his friends were killed. She was my first, you might say. If you don't count *them*. It was when I heard about her death that I got the idea of starting the CFS. Now it's my life." He said it matter-of-factly. "You interested in Sondra Turette? She was a social worker at Johns Hopkins."

Another social worker! Sabina was right! I said, "I'm interested."

"Student placement, actually," Spinks went on. "But she was no kid. She'd gone back to school at the age of forty or thereabouts. Makes you think there must have been something unusual about her, doesn't it? Kind of a waste. Another thing—"

I had an idea I knew what was coming.

"She'd gotten married only a short time before she was killed." He paused, while a speculative look came into his mild eyes. "Funny thing—that Bowie woman hadn't been married long, either." His expression grew worried. "Odd, don't you think? I've been meaning to check back—" He waved vaguely toward the filing cabinet. "Been too busy, though. We've got a bill in committee. So. Maybe *that's* why you're here." The pink-rimmed eyes gazed thoughtfully into mine.

"That's why I'm here. But I hope you'll keep it to yourself." And I explained to him about the investigation we were engaged in, while he listened intently and made a few notes. He was especially interested in Ruthann Duncan's death on Long Island, which he hadn't heard of.

"See?" he said when I'd finished, and there was a hint of animation in his whispery voice. "What did I tell you about enlightened self-interest? This could add a whole new dimension to our lobbying campaign—unguarded railroad crossings serving as an invitation to murder!" He added regretfully, "Too bad you didn't come and see me before I got the newsletter pasted up."

"Wait a minute, Mr. Spinks. We wouldn't want any publicity. Not right now."

"Why not?" A gentle stubbornness settled around his jaw. "The timing couldn't be better. Our bill should be coming up for a vote in committee in about ten days."

"But we're tracking a killer, Mr. Spinks. If he finds out we're after him we may not catch him."

Spinks shook his head. "The greatest good for the greatest number, Mr. Newman. Care to stay for lunch?"

I had a feeling it wouldn't do any good to try and pressure him. "Okay. Sure. Ah—what do you mean, the greatest good for the greatest number?"

He cleared a space for us to eat, gathering up the papers spread out on the table and stacking them in a pile. "We regard this bill as a piece of model legislation. We're hoping that, once Maryland passes it, certain other states will do the same."

"Who wrote the bill?"

"I did." That didn't surprise me. He went into the kitchen and returned in a moment with a handful of eggs and a jar of mayonnaise. "You might say, 'Why Maryland?' and you'd be right. Accidents at railroad crossings are a bigger problem in some of the other states." He brought out a bowl of apples, a couple of napkins, a can of string beans, a can opener, and two forks. "However, Maryland is where I happen to live. You have to start someplace." He opened the can of string beans and then pulled a garbage can up to the table. "Let's eat," he said.

The eggs were hard-boiled. We cracked them on the table and dropped the shells directly into the garbage can.

"Saves a lot of time," said Spinks. "I try to avoid using plates. You'd be surprised how much time people waste washing dishes. Inefficient. Not to mention the waste of water." He dipped his egg into the mayonnaise jar. "I like a little mayonnaise on a hard-boiled egg. Help yourself if you want some."

I dipped my egg into the jar and thought about the lunch from Zabar's I'd missed out on yesterday. Riverdale, MD, and Riverside Drive might have existed on separate planets, and not just in the food department.

"Sometimes I miss tuna fish. I'm a vegetarian but, I don't know, canned tuna seems like kind of a gray area." He ate a string bean from the can. "That's not really logical, I know." He ate another string bean. "Still, I might go back to tuna fish. Have some string beans."

"Thanks." I forked a couple out of the can.

"Nice to have company." His eyes drifted off to the archery trophies. "You know a funny thing? The only person I ever hit in my life was the one I loved best." He shook his head. "I try to be nonviolent, but—" He shook it again, looking baffled. "My son gravitated toward violent sports, for some reason. Hockey, football, motorcycles— It used to bother me, I just couldn't understand it. We had a lot of arguments." The weak eyes blinked moistly. Spinks helped himself to a spotty-looking apple. "Organic," he pointed out. He took a bite and chewed it. "I was a conscientious objector in World War II."

"Did you go to jail?"

He nodded.

"Was it bad?"

"Not too bad. After a while they let us work as medical orderlies."

We ate a couple of apples apiece. They were quite tasty.

After we had finished, Spinks tossed the empty string bean can in the garbage can. He rubbed the table with his napkin and tossed the napkin in the trash. I threw mine in, too. "Two forks to wash," he said, sounding pleased. "That's all. If you hadn't been here I wouldn't even have bothered with a fork."

"It's—efficient. Like you said."

"More people should try it." He carried the mayonnaise jar, the can opener, and the bowl with the remaining apples into the kitchen. "Trouble is, they don't think things through." I heard the refrigerator door open and close.

Spinks came back into the living room and sat down at the table again. I waited. "Well," he said finally. "I've thought it over. It's nice that you haven't been pushy. I hate—that is, I don't like it when somebody tries to push me. You want to catch a murderer. I see your point of view, it's valid. People like that should be put away. I guess I can hold off." He looked regretful. "But you'll let me know as soon as I can use the information?"

"Absolutely," I said. "That's a promise. Thanks for an interesting lunch. Would you mind if I stayed a little longer and looked through your file of clippings?"

"Not at all, only you'll have to do it on your own, I have a newsletter to run off. By the way, if you'd like to make a contribution, we're tax deductible."

I wrote out a check for twenty-five dollars. I figured Donna could afford it.

Twenty-four

Sabina had put a map of the United States on her wall. As I walked into her office she was skewering Stony Brook with a red pushpin; Bowie had already received the same treatment.

"Ah, Vic," she said when she saw me. "Well?"

I took off my coat and dropped it on a chair. "I had some day, wait till you hear! Hey, even my obnoxious neighbor Paul Geissdorf wished me good morning! Let me tell you, those guys in the white coats deserve a lot of credit."

She looked at me, frowning. "What are you talking about? Didn't you see Arnold Spinks?"

"That I did. And I hit the jackpot. You got three more pushpins?"

"Three!"

"We're starting to get somewhere."

"Three," she repeated, and her blue eyes flashed. "Let's hear what you've got."

I consulted my notes. "I've got a lady named Ilene Vance, in Wilkes-Barre, Pennsylvania. A social worker."

"Aha!"

"Also, a social work trainee in Baltimore, named Sondra Turette. Plus, a third woman in Danbury, Connecticut—I don't know her name, because she hadn't been identified as of the time the article in Arnold Spinks's file was written. All three were killed when their cars stalled on the railroad tracks."

"Good work! Excellent!" She took out three red pushpins. As she stuck them into Danbury, Wilkes-Barre, and Baltimore, her expression was grim but triumphant. "Let's sit down, I want to hear about your visit to Mr. Spinks. And don't leave anything out."

I gave her a full report, including a description of the lunch I'd had with Spinks, which appalled her. Then I handed her the copies I'd made of the clippings from the file. She studied them carefully, making notes on a piece of paper as she sat at her desk. I waited.

"It's coming together," she said finally. Picking up the piece of paper, on which she'd written a list, she read aloud:

1. Sondra Turette, social worker, recently married. Baltimore, June 1981.
2. Ilene Vance, social worker. Wilkes-Barre, February 1982. (Nine months.)
3. Unidentified woman in Danbury, September 1982. (Seven months.)
4. Ruthann Duncan, social worker, recently married. Stony Brook, May 1984. (Twenty months.)
5. Fran O'Donnell, social worker, recently married. Bowie, July 1985. (Fourteen months.)

"The months," she said, "indicate the time elapsed between a particular death and the death of the preceding known victim." She studied the list. "There's no longer any doubt in my mind that Keith Browdy has been deliberately seeking out social workers, most likely because he holds some kind of grudge against the profession, marrying them, murdering them, and inheriting

173

their property. And, almost certainly, he meets them through the Personals."

"Hey, wait," I said. "What about the guy Ruthann dated in Toronto? Couldn't Browdy be a social worker himself? Couldn't he meet his victims at conventions?"

"Not bad, Vic." She shook her head. "But incorrect, unfortunately. I spoke on the phone to two members of the Missouri delegation to the Toronto convention. The man Ruthann Ellis became friendly with was quite well-known in the organization as a former alcoholic who ran a residential treatment center for prominent alcoholics outside St. Louis."

"Did you say, 'was'?"

She nodded. "That's right. He died of leukemia in January, 1983, four months before Ruthann Ellis was killed and a year and a half before Fran O'Donnell's death."

So much for that lead. "Any possibility his death was faked?"

"None. One of my informants visited him in the hospital. Both of them went to his funeral." She paused. "There was an open casket ceremony."

"Damn! I guess that's pretty conclusive. You know, I really thought he was the one."

She shook her head. "Afraid not. It's too bad, because he'd have been easy to locate. However—" She leaned back and picked up the glass paperweight, holding it up to the light. "At least we're in a better position to form a theory about how our murderer operates." Thoughtfully, she studied the swirls of color inside the glass. "My guess is that Mr. Browdy reads the Personal columns in different parts of the country—or at least on the eastern seaboard, which seems to be where he's active— until he finds the type of ad he's looking for. Ruthann's ad specified she was a social worker. Let's say the others did, too— in fact, they must have. It also said she had no dependents, and was looking for a man who was a professional. That gave him the information he needed about how to approach her; he claimed to be a lawyer. I'd be willing to bet your friend Fran advertised for a man who was well-travelled and had many interests." She put down the list. "Are you familiar with a playwright named Pirandello?"

"Don't think so. Broadway playwright?"

"No, he was an Italian whose work was quite well known some years ago. Experimental—he had a theory that people's personalities are so fluid as to be practically nonexistent, and the way they behave is mostly a reaction to the situation they happen to be in and the expectations of other people. Pirandello would have been fascinated by Keith Browdy, because seemingly Mr. Browdy knows how to transform himself into whatever his victims need and want. He's supremely skilled at it. He must be. How else could he have persuaded all these different women to marry him, and in such a short time—only two or three months, in Fran's case. Ruthann Ellis hadn't known him long, either." She paused. "Of course once he marries them, he needs a bit more time to talk them into writing wills in his favor. Say another month or two. I'm speculating here, because I'm trying to determine how many women he may have killed, in the four and a half years since the death of Sondra Turette, his first victim that we know of." She made a note. "It would take him a certain amount of time to locate suitable candidates. And he must have courted at least a few women who refused to marry him."

"The ones who got away," I said. "It comes to about six months per victim, at a minimum. In other words, it's possible he's killed as many as nine women in the last four and a half years."

Sabina shuddered. "I hope not. There may be other, unknown factors that slow him down."

I said, "You know, it's almost exactly six months since Fran O'Donnell died." We looked at each other. "You think he could be getting ready to make another kill?"

She got up and went over to the map on the bulletin board. "I don't know," she said slowly. "On the whole, I'm inclined to doubt it, because I think you frightened him badly, Victor—judging from the way he abandoned the money remaining in

Fran's bank account, and the house. My guess is he's lying low, and he'll be extremely cautious for a while."

"But how long? And what if he's running out of money?"

"He must have salted away quite a bit by now."

"According to Fran, he liked to play the races. She said she thought he overdid it, which means gambling wasn't a part of his Pirandello act, it was genuine."

"Good point. In that case, he could be running low already." She revolved the glass paperweight in her fingers and said slowly, "You know, this could be an excellent time to set a trap for him, if only we had some idea of where he is. He has to have a hidey-hole somewhere—a place to keep his belongings, a place he runs back to." She stood up and went to the map, studying it with her back to me. Suddenly she slapped it with her hand. "He's here! Somewhere on the eastern seaboard between Boston and Washington!"

"You're talking about four hundred and fifty miles, Sabina."

Her shoulders drooped. "I know. I know. And in that four hundred and fifty miles live how many million people?" She turned, walking unseeingly past her desk, and stepped across the stone threshold into the cloister. Clasping her hands behind her back, she began to pace slowly around the arched colonnade. I didn't move. After she'd made half a dozen circuits she paused. There was a faraway look in her eyes. "Victor."

"Yes?"

"What was it you said about that troublesome neighbor of yours?"

"Neighbor?"

"Yes. You mentioned something when you first came in."

"You mean Geissdorf? Just that he said hello to me this morning—why?"

"Geissdorf," she breathed. "How could I have forgotten about him?"

"I don't see—"

She resumed pacing. After a few more circuits, she stepped back into the office. Her eyes had lost their faraway look and were glittering with intensity.

"Vic, I've been stupid," she said brusquely. "I overlooked something. Paul Geissdorf searches through people's trash—remember? Fran said so. And sometimes people throw away things that can be very revealing. Vic, I want you to visit your neighbor."

"Visit Geissdorf?" I shook my head. "Uh uh, I've spent twenty years avoiding the guy! I don't want to visit Geissdorf, he's crazy. Paranoid. He won't give me the time of day."

"He said good morning, didn't he?"

"I know, but—"

"Visit him!"

Twenty-five

Ida Geissdorf answered the door. "Why," she said when she saw me, "it's Vicky! What do—I mean, come in. Come right in!" Awkwardly, she stepped aside and I went in. The living room was painfully neat, just as it had been the few times I'd been in the house during my childhood. The couch and the two matching chairs were covered by the same clear plastic material, now slightly yellowed, that showed the flowered upholstery underneath. When I sat down in one of the armchairs, the plastic felt cold and slippery, the way I remembered it. I said, "I'm sorry to bother you, Mrs. Geissdorf."

Ida Geissdorf perched on the edge of the couch—knees close together, feet side by side, hands clasped primly in her lap—and gave me a bright, uncertain smile. "Oh, no bother." She stared at me, the smile flickering on her pale, chapped lips as if she wasn't quite sure when to turn it off. She had a small, pouchy face with a pointed nose like a puppet's, and anxious, eager-to-please eyes set close together. Like the living room, she seemed to have changed very little in twenty years. She still wore a neat dark skirt and a white blouse with a string of imitation pearls peeping out from under the collar, nylon stockings, and what I'd always thought of as "old lady shoes"—black, with laces up the front and stout, medium-height heels.

I said, "I'd like to see Mr. Geissdorf, please. Is he home?"

She looked surprised. "He's taking a shower." Nervously she glanced toward the stairs that led to the second floor. "But don't run away, we don't have that many visitors. I thought you were the Jehovah's Witness."

I stood up. "Well, maybe I'll come back in an hour or so."

"No, stay, I'll make coffee. Or I could make tea."

"No, really—"

She lowered her voice and said, with a glance up the stairs. "My husband was in the hospital, I guess you heard."

"Yes. Sorry to hear it."

"It was a blessing in disguise. He's so much better." She gave me a bright, emphatic smile. "The medication is helping him. Only"—the smile died—"I'm kind of afraid he'll stop taking it." She leaned forward and whispered, "When you see him, if you get a chance would you try and get him to take his pills? You know, if it comes up naturally in the conversation? Just drop a hint."

"Ida, who's that you're talking to? You're talking to somebody, I can hear you." It was the loud, harsh voice of Paul Geissdorf, coming from the top of the stairs.

Fear flickered in her eyes. "It's just Vicky Newman, dear," she said in a cheery, sing-song voice, as if reassuring a child. "Vicky from across the street."

The thought occurred to me that I would hate to have somebody talk to me in that voice every day.

A pair of naked, hairy legs appeared on the steps. Geissdorf was coming downstairs in a terrycloth bathrobe that skimmed the tops of his knobby knees. "What do *you* want?" he growled when he saw me.

Ida rose and fluttered toward him. "That's no way to make a

visitor feel at home, Paul." To me she said, "Don't mind him, he doesn't mean anything." She confronted her husband. "Paul, don't you think we should have coffee? Maybe I could make some. Yes, I will." She hesitated. "You'll be all right?"

He scowled at her, a wizened, white-haired man a good deal older than she, with a face that flamed bright pink, as if he were on the verge of having a fit or flying into a rage. "You think I'm going to run out in the street in my bathrobe in the middle of January, is that it?" he demanded. "Sure I'll be all right!"

Before his hospitalization, I recalled, he'd run around the neighborhood naked, or so Lester had said.

"Well, I know you'll be all right, the thought never crossed my mind. Did you take your pill after lunch?"

"Not yet. Will you get off my back about the pill?"

"It's four o'clock." She looked to me for reinforcements, but I was staying out of it. She turned back to her husband. "Paul, you said you'd take it. The doctor—"

"I told you, get off my back! What's the matter, you deaf? I'll take it when I'm good and ready."

"Well—" Uncertainly, she looked back and forth between the two of us. "I'll make the coffee."

She sidled out of the room. Geissdorf said, "Damn woman drives me crazy."

"I'm sure she means well."

"What the hell do *you* know?"

A long silence followed, in which I tried to think of some approach to Geissdorf that might work.

He said, "I guess you heard I was in the hospital. I guess everybody in Bowie knows my business by now." He glared at me.

"Well—Bowie's a small town."

He folded his arms. "What do you want here, anyway?"

"Just wanted to ask you a couple of questions, Mr. Geissdorf."

His face turned a shade darker, and then he frowned as if he'd just remembered something. "Look, I didn't mean that like it sounded. Doctor said I should open myself up to people. Group said the same thing. You got questions? Go ahead, let's hear them. Maybe I'll answer, maybe I won't."

"Thanks, Mr. Geissdorf." I cleared my throat. "Do you remember a man called Keith Browdy? He married Fran O'Donnell, lived in her house last summer?"

"You mean to say he *married* that homely old prune? Must have been after her money."

"You're right." He looked surprised, as if he wasn't used to being agreed with. "I'm afraid that's exactly what he married her for. And after that—well, he murdered her."

"You don't say!" He looked interested. "Murdered her! Well, well. Murdered her, did he?" He mulled it over. "Tell you, that son of a bitch, nothing he did could surprise me. Would you believe he gave that mangy cur of his the run of my yard? I told him, 'Keep that dog tied up or one fine day you won't *have* a dog!'" He added suspiciously, "What makes you say it was murder? What I heard, it was an accident in that Toyota of hers. I could believe it, a sardine can on wheels like the rest of those foreign cars. Anyway, the damn woman couldn't drive, used to leave tire tracks on her own lawn, pulling out of her driveway. I ask you. And now the house is standing empty, probably falling apart—why don't they sell it? Come summer when the grass starts growing, what do you think that place is going to look like? It's gonna look like hell, send all our property values down." He shook his head. "Nobody gives a shit for the little man."

"Mr. Geissdorf, I'm investigating Fran's murder. I'm a detective. I don't know if you knew that?"

"Heard it," he admitted grudgingly.

"I know you didn't care for Keith Browdy, and it looks like you had good reason. I heard when his dog dug up your petunias he didn't even apologize."

"Forget apologize! The bastard tried to punch me in the nose is all the apology I got!"

"I wondered—do you know anything about Browdy that maybe could help us find him?"

"Why should I know anything?"

This was the tricky part. "Well, I heard—I'm not sure if this is right, exactly—about you being into recycling. I mean, people throw away all kinds of good stuff. It's incredibly wasteful, when you think of it. I heard—sometimes you were able to rescue some of it. . . ."

I looked him in the eye. He thought over what I'd said.

He said, "You want to catch that son of a bitch, throw him behind bars—right?"

"That's right."

He thought some more. Then he said, "Come upstairs."

We went up to the attic. The place, which had an unpleasant smell, was full of dust and spiders, castoff odds and ends, and a row of black plastic garbage bags with labels stuck on them.

"I don't let anybody up here," Geissdorf said. "You're the first."

"Thanks, Mr. Geissdorf. It's an honor."

"Wife keeps after me, wants to come up here and run the vacuum cleaner. I don't let her, though." As he spoke he was rummaging among the plastic bags. He dragged one out that was labelled 'F. O'Donnell,' and handed it to me. "Here, keep it. I don't need it now that both of them are gone."

We went back downstairs. Ida was waiting for us with coffee. "Where *were* you?" she said to her husband. "Did you take him in the *attic*?"

Geissdorf growled, "Never mind. He's leaving."

"But the coffee—"

Ignoring her, Geissdorf prodded me toward the door.

I said, "Thanks a lot, Mr. Geissdorf. Sorry I can't stay for coffee, Mrs. Geissdorf."

Geissdorf said, "Come on, come on, you got what you came for. Now beat it."

As I stepped outside I heard her ask again, "Paul, did you take him in the *attic*?"

"Just pour me a cup of the damn coffee, willya? And shut your trap." The door closed behind me.

Twenty-six

Sabina's eyes gleamed as I handed her the bag. "Bravo, Vic. Well done!" she said. "Perhaps—the garage?"

I carried the bag to the garage for her. Then I spread newspapers on the workbench and laid the bag on it, while she wrapped herself in an apron and drew on a pair of rubber gloves. The bag was closed with a wire twist-tie. She loosened the tie and laid it carefully aside; then she opened the bag, wrinkling her nose at the musty smell. Actually it could have smelled worse, considering the garbage was half a year old.

She looked inside. With one gloved hand she gently stirred the contents. "Paper, mostly, except for these." She extracted a few empty Pepsi cans, speckled with a blackish grit. "Coffee grounds," she said. "Orange peels." These she lined up at the edge of the workbench. Then she began carefully removing newspapers and what looked like mostly third-class mail—catalogues, appeals from charities, announcements of sales. There were envelopes that had contained bills from Pepco, Radio

Shack, the C & P phone company, Hecht's department store, all either with Fran's name on them or with those transparent windows. A crossword puzzle torn from a newspaper and filled out in ink. Curled-up sheets of photographic paper. "All right," she said, her hands busy. "This is going to take some time. You'd better be on your way to Baltimore."

"Am I going to Baltimore?"

She nodded without looking up. "That's right, to make inquiries at Johns Hopkins. About Sondra Turette. You remember—the woman who was there as a social work trainee when her car was hit by a train."

"You think I'll get anything? It was five years ago, Sabina." I had the feeling—it was becoming only too familiar—that all I would accomplish by driving the forty-five miles to Baltimore, was to wind up in another blind alley.

"You never know," she said. "Better hurry, or the clinic will be closed when you get there."

"Well," I said. "You're the boss."

"That's right, Victor." She glanced at her watch. "So get moving."

Johns Hopkins hospital sprawls over a dozen blocks, and it isn't the easiest place to find your way in if you don't know where you're going. I wandered around for a while, trying to find the adolescent psychiatric clinic. Something kept nagging at me, like an elusive memory—something to do with the stuff Sabina had been taking out of the garbage bag. I kept trying to remember what it was, without success.

Eventually I was directed to the office of the social work supervisor, Mrs. Ochimura. She was getting ready to leave for the day and didn't ask me to sit down.

"Sondra Turette," she said. "I've never heard of her, I'm afraid I can't help you." She was a spare, severe-looking woman of Oriental descent and indeterminate age, who was stashing charts in an attaché case, no doubt to take home with her. No rest for the weary. Mrs. Ochimura was definitely one of the weary. There were dark rings under her eyes and she kept squaring her thin shoulders as if to keep them from sagging.

"Somebody must have heard of her," I said.

"Hopkins is a teaching hospital, Mr.—Newman?" she said in a tired voice. "Students come and go constantly."

"Still, this was only five years ago."

"I accepted this position three years ago, so . . ." She shrugged.

"Well, is there someone around who's been here longer?"

"They've all gone home."

"Who was the social work supervisor before you came?"

"Gertrude Becker. She supervised the social work students for thirty-five years." She seemed to find the idea appalling.

"Is there any way I could speak to her?"

"I doubt it." Mrs. Ochimura put on her coat. "She's very old and I understand she's quite ill. I'm sorry, Mr. Newman, but my husband is waiting in the parking lot."

"Could you give me Gertrude Becker's phone number?"

"That wouldn't be possible, but if you care to leave your name and number . . ."

I wrote them down while she stood beside me jingling her keys. Then, picking up her attaché case, she led me out of the office, locked the door, and hurried away.

I hunted up a telephone booth with a phone book. Sure enough, Gertrude Becker was in the book. I wrote down her address, started retracing my steps, and eventually managed to locate my car.

Gertrude Becker lived in a narrow, brick row house that looked at least a hundred years old. Somebody had tossed a couple of empty beer cans into the tiny, neat garden of ivy and azalea bushes out front. I leaned over the low wrought-iron fence and picked up the cans. A large woman with her back to me was scrubbing one of the three stone steps that led to the front door.

"Hi," I said. She turned around, and I handed her the cans. "Looks like somebody left you a present."

"Happens all the time," she said. "What can I do for you?" She was about forty, with a shiny, pleasant face and an expression of solid competence.

"I'm looking for Gertrude Becker."

"What for?"

"You know her?"

"I should. I'm her daughter."

There was a loud banging on the front window from inside the house. I looked up and saw what looked like the tip of a cane hammering on the glass, hard. I said, "Hey, that's gonna break the glass."

The woman sighed. "Tell me about it. I've replaced so many panes of glass by now I could get my glazier's license."

"Your mother?"

"You guessed it." She raised her voice. "Coming, Mom! I'm coming! Hold your horses!" She sighed. "Probably has to go to the bathroom. You said you wanted to see her. What about?"

"Mrs. Ochimura at Johns Hopkins gave me her name. I'm trying to find out about a woman who used to be a social worker at the hospital. I'm a private detective—Vic Newman's the name."

"You want to talk to her about Hopkins? You come right in. My mother is bored out of her gourd. She also happens to be a very sick lady, so if she starts to get tired I'm going to throw you out. You got it?" I nodded. "Fine." She picked up her scrub bucket. "Oh, and don't be surprised if she asks you to kill her."

"To what?" I didn't think I'd heard her right.

"Kill her. Probably want you to bring her poison. Just tell her it's against the law and you can't do it. She'd like to die and I can't really blame her, but that's one thing I'm not prepared to do for her. So she's angry at me. Angry at God, I should say; I'm just a handy target." She sighed. "By the way, my name is Mary Beth."

"Hi, Mary Beth."

"Follow me."

We went inside.

From the direction of the window there came a tremulous clicking. It turned into a banging. There was a wheelchair by the window, and in it a tiny, ancient, gnomelike figure, hunched over so that her chin was only inches from her knees. One dangling hand shook convulsively; the other grasped a cane, which she was banging furiously on the floor.

"Okay, you can stop banging," Mary Beth said. "I'm here."

I stared at the rheumy, milky eyes and the sagging mouth from which saliva dribbled, and thought, Oh no. Mrs. Becker appeared demented, and my hopes of obtaining any useful information drained away. But I could hardly just turn around and leave.

The old woman stopped banging her cane, and the clicking sound started again as the cane, held in her shaking hand, came to rest against the wheel of her chair.

"Bathroom?" said Mary Beth.

Gertrude Becker nodded. Then she seemed to notice me. She took a couple of gasping breaths—"hunh! hunh!"—as if pumping up her lungs like a bellows. "Who's he?" she wheezed.

"He's here from Johns Hopkins."

"Johns Hopkins." A spark of interest came into the watery eyes. "What for?"

"I guess he'll tell you himself. Let's go to the bathroom first."

"Stupid girl!" The old woman swiveled her head in my direction. "Who are you?"

"My name's Vic Newman."

"Hmph. That doesn't tell me much."

Mary Beth sighed. "Bathroom, Mom." She wheeled her mother away. This time, the old woman didn't protest.

I looked around the dining room where I was standing. It was dollhouse size, barely big enough for a table and chairs. The adjoining living room wasn't much larger, but a hospital bed had been crammed into it. A few nice-looking antiques had been pushed against a wall.

"I gave her a pill," Mary Beth said, when she returned with the wheelchair. "She should be fine for a while. You can talk in here."

"Don't call me 'she'! I'm not an inanimate object!"

"I'll say you're not."

I pulled a chair out from the table and sat down. The daughter went into the living room where she could keep an eye on us, picked up what looked like a half-finished sweater, and started to knit.

Gertrude Becker raised her head and we stared at each other. I couldn't tell how much she could see out of those milky eyes. She looked completely blind, but apparently wasn't. "What can I do for you, young man?" she wheezed.

"I'm a private detective," I said, not that there seemed much point to it. "I'm trying to obtain any information I can about a woman named Sondra Turette."

"You're not from Hopkins?" Mrs. Becker seemed disappointed.

"Not exactly. I was just there, though. Mrs. Ochimura gave me your name."

"Ochimura!" the old woman sniffed. "*She* won't last."

"I understand Sondra Turette was a social work trainee while you were supervisor. Do you remember her?"

Mrs. Becker's head kept bobbing up and down. She raised a wad of tissues in her shaking hand and dabbed at her chin. "Sondra. Yes."

"You remember her?"

My skepticism must have showed in my voice, because she wheezed, "Young man. The brain still works."

"I didn't—"

"She was a hippie."

"A what?"

"You deaf? A hippie. Lived in a commune. Decided to be a social worker and went back to school. Took out a loan, worked nights as a cocktail waitress. She was a thorn in my side."

"Why?"

"A rebel. Identified too much with the kids. Wore Indian love beads, no bra!" She gave a couple of deep wheezes— "Hunh! Hunh!"—and I realized she was laughing. "No bra, around adolescent boys! I put a stop to *that*! My, Sondra was furious! Good though, with kids. Adolescents—a tough population. The toughest, I always used to say. Takes a special knack to work with them. Sondra had it, bra or no bra." Slowly, tremulously she shook her head. "Died in an accident. What a waste!" She kept shaking her head. "Could have been outstanding."

"I hear she got married not long before her death," I said. Gertrude Becker raised her quivering chin, and I had the feeling she was becoming more interested. "Did you ever meet her husband, do you know anything about him?"

"Oh, him."

"You remember him?"

"I certainly should."

"But do you?"

"I just said I did."

"What do you remember about him?"

"Plenty. Too much! I told her she was making a big mistake, but— You ever try giving a hippie advice?"

"I don't think so."

"That's smart. It's a waste of time." She gave a couple of rasping coughs, as if clearing her air passages.

I said, "Do you mean you told Sondra Turette it was a mistake to marry this person?"

"Just said so, didn't I? How many times do I have to repeat myself?"

"I'm sorry, Mrs. Becker, I'm trying to make sure I understand. Why didn't you think she should marry him?"

"Because he was one of our boys. And one of our worst."

"Your boys?"

"He'd been a patient in the clinic!" she said irritably. "Why don't you pay attention? This was long, long before Sondra came. Baltimore boy, pathology galore. Oh yes, he was famous at Phipps in his day."

"You mean you actually *knew* him?"

"Everybody knew him." She chortled—hunh! hunh! "The famous Royce! Not one of Sondra's brighter ideas, marrying Royce."

I took out a pad and started making rapid notes. Was it possible I'd finally found the link to Keith Browdy's past we'd been searching for? "Royce was his name? What was his last name?"

She furrowed her brow, thinking. "Can't remember. Rats! I never could remember names. But faces—that's another story. I've never forgotten a face in my life. He came to pick up Sondra one day, and I recognized him right away. He still looked young. And handsome—oh my, yes. Probably made a pact with the devil, like what's-his-name."

"You mean *The Picture of Dorian Gray?*"

"That's what I said, isn't it?" Her head waggled faster. "The famous Royce! My, my, my."

"What was he famous for?"

"Great teaching case. Guess you don't know what that means. Every spring, new social work students would arrive, green as the grass. One of them would always get Royce. The lucky one!" She gave her wheezing cackle. "*They* didn't think so. But they *were* lucky. Survive Royce, they could handle anything."

"He was a tough case?"

"Real sociopath. Little con man. And that angel face! Suck them right in, get them feeling sorry for him, get their rescue fantasies going—then the fun started! Jumped the poor girls through every hoop in the book."

"What did he do?"

"The gamut. Lied. Set fires. Stole. Made trouble you wouldn't believe in the foster families, always with that innocent smile on his face."

I remembered what Browdy had said to Mrs. Atkins at the Stony Brook agency. "Royce was in foster care, then?"

"From the age of seven on. One family after another. Tested them to the limit. Past the limit. Bounce him back to us. One family, he doused the cat with lighter fluid, set it on fire. Jealous of the attention. Another family, he stole all the grandmother's jewelry. Not that he admitted it, and there wasn't any proof. But he was the one, all right. Things like that. Royce was bright, and somehow he always managed to stay out of correctional institutions. My girls would go to bat for him, testify he had 'potential'—oh, they gave their all. Well, they were students, still had a lot to learn. People love to sneer at social workers, you ever notice that? Like to see *them* tackle our cases! They call us names—bleeding heart, lady bountiful—if you want to know why, I'll tell you in one word. We're women! When a man does what *we* do, he's a hero. A saint. Hunh! Ever notice?"

"What about Mother Teresa?"

"The exception proves the rule, young man," she said tartly, and started coughing.

"Well—you could have a point. Anyway, Royce—"

She waved her tremulous hand, still coughing, and dabbed her mouth with the wad of tissues. "I could tell you stories all day about him. We placed him once with a rural family—one of the girls figured, get him out of the big city."

"And?"

"It worked, at first. He liked the country. Had a dog." She paused. "Loved that dog, probably the only thing he ever did love as long as I knew him. Couldn't love people—didn't have it in him. Then he got angry, and that was the end of it. Knocked over all the beehives with a stick." She chuckled. "Hunh! Hunh! That one backfired, oh my, yes. He wound up in the hospital and nearly died."

I took out the photograph of Browdy, wishing it were clearer. "Mrs. Becker, I'd like to show you a picture."

"Doubt I can see it, young man. Cataracts. Growing old is no picnic."

"Try."

She took the photograph in her tremulous hand and squinted at it, holding it up close and then further away. "Can't make it out," she said, and handed it back to me. "Mary Beth!"

"What, Mom?"

"Make the young man some tea."

Mary Beth said, "Mr. Newman, you want tea?"

"Make it!"

The daughter got up and went into the kitchen. Gertrude Becker's hand shot out and gripped my arm. She tugged me toward her, and as I leaned closer I could feel her constant tremor, like the hum of a machine. "Would you do me a favor?"

"Sure. What can I do?"

"I have money. Diamond ring, worth a lot." Looking down at the hand clutching my arm, I saw a ring with a large, square-cut diamond on one of her bony fingers. "You're a detective, you must have a gun. Kill me. Please," she whispered urgently. "I want to die! No kind of a life—for me, for Mary Beth. Break in! I'll tell you the best time. Shoot me, take the ring. Take anything you want!"

"Mrs. Becker, I couldn't do that."

"Please!"

"You don't mean it."

"Yes. Yes! Would *you* want this life?"

I couldn't answer her.

"Then poison! Come and see me. Bring something. Pills, anything!"

"I couldn't, Mrs. Becker. It's against the law, I'd wind up in jail."

She sank back. "I'm very disappointed. In *you!*" she hissed.

"I'm sorry. Really." There was a silence. "Mrs. Becker, if I could just ask you a few more questions."

She shrugged.

I said, "You said Royce got into foster care when he was seven. Why?"

"Psychotic mother—hospitalized. Chronic schizophrenic." She seemed to have sunk into herself.

"And his father?"

She shook her head. "That was a bad situation. Father locked him in a closet and never came back. Neighbor heard him crying. He was a mass of bruises, scars all down his back—that's how he got into the system." She started coughing. "Stayed 'til he was fifteen." She gave a whooping kind of a gasp. The thin shoulders shook till I was afraid she was going to fall out of the wheelchair. I grabbed her; she couldn't stop coughing.

Mary Beth came running out of the kitchen with a glass of water. She thrust the glass at me, jerked her mother upright, and began pounding her on the back. Then she held the glass to the old woman's lips. After a couple of sips, the coughing tapered off. Mary Beth lowered her mother back into the wheelchair.

"It's too much talking, she's had enough for today. You been reminiscing about Hopkins, Mom? You been talking up a storm? This has been a treat for her, Mr. Newman."

"Stupid girl," muttered Mrs. Becker. "Think you know everything."

I stood up. "Thanks a lot, Mrs. Becker. Thank you, Mary Beth." The old woman started coughing again. "Will she be okay?"

"She gets like this sometimes. Don't worry." Holding the glass to her mother's lips with one hand, Mary Beth waved me away.

Twenty-seven

 I found Sabina playing chess with Bruno. "I've got news," I said.

"Ssh!" She was leaning over the board intently.

"This news is big."

"It can wait two minutes." I could see the game was almost over; there were hardly any pieces left on the board.

"But—"

"Ssh! I'm going to win this one!" Her hand hovered above the pieces, poised to pounce. For some reason she still hasn't given up hope of one day beating Bruno at chess, though he always wins. He's offered her odds, but she won't take them— she figures winning with odds doesn't count. Bruno was stroking his beard in deep concentration, his eyes on the board, and I doubted he'd seen me come in. Her hand swooped down and snatched up a piece. "Ha!" she said, throwing Bruno a triumphant look.

Calmly, he nudged a pawn forward.

She gave an agonized cry and shoved the board away. "I don't have time to finish this stupid game, Vic has to report."

"I win."

She stood up. "You don't win. The game is adjourned."

She stalked from the room and I followed her. Behind us Bruno repeated, in a satisfied voice, "I win." I heard the clicking of the pieces as he began to set them up again.

She was still fuming as we walked through the cloister, and I could tell the sound of the fountain wasn't doing as good a job as usual of calming her down. When we reached her office she sat down at the desk, folded her arms, and scowled at me. Finally she said, "Well? What's this so-called big news?"

"I didn't think you were interested."

"Don't be childish. Just tell me."

"It so happens I've found somebody who knew Keith Browdy as a child."

"What!" She jerked forward in her chair. "Why didn't you say so right away?"

"I tried, Sabina. You wouldn't let me."

"Nonsense! Of course I'd have let you if you'd told me it was really important! I expect you to use your judgment, Vic. That's what I pay you for. Give me the whole story. Start at the beginning, and don't leave anything out."

I delivered a full report on my visit to Gertrude Becker. She listened, enthralled. "Wonderful," she breathed. "The pieces are coming together, and they fit, they all fit!" She stood up. "Let's walk." We went into the cloister and paced side by side around the arched colonnade, our footsteps echoing on the stone pavement. I glanced at her face and saw that she was deep in thought. Finally she stopped walking and spoke. "You know, I'm starting to feel this series of crimes could have begun in Baltimore." She nodded to herself. "Yes, right there at Johns Hopkins. I'm still not sure exactly how." She paced for a few moments and stopped again. "At least we *do* know the adolescent psychiatric clinic was the focal point of Browdy's childhood. And we know his childhood was absolutely horrendous— not that this explains the fact that he grew up to be a murderer, nothing really *explains* that kind of evil. Yet it does fit." She resumed walking. "He never had a stable home, he was constantly moving from one foster home to another. The only place he kept coming back to was the clinic. And the clinic was where Sondra Turette worked, years later. Is it only a coincidence that she was his first victim, as far as we know?" She paused beside one of the stone columns that separated the walkway from the garden with the fountain in the middle. Absentmindedly, she smoothed the column with her hand. "Suppose he just happened to revisit the clinic one day—on impulse, maybe, as he was passing through Baltimore—and that was how the two of them met."

"Why do you say 'passing through' Baltimore? Doesn't he live there?"

She looked at me in surprise. "You think he still lives in Baltimore, after twenty-five years?"

"Why not? Don't I still live in Bowie?" I added excitedly, "I bet that's where he is right now—in Baltimore! And I was there today! I could have passed him on the street!"

"Well—possibly."

"You don't think so? Why not?"

She started walking again. "You haven't asked me if I found anything in that bag."

"Bag? Oh, the garbage bag. Well, did you?"

She didn't answer right away. We reached the threshold of her office and she crossed it and headed for the file cabinet. "Not a great deal. But there was this." She took a clear plastic folder out of a file drawer. "What do you think of it?" She handed me the folder. Inside was a sheet torn from a newspaper, about a quarter of a page.

I examined it. "Used car ads on one side, none of them circled or marked in any way." I turned the folder over. "Crossword puzzle on the other, filled out in ink. Plus a few news items of no particular interest: Jennifer Lee Clifton has been named to the Dean's List with a B average, hey, good for Jennifer—"

Crossword puzzle. Was that what had been teasing my memory? I said slowly, "Where have I seen a crossword puzzle before?"

"You don't remember? Think back. The condolence call you—"

The memory returned. "That's right! There was a magazine on the armchair, open to the crossword puzzle. Browdy seemed to have been working on it." I tapped the folder. "You think he did this?"

"That's what I've been wondering. Did Fran like crosswords?"

"Not that I know of. I doubt it, actually. She used to say she couldn't spell."

"Then probably it was Browdy. Royce, I suppose we should call him, since that seems to be his real name."

"Wait, how about Pudge? She was living there around that time."

Sabina shook her head. "I gave Miss Poge a call this afternoon. She told me she considers crossword puzzles a waste of the all-too-brief time God has given us. By the way, have you noticed the name of the newspaper?"

I hadn't. When I looked, I saw it was printed in small letters in one corner. "The Cecil *Whig*? What the heck is that? Sounds like a leftover from the Revolutionary War."

"In a sense, it is. I made a call to the public library today. I was told that the *Whig* is the newspaper of Cecil County, Maryland. As you may or may not know, Cecil is one of the oldest counties in the state, with settlements on the Chesapeake Bay dating back to the seventeenth century. How familiar are you with the area?"

"Not very."

She nodded. "Like most people—yet you drive through it every time you go to New York. You don't see the real Cecil County unless you leave the highway." She paused and then remarked after a moment, "You know, Vic, Cecil County is within a couple of hours' drive of Washington, Baltimore, Wilmington, Philadelphia—even New York. Convenient, don't you think? Yet at the same time it's off the beaten track, and parts of it are still fifty years in the past—fishing, duck hunting, sleepy little villages—though I understand the land developers are starting to make inroads. Inevitable, I suppose, though it seems a pity."

"All that's interesting," I said. "But I don't see what it has to do with the case."

She leaned forward. "Tell me this. What was Royce doing with a crossword puzzle from the Cecil *Whig*? What's his connection with Cecil County?"

I shook my head. "Don't ask me. Aren't you making kind of a big deal out of this? The paper could have been lying around anywhere, and he picked it up because he saw the puzzle and wanted to do it."

"*I've* never seen the Cecil *Whig* 'lying around anywhere,' have you?"

"Well, no."

Her eyes gleamed. "Suggestive, isn't it?" She stood up and went to the map of the eastern seaboard with the red pushpins in it. "Vic, I'm wondering if finding this scrap of newspaper could be the breakthrough we've been looking for. Maybe Royce's hidey-hole is in Cecil County." She picked up a black pushpin and stabbed it into the narrow head of the Chesapeake Bay. "Yes! I have a hunch he could be right *here* somewhere."

I couldn't help feeling skeptical. "It's pretty flimsy evidence, Sabina. I mean, there's no *proof* Royce did this puzzle. Maybe a visitor brought it to the house, or—"

"Well, Royce has to be *somewhere*." She broke off as if a thought had struck her. "Vic. I believe Gertrude Becker told you Royce was a patient at Hopkins until he was fifteen. What happened after that?"

"She didn't say."

"Call and ask her."

"Now? Won't she be asleep?"

She looked at her watch. "It's only nine o'clock. Try."

I dialed Mrs. Becker's number. Mary Beth answered, and I asked if her mother was still awake.

"She's up, yes." Mary Beth sounded harassed. "She's not feeling well."

"Could I possibly talk to her?"

Her voice sharpened. "She's not well, Mr. Newman. She overdid it today, I shouldn't have let her—" In the background I could hear her coughing.

"Please, Mary Beth, it's very important. If you don't want me to speak to her, could *you* ask her one question? Just one?"

"Well—" The coughing slackened off. Mary Beth said reluctantly, "What's your question?"

"Ask her what happened to Royce. Why did he stop coming to the clinic? Please."

"I think that's *two* questions, but—oh, hold on."

The line was silent for so long I was beginning to wonder if Mary Beth had hung up on me, when I heard her voice again. "My mother says they closed the case after a new set of foster parents he'd been assigned to left town. They took Royce with them. Goodbye, Mr.—"

"Mary Beth, wait! Just one more question, I promise it's the last. Does she know where they went?"

"I've answered one question and that's it." In the background there was coughing again, and words I couldn't make out. Finally Mary Beth sighed and I heard her say, "All right, all right. He wants to know where they went." Another silence followed. I covered the receiver and whispered to Sabina, "The foster family Royce was staying with moved out of Baltimore and took him with them."

Sabina nodded tensely.

"Mr. Newman?" Mary Beth was back on the line. "Mother says to tell you one of the social workers tried to make a home visit, after Royce stopped coming to the clinic, and she spoke to the neighbors. They told her the family had moved up around Elkton. That's all she knows. All. Goodbye." She hung up.

Sabina said, "Well?"

I got up and went over to the map. I pulled out the black pushpin and thrust it in again, half an inch to the east of where she'd stuck it. "According to the neighbors, the family moved up near Elkton."

"Aha."

Her eyes met mine and then swiveled toward the map.

Elkton is the capital of Cecil County.

Three

SABINA

Twenty-eight

Next morning we were on the highway, heading north toward Elkton. I was driving, while Sabina sat huddled in her coat with the big fur collar, complaining because the heater was on the blink. "Bruno just took the car in for a checkup," she said.

"Mechanic must have missed something. Or he crossed a couple of wires while he was fixing something else."

"The amount of sheer incompetence in this world is appalling," she fumed, and sneezed. "I'll probably come down with the flu, if not pneumonia." I cut in front of a pickup truck and didn't say anything. She was trying to play on my sympathies because she knew I was pissed about her plan and this was making her nervous. After a while, she said in a sweetly reasonable voice, "Now, Victor. I know you're just acting this way because you're concerned about me. And I appreciate that. But we have to discuss the situation, we have to make decisions."

"I wish you'd told me this cockamamie idea of yours before we left Georgetown, so I could have had Bruno talk some sense into you."

The sweetness drained out of her voice like syrup from a punctured can. "Watch it—I'm your boss, remember? As a matter of fact, I refrained from mentioning it, on purpose. There are certain things Bruno can't handle."

"Yeah? Well, I can't handle them either. As far as I'm concerned, this guy's a snake in human form. And you're gonna be the tethered goat—the whole idea's crazy!"

"On the contrary, it's the only thing that might work. Or can you think of an alternative?"

I mulled it over and didn't answer.

She settled back. "All right then, let's get down to business. We're going to assume our quarry is somewhere in Cecil County, lying low. It's not that big an area, perhaps a hundred and fifty square miles, but it's certainly large enough to hide a man whose last name we don't know. Therefore we'll have to lure him out. The best way to do it, unless, of course, you have a better suggestion?"—I didn't, and she knew it—"is through the Personals. Right? He's certainly in the habit of reading them, by now it must be second nature. So—we place an ad and wait for a reply."

"And then you go out on a date with him. Great! And then he bumps you off and I have to find another job." I shook my head, and passed a car that was putt-putting up the Baltimore-Washington Parkway at forty miles an hour. I gave the guy the finger and yelled, "Why don't you buy a bike?"

"A hostile driver is an unsafe driver, Victor," Sabina admonished.

"*You're* telling *me* about unsafe?" I pressed my foot down on the accelerator, hard. Let *her* be scared, for a change. "Okay, so Royce is lying low. What makes you think he'll answer your ad? If Cecil County is his hidey-hole, it's got to be the one place he *won't* stage any 'accidents' in."

"True. But he'll answer my ad because it'll be irresistible. Even if he's hiding out at the moment, that doesn't mean he isn't doing a little research with an eye to the future."

"Well—I guess that's possible."

"So we compose an ad. We place it in whatever publication the citizens of Cecil County use for this purpose—we'll find out what that is when we get there. Then we wait for replies. In the meantime—in fact, today—we'll rent an apartment. And have a telephone installed."

"A motel would be simpler."

"Simpler, but not better. When and if Royce calls, I don't want him reaching a switchboard. That would make him suspicious. The woman who's placing this ad would have a residential phone."

"I still don't see why he should contact a woman who lives in Cecil County, if he wants to keep his hidey-hole safe."

"Because this particular woman is in the area temporarily. She's taking some specialized courses in the social work field at the University of Delaware, which is right across the state line in Newark, only five miles from Elkton. Naturally she'd like to meet some people, she's lonely—after all, she's older than most of the student body. She's at the university for the spring semester, and then she plans to return home."

"Which is where?"

"Let's see. How about Richmond, Virginia?"

"You don't have a southern drawl."

"True. How about Boston?"

"You don't sound like a Bostonian, either."

"Well then, anyplace. New Jersey."

"Yeah. You could come from New Jersey. You're the type."

"Don't be surly. Oh, and would you please refrain from driving above the speed limit? I see a police car peeking out behind that blue spruce."

I slowed down to fifty-five. "By the way, there's no social work school at the University of Delaware."

"What! Are you sure?"

"Positive. I knew a woman from Wilmington once who was studying social work. She had to commute to Baltimore."

"Hm." She huddled deeper into her fur collar. After a while

she said, "Well, it doesn't matter. I could be taking psychology courses. School counseling. I'll think of something."

We crossed the Susquehanna River and left Route 95 for the old Pulaski Highway, passing Bud's Body Shop and the Tabernacle of the Spoken Word en route, plus an incredible number of rusty Dr. Pepper signs. Bulldozers were roaring in the woods, clearing tracts the size of shopping centers and housing developments. I stopped at a general store and picked up an assortment of the local papers, but none of them, including the Cecil *Whig*, carried Personals in their classified ads, to Sabina's disappointment.

We continued down the Pulaski. Sabina had a map in her hand, but it wasn't much help because the smaller roads we were passing weren't on it. She peered out the window as we passed a sign. "Winch Road," she read, and a moment later, "Razor Strap Road. Where on earth are we?"

"All I can tell you is, on the way toward Elkton." Wasn't there something about Elkton I was forgetting, something special?

"Well, don't rush," said Sabina, as I stepped on the gas. "There's no reason to believe Royce is actually *in* Elkton. Let's get off the beaten track."

"We are off it."

"Further off."

I turned down Red Toad Road and bumped along in the direction of the Chesapeake Bay. It was very quiet once we'd left the Pulaski, and we didn't see anybody around. We passed low, frame houses with pickup trucks in front and piles of rubbish out back, and trailers set up on piers covered with shiny sheets of aluminum that were stamped to look like concrete blocks. Between the houses stretched patches of swampland and stands of leafless trees, and beyond them we caught glimpses of the bay. Dogs barked fiercely and chased our car, leaping up at the windows. Overhead, hawks were wheeling in a cold gray sky.

"I could imagine Royce in one of these houses," Sabina said thoughtfully.

"Really? Doesn't he have more expensive tastes?"

"Only superficially. Look at the way he was living in Fran's house. Dirty dishes, pots on the table, dead plants dropping their leaves on the floor—that's what he's basically comfortable with." She looked at her watch. "Let's find a place to stop for lunch—someplace ordinary."

"That should be easy." I slowed down alongside a historical marker that said George Washington had passed through the area in 1795. Nearby stood a crumbling building with a home-made sign out front: SWEET DADDY'S RIBS. I said, "How about this?"

She shuddered. "I'm afraid it looks perfect."

We went in. The place was gloomy and we were the only customers. The waitress who came to our table was a timid, anemic-looking girl of seventeen. I said, "Hi, are you Sweet Daddy's daughter?"

"Huh?"

"Never mind. Give me the ribs."

Sabina nudged me and hissed, "The chicken might be safer."

"Hey, I thought you wanted to live dangerously. Have the ribs!"

She thought that over. "Well—perhaps you're right. More indigenous." The waitress puckered her brow. "I'll try the ribs, too. Oh, and Miss, may I ask you a question?"

"It's down the hall."

"That's good to know, but my question was on a different topic. Tell me"—she smiled carefully—"if you were living in Cecil County—"

The waitress looked confused. "I am," she said. "I mean, I do."

"Of course you do. But we don't, you see. We're just passing through, that's why we need information. Now. Suppose you wanted to place an ad in the Personals column—you know, to meet someone." The girl seemed baffled. "Of the opposite sex. *You* know. A man."

Enlightenment dawned. "Oh, I would never do *that!*" She sounded horrified.

"I don't mean *you*, specifically. I mean, *one*. Anyone. Where would someone place such an ad, if one happened to live in Cecil County?"

"I wouldn't think of such a thing! This is a quiet place, people go to church, we don't have bank robberies or—or—" Imagination failed her. "I better give him your order." She scuttled off to the kitchen.

The ribs were tasty—Daddy's sauce was loaded with Tabasco—and I enjoyed every dripping morsel although I did get a few spots on my clothes. Sabina's, naturally, stayed immaculate. The waitress did her best not to linger, but Sabina managed to snag her when she brought us the bill. "I hope you understand I didn't mean anything personal when I asked you that question before. We're just—ah, conducting research for a book." She smiled winningly.

"On the singles scene in Cecil County," I put in.

The waitress's eyes grew bigger. "I don't think we have one. Honestly."

Sabina frowned. "So if somebody wanted to advertise to meet someone, in order to improve his social life, you don't know where he could place such an ad? Is that correct?"

The girl shook her head firmly. "Nothing like that goes on around here."

"A complete and total waste of time," snapped Sabina, as we got into the car.

"Oh, I don't know. The ribs were great."

"Greasy, I thought."

"Ribs are supposed to be greasy." I pulled out of the parking lot into the road. "Okay, where to?"

"Elkton." She sounded discouraged.

I suddenly remembered what it was about Elkton. "Say, isn't that the place where people go to get married?"

"Used to."

"There's no waiting period or something like that?"

"Not anymore, they've changed the law. Couples used to come by the thousands at one time—it was quite a lucrative business. But now Elkton's just another sleepy country town."

It turned out to be slightly more than that, since after all it was the county seat. Traffic was screwed up due to road construction, but eventually we found ourselves driving slowly down the ten blocks that made up Main Street, past a sprinkling of restored Victorian houses and the new County Courthouse. Only one of the old wedding chapels was still open for business, a dreary structure with a fake stone front. I don't know why, but Elkton depressed me. Maybe it was the thought of all those couples rushing off to get married. Maybe it was because I started wondering why I'd never felt the urge to do likewise. When we got to the outskirts of town, I pulled off the road and said, "Sabina, would you please tell me what we're doing here? I'm tired of driving around. What's the point?"

She stared out the window, her gloved hands gripping her pocketbook. "He's not far away, Vic, I feel it. We're right on his track."

"Since when did you develop ESP?" I shook my head. "Sabina, this case is making you a little weird. Okay, suppose for the sake of argument we say you're right. How do we find him? That's what I want to know."

"Human nature is no different here than the rest of the country, I don't care *what* that idiotic girl said. There must be a Personals column."

"Fine. Where?"

She burrowed deeper into her coat and went into one of her trances. I'd parked in the shade of a dense stand of pines, and with the heater on the blink the car was freezing; by the time she finally spoke, my teeth were starting to chatter.

"Seven-Eleven."

"What?"

"Seven-Eleven!"

I should have known. She has this theory that if you want to put your finger on the pulse of America, a 7-Eleven is the place to do it. Personally, I just think of them as sources of bread and such when the regular stores are closed. "Whatever you say. Any particular one?"

"They're interchangeable. Find the nearest one."

It didn't take long. There was a big 7-Eleven on the Pulaski Highway, across from a gas station. I parked and went inside. It had the usual magazine rack, but none of the publications looked promising. Picking up a copy of *Newsweek*, I went to the counter where the cashier, a brassy blonde in her late thirties, was painting her fingernails red.

"Business must be slow," I said.

"It's not slow," she said, and blew on her nails. "It's dead. I don't know what it is with today."

"Must get kind of boring."

She rolled her eyes upward. "Dullsville, totally."

"Too bad. Listen, could I ask you a question?"

"Honey, you can ask me anything." She shook her hands in the air to dry them, and gave me an innocent stare out of blue eyes ringed heavily with eyeliner.

"You're a sweetheart," I said. "How come I never meet girls like you? Which brings me to my question. I'm new in the area and I'd like to put an ad in the Personals, make a few friends— you know, the whole bit."

The eyes focused on me more sharply. "Honey, you don't need the Personals. I mean, you're not uncute."

"Thanks, but I thought I'd try it. Only trouble is, I don't know where to place the ad. Where do people around here do it?"

She shook her head. "Really, you don't need that. Plenty of women would go out with you if you asked them."

"Well, I still think I might try an ad. I'm kind of shy."

"That's cute," she said. "I like shy guys." She waited expectantly. I looked out the window. Her voice hardened. "You're not the brightest, you know that? Try the *Grapevine*. There's a stack of them over there in that milk crate—guy just dropped them off."

"Aha!" cried Sabina triumphantly, when I got back to the car. "Give me that!" She snatched it from my hand.

I slid behind the wheel. "Did you realize I'm not uncute?"

"You're not what?"

"Uncute. According to the cashier."

She gave me a look of disgust. "Sometimes I despair for the future of the English language. Please don't tell me things like that, they upset me." She opened the *Grapevine*.

I said, "Sabina, now that we've located the damn paper, I have to say again I don't like this idea. I really mean it."

She swiveled to face me. "Victor, I've been extremely patient. You've already expressed your objections, and I think you're overreacting. In the first place, Royce may not even *be* in Cecil County. If he is and we place an ad, he may not read it. Or he may read it and decide not to answer it. So you see, it's premature to worry. Anyway, I promise to be *extremely* careful. Now I don't want to hear any more about it." She began to turn the pages. The *Grapevine* resembled a tabloid newspaper, and consisted entirely of classified ads, mostly for cars people were trying to sell. She leafed through the pages, skimming the ads. "Ah, here we are. The Personals!"

I was looking over her shoulder. "Yeah, right after 'Cemetery Lots.' Not too reassuring."

"Victor," she said warningly, and began to read. "Listen to this. 'Short, fat, ugly, unsuccessful, lazy man, who doesn't enjoy anything life offers, is looking for a similar female.'" She shook her head. "Extraordinary."

"For real?"

"Yes, it's right here."

"They can't all be like that."

She skimmed the page. "Let's see. 'Married man looking for a little daytime action.' Hm. 'Refined educated couple seeks same, send measurements.' Oh here's one that sounds more in our line. 'SPECIAL LADY—Professional and intelligent yet sensitive and caring, this attractive brunette seeks tall, very attractive, conservative gentleman, 35-50, successful, well-educated nonsmoker for long walks, sailing, and evenings by the fire.'" She turned to me. "That's the sort of thing we need to come up with. Let's write one." Opening her handbag, she rummaged for paper and pencil.

I mused, "Long walks, sailing, and evenings by the fire— Let me see that last ad."

"You're too young for her, Victor. All right, how does this sound? 'Attractive, 40ish social worker, in Elkton temporarily'— Vic, do you think I should say attractive?"

"You can say anything you want."

"That's not what I meant. I don't want him to get a shock when he meets me."

"You know damn well he won't get a shock. Sabina, when Bruno hears about this . . ."

"I don't want you mentioning this project to Bruno."

"But—"

"That's an order. Let's see . . ." She chewed thoughtfully on her pencil. "What do you think of scuba diving?" she said finally.

"Never tried it. Why?"

"No, I mean, to put in the ad. If we give this fictitious woman some specific interest, it'll help us weed out the replies. Royce being Royce, he'd certainly write that scuba diving is his favorite activity—you see what I mean?"

I shook my head. "Scuba diving is too extreme. How many middle-aged social workers are into scuba diving?"

"You're right. We'd better come up with something else."

We drove for a while. I said, "Skiing?"

"Possibly. Perhaps a bit too athletic. Tennis? But if Royce doesn't play, that might discourage him. He might think she'd expect to have a game with him now and then. Let's see—"

We drove some more.

"Museum going!" she said finally. "Anybody can go to a museum, that doesn't take special skills."

"Museum going sounds good to me."

She scribbled a few more words and then read me her ad.

VISITOR TO ELKTON—*Attractive 40ish D/W/F social worker, here till June, old-fashioned, reserved yet affectionate, seeks educated, sincere man for museum going, friendship, possible ongoing romance.*

I said, "Well—it's pretty good. 'Sincere'—that's a nice touch. Frankly I don't see the need for 'affectionate.'"

"I'd have thought it was obvious. The word 'affectionate,' together with 'old-fashioned' and 'reserved,' conveys the message that this woman doesn't make friends easily, is hungry for love—hence vulnerable—and probably is very interested in marriage. You see?"

"Well—"

"Let's find a post office and send in the ad. And we'll rent a box for the replies. I imagine they'll start coming in ten days or two weeks. We'll find a furnished apartment—there are some in the *Grapevine*—and order a phone."

"And then?"

"We'll go back to Washington. And wait."

Twenty-nine

 Two and a half weeks later I found myself in a garden apartment near Elkton, bogged down in a jigsaw puzzle and waiting for Sabina to come back from the post office.

The puzzle I was trying to do showed a picture of a million different desserts, all made out of chocolate. Abby Rademacher, who was holding the fort while we were out of town, and who happens to be a chocolate addict, had bought the puzzle during a relapse, but God finally gave her the strength, or so she claimed, to give it to me as a Christmas present. I'd thought it would be a good thing to take to Elkton for the times I'd have to spend waiting around for something to happen, but I was beginning to think I'd been wrong. Every piece of the damn puzzle was more or less brown, and it was getting to me.

I'd made some headway by the time Sabina's key turned in the lock. The edges were done and I was collecting pieces for the chocolate mousse, which had a dab of whipped cream on top. I was counting on the whipped cream to help.

"Vic!" The door opened. "It's just extraordinary! This whole envelope is full of letters!"

"Terrific," I said sourly.

She came into the kitchen and dropped a manila envelope on the counter. "Must you do that puzzle on the kitchen table?"

"There isn't anywhere else."

"Why not the table in front of the couch?" She draped the jacket she'd been wearing over a chair. "Have you been outside?"

"No. And the coffee table is too small. Any of the letters seem promising?"

"I thought we'd open them together. You should go out, it's like spring." It was February, but the weather had suddenly turned warm.

"Spring, when a serial killer's fancy lightly turns to thoughts of love? Love, followed by murder, followed by me being out of a job?"

Sabina folded her arms. "Victor." She glared at me in exasperation. "I'm tired of putting up with your sulking. I'm a private detective, and there are certain risks in the profession, and if you can't accept that simple fact perhaps you should look for another kind of work." I could tell from the way the pupils in her blue eyes had shrunk to tiny points that she wasn't kidding. "Now that we're here in Elkton I intend to focus all my attention on the job of catching a killer, and I have no time to spare for humoring you—understand?"

"Yes, ma'am."

She tore open the manila envelope. "I expect you to back me up, no questions asked. Have I made myself clear?" Her voice dripped icicles.

"Okay, okay." She pushed aside some of the puzzle pieces and dumped out the letters. I said, "Those pieces you just moved happen to have been the mousse I was putting together."

She leaned over the table, glanced at the picture on the cover of the box, picked up one of the pieces she'd moved and said,

"This isn't the mousse, it's the eclair. So is this and this and this—"

I opened the first letter and read aloud. "'Dear Visitor to Elkton, I am a married man but—'"

"Go on to the next one."

"My God, you've put the whole eclair together! How do you do it so fast?"

"You just get the gestalt in your head and then it's easy."

"That's a big help."

"Are we going through these letters or not?" She started putting the mousse together.

"I'd rather do it in the living room."

We went inside and sat down on the couch.

We'd received twelve replies, and a couple obviously were from cranks. Of the rest, most seemed unlikely to have been written by Royce, for one reason or another.

There were three possibilities remaining. All were brief notes from men who claimed to be educated, middle-aged museum lovers, and each enclosed a phone number.

"All right, let me try Herman Schmidt," Sabina said, reaching for the phone. "You listen in on the extension. Nod if you recognize the voice."

"I'm not sure I'd know his voice," I said. "It's been six months, and I don't recall anything special about it."

She was dialing. "Try."

Eliminating Herman Schmidt was easy because he had a faint trace of an accent. I shook my head and mouthed, "Accent."

Sabina said into the receiver, "Oh, there's someone at the door, I'll have to call you back," and hung up. "See?" she said, and picked up the next letter. "You could tell. Now let's try F. Chauncey Randall."

F. Chauncey wasn't home. He had an answering machine, and the voice that delivered the message didn't tell me anything, pro or con. Sabina cooed into the receiver, "This is the Visitor to Elkton, thank you for your letter. Perhaps we could chat some time?" She left our phone number.

The third letter writer had a nasal voice that I was certain didn't belong to the man I'd met at Fran's house.

"So. Where does that leave us? Should we try some of the guys we've eliminated?"

She shook her head. "No. Let's wait for F. Chauncey Randall to call. And we may get more letters."

"F. Chauncey's not the one. The name sounds so phony it has to be real." I picked up his letter and read it again.

Dear Visitor to Elkton:

I am a civil engineer, age 41, never married but still looking for that "special someone." I read your ad in the Grapevine *and would be happy to meet you and show you some real old-fashioned "Cecil County hospitality," since you're an old-fashioned girl! I promise you won't forget it in a hurry! It so happens I'm a museum buff also. Quite a coincidence, don't you think? I've got a feeling we have a lot in common, especially since your ad mentioned "affection" and that's something I can definitely relate to! Not that I would have to be on the receiving end all the time, in fact I wouldn't mind giving plenty of same to the "right person"!*

Hoping to hear from you,

Sincerely,
F. Chauncey Randall

I shook my head. "Too many exclamation points. Too many quotation marks."

"Murderers don't have to be great prose stylists, Vic."

Time passed. F. Chauncey Randall didn't call back. We worked on the puzzle. She was so damn good I felt like hinting around that it was *my* puzzle and maybe there was something else she could do to pass the time; only I was afraid I'd sound petty. By the time the phone finally rang, I was feeling pretty frustrated. As soon as we heard it we both jumped up and rushed into the living room, and when she gave the signal, we simultaneously picked up the two extensions.

"Hello," she cooed.

"Hello, is this—ah, the Visitor to Elkton?" A man's voice.

"Why yes, it is."

He laughed. "I felt kind of silly saying that. I mean, what if it wasn't? This is F. Chauncey Randall. You've got a sexy voice, anybody ever tell you that?"

"Oh—maybe one or two, Mr. Randall." She raised her eyebrows at me questioningly.

I shrugged. I couldn't tell if it was him or not.

"My friends call me Chuck," he said. "What's your name, sweet-face?"

"Sylvia."

They chit-chatted a couple more minutes, and Sabina put her hand over the receiver and hissed, "Well?"

I shrugged again. F. Chauncey had an average kind of voice. It didn't stir any memories, but it didn't jar any either. I mouthed, "Better meet him."

They arranged to have a drink at a place called Hernando's Hideaway. He told her he was tall and had blond hair (a description that would fit not only the guy we were looking for but a goodly percentage of the male population), and that he'd be wearing a blue suit and a yellow paisley tie. She told him she was medium height and had brown hair she wore in a chignon, and would have on a black suit and a pink blouse. Then all three of us hung up.

I drove Sabina to meet F. Chauncey. She was looking great, in a black satin suit with a boxy jacket that disguised the fact that her waist wasn't what you'd call slim any more, and a short skirt that showed off her truly excellent legs. As usual, she was wearing spike-heeled shoes, this particular pair being black patent leather.

Belted into the passenger seat beside me, she clutched a patent leather handbag that contained her Sterling pocketgun, which although on the light side is capable of delivering quite a punch. "Where is this place?" she said, staring out into the darkness. We'd just crossed a river.

"Don't ask me, I'm following F. Chauncey's directions. I think we're near Havre de Grace. Nervous?"

"Somewhat."

"You'll be okay," I said. "Just don't leave the bar with the guy." We'd agreed that if F. Chauncey turned out to be Royce, Sabina would make a follow-up date and bring uniformed reinforcements. We had enough facts now to go to the police—five middle-aged, recently married social workers, killed in identical "accidents" in four and a half years. This had to be more than coincidence.

"It's not that I'm *afraid*. Just—nervous."

"What's the difference?" I turned left at a Texaco station.

"I don't feel in *danger*—"

"You don't mean you're nervous because you're going out on a date?" I kept my eyes front and tried not to smile.

"I fail to see the humor."

"Sorry. I guess it's only natural—you and Bruno have been married a long time."

"Seven years."

"That's all?" The highway we were on had narrowed to two lanes lined with tacky little businesses, most of them closed for the night.

"That's all. It's not as if I know nothing about being single, Vic. When I met Bruno I'd been a widow for eight years, so I know enough about the single life to dislike it intensely. Such a waste of energy, always trying to find someone! Don't *you* ever—"

"Wait," I said. "I think we're here." I slowed down but didn't stop. Neon flashed on and off. Apparently, Hernando's Hideaway was the cocktail lounge of the Deluxe Budget Motel. "Hey, I like it," I said. "This guy's got class."

"Good God." I drove down the road a short distance and

pulled into the parking lot of a Dairy Delite. Through the plate-glass window I could see the place was empty except for a woman in a pink uniform, passing a rag over the counter as if her thoughts were elsewhere.

We got out of the car. Sabina climbed back in on the driver's side, stepped on the gas, and made a U-turn. I started walking back toward the motel along the edge of the highway. F. Chauncey had said he would wait for her in the bar, but we were taking no chances of his seeing her arrive at the motel with me.

Hernando's Hideaway was a place, like the one in the song, where lights were low. That helped, because I didn't want Sabina's date catching sight of me. If I could recognize Royce, he could recognize me. But as soon as I saw Sabina squeezed into a tiny booth next to a guy whose hair had been slicked back with goo, I knew I could relax. F. Chauncey Randall wasn't Royce.

Another blind alley.

I meandered over to the bar and ordered a beer. Might as well get something out of the evening. The room was dense with people and an intense band was blasting away on a stage barely big enough to accommodate the musicians. I asked a youngish brunette who was twitching on her bar stool in synch with the beat if she'd care to dance, and a moment later we were out on the floor. It felt good to be in motion after a day spent picking up little pieces of cardboard, all of them brown.

We danced the whole set. Once Sabina saw I'd dropped my cover, she knew, of course, that her date wasn't Royce. She gave me a dirty look as my partner and I maneuvered athletically past her table. F. Chauncey's arm was around Sabina, and she was removing his hand from her knee. I figured she was a big girl and could take care of herself.

During the break I went over to their table. F. Chauncey was trying to play footsie while she kept edging her feet into the aisle. "Sylvia!" I said. "I *thought* it was you. Hey, what are you doing here?"

"Taking courses at the university," she said, smiling through her teeth. "What are *you* doing here?"

"Attending a meeting." I leaned over the table and stuck out my hand in F. Chauncey's direction. "Name's Vic," I said. "Sylvia and I used to work at the same agency."

"Name's Chuck," he said, and slid his arm around her shoulders.

She shook him off and rose. "Thanks for the drink, Chuck. I'll give you a call one of these days."

"Wait a minute!"

I looked from her to F. Chauncey and back again. "Oh, you mean you two aren't—"

"Chuck and I," she said firmly, "have only just met. Vic, I'm starving, could I interest you in dinner?"

"Sure could." I threw F. Chauncey an apologetic shrug as she took my arm. "Sorry . . . old friends, you know—" We made our getaway.

I steered her down the hall, making light conversation. "Seems like a swell guy. Friendly and all—" We reached the lobby of the motel, blinking in the sudden brightness. "I hope he told you what he puts on his hair, I'd like to try it, probably make a big hit with the girls."

As soon as we reached the parking lot, she jerked her elbow out of my hand. "How could you—*dance!*"

"Studied at Arthur Murray's—no, seriously, I really needed the exercise. Band wasn't bad, as a matter of fact. Why didn't you give it a whirl yourself?"

"Dance? I? With him? He was a wolf!"

"Wolf?"

"His hands were in constant motion! You saw what was going on, why'd it take you so long to come over?"

"I knew you could handle him." We got into the car and I backed it out of the space. "I mean, this whole thing was your idea, Sabina. I opposed it, if you recall. But we private detectives have to take certain risks—"

"Drive," she said.

"Surely you expected—"

"That's enough. Drive!"

Thirty

It was three and a half weeks since the ad had appeared, the Visitor to Elkton had received a total of twenty-one letters, and Sabina had gone out with a second man who'd turned out not to be Royce. F. Chauncey kept calling and asking for another date, even though Sabina had told him in no uncertain terms she wasn't interested. We were running up an enormous bill on Donna MacNiece's account, not that Donna seemed particularly disturbed when Sabina called her to discuss it. Guess those old tobacco barons really made a pile, before the Surgeon General spoiled their fun. As far as I could see, all we seemed to have accomplished since coming to Elkton was to raise false hopes in F. Chauncey and fulfill one of my lifelong ambitions: to read *Crime and Punishment* from beginning to end.

Sabina wasn't ready to give up yet. The response rate to the ad had tapered off, but she was talking about placing another ad, claiming there'd been no flaw in the chain of reasoning that had led us to Elkton. I had a hunch the real reason was that she'd run out of ideas for finding Royce.

Personally, I thought it was time to go home. Sabina was the boss, though; so I drove up to Newark, located a bookstore near the University of Delaware, bought myself a copy of *War and Peace*, and hunkered down to wait some more.

"Vic!"

It was Sabina, back from the post office with an envelope in her hand.

"You got a letter." The news didn't excite me. All the letters we'd been receiving led in the same direction: nowhere.

She slipped out of her jacket and dropped down beside me on the couch, where I was sitting with my book. "Not *a* letter, Vic. I think—*the* letter!" Her voice was shaking with suppressed emotion.

"You don't mean—"

"I think so!" She waved the envelope at me. "Persistence! Isn't that what I always say? It's persistence that pays off!"

The telephone began to ring. I said, "Probably F. Chauncey. Now *there's* persistence."

She groaned. "Why can't the wretched man leave me in peace?"

"Your fatal charm."

"Would you please get it?"

I reached for the phone. "Hello?" Yep, it was him. "No, you can't speak to Sylvia. Uh-huh. Nope. Yes, this is Vic. You're right, it *was* fishy the way I showed up. Uh-huh. Uh-huh." I let him run on for a while. "Listen, Sylvia and I are having a hot affair, so don't call back anymore, okay?" I hung up.

Sabina blushed. "Thank you, Victor. Did you have to be quite so direct?"

"I used my best judgment."

"Well—I guess that's what I pay you for."

"That's what you pay me for." There was a silence that could have gotten uncomfortable if it had lasted longer. There's always been a little chemistry between me and Sabina, especially in situations like this when we're together day and night; but we both think it's better not to push it. At least, we haven't done so yet. I said, "What about that letter?"

"Oh, the letter." She took it out of the envelope, holding it by the edges, and opened it up. It had been typed on ordinary white paper and mailed in a plain white envelope. The return address was a box number at the main post office in Wilmington, Delaware.

I said, "Wilmington?"

"Why not? Wilmington is only twenty miles away. It's the nearest city big enough to have a post office where a box holder needn't worry about being recognized."

We read the letter.

Dear Visitor to Elkton:

I read your ad in the Grapevine *with great interest. Having spent much time travelling in connection with my work, I comprehend full well how lonely it can be when one is in an unfamiliar locale.*

I, like yourself, am in my forties, but chronological age is insignificant to me. What counts is what is inside a person, emotionally and spiritually. You, I gather, from your interest in museums (an interest I definitely share) are a cultured and classy lady. If you are "reserved," as you say in your ad, it will be my delightful avocation to draw you out. As for being "old-fashioned," I am that way myself. It seems we are on the same wave length.

I possess a Master's Degree in Library Science from Harvard University and labored for a number of years as a librarian, but although I thrive in the presence of learned volumes I was eventually forced to conclude that this was not sufficiently remunerative, so I resumed my educational endeavors and earned a Master's in Business Administration from the University of Delaware. I now have my own business as a consultant in the software field (the reason I travel so extensively, as alluded to above).

. *According to your ad, you are divorced. I, too, find myself in that situation, having separated from my former wife approximately three years ago. Do you at least have the support of a close and affectionate family? My wife and I were childless and all my relatives are either deceased or geographically remote, so there are times when I find myself envying those who are fortunate enough to possess a family life. I would definitely consider remarriage if I met a compatible lady who cherished love and affection.*

I would be honored if you allowed me to make your stay in Elkton more enjoyable, and hope you will be moved to write me at the above box number, including your telephone number, and if possible a photograph so I can recognize you when we meet. Have you already visited the Wyeth Museum in Chadd's Ford, which is not far from here? If the answer is no, perhaps you will allow me to escort you there when we get together.

Yours very sincerely (yes, I am sincere, but hope you will conclude that for yourself before too long).

Elliott Martin

The name "Elliott Martin," like the rest of the letter, was typed.

"You see?" said Sabina. "Isn't this letter perfect? Too perfect? You notice he addresses every single point raised in the ad. Our fictitious social worker wants a man who is educated? Very well, Mr. Martin has not one but *two* master's degrees, one of them from—where else?—Harvard! Yet the tone of the letter doesn't suggest an educated man to me—certainly not a Harvard librarian."

"Why not? Look at this vocabulary—'enterprising.'" I said. "And how about 'remunerative'?"

She shook her head. "That's just it, there are too many big words. 'Resumed my educational endeavors'! Why doesn't he just say he went back to school? This is the letter of a sketchily educated man who thinks long words are impressive." She re-read it, slowly and carefully. "And look at the information he offers about himself. He's divorced and has no family, is self-employed, and travels frequently—matters that are hard to check, matters that could also make things easier for him later. And did you notice he asks only one personal question in the entire letter: Does she have close family ties? Of all the possible questions in the world, why that one? Because he wants to know whether there are relatives who might raise awkward questions if something happened to her. I'm convinced this is the man we're after. What do you think?"

I recalled the man I'd met six months ago in Fran's house, the man who'd called himself Keith Browdy, and tried to imagine him writing this letter.

And I could.

There was something about them, the man and the letter, that had the same feel—a kind of plausibility that was almost but not quite convincing. A lack of genuine feeling. It was a hard thing to put into words. I said, "I agree with you."

Sabina was still studying the letter. "Notice that he offers to take this woman he's never laid eyes on all the way to Chadd's Ford. A neat little Pirandello touch, calculated to appeal to a lady who loves museums. Why isn't Mr. Martin even the slightest bit tentative? Wouldn't it be more normal for him to want to find out whether she's attractive before suggesting such a lengthy outing? Why doesn't he ask her to meet him for a drink?"

"Because he doesn't care if she's attractive." After the long, discouraging chase, could we finally be closing in on our quarry? "Because as long as she doesn't have any close ties, he's going after her!" I could feel excitement beginning to build.

"Exactly!"

"So—now that he's taken the bait, I guess you have to call him." I still didn't like the plan of attack.

"I can't, Vic. Didn't you notice? There's no phone number—only a post office box." She gave a little smile. "Mr.

Elliott Martin knows phone numbers can be traced, and he intends to remain in control of his future relationship with the Visitor to Elkton—totally! Well, we'll see about that. Why don't you put up the kettle, while I write Mr. Martin a note."

It didn't take her long. Before she sealed the letter she enclosed a photograph Bruno had taken of her at the National Arboretum during azalea time. It showed her gazing at a spray of blossoms with a deceptive expression of pensive sweetness. "This picture takes ten years off my age," she gloated as she licked the flap of the envelope.

I said, "Now we mail the letter and wait?"

"Correct."

"There's too much waiting in this case."

"You're young, Vic. In time, you'll learn to cultivate patience."

Thirty-one

The plan was that we would wait for Elliott Martin to call, and when he did I would listen in on the extension while Sabina made an appointment to meet him in some public place. If I could make a positive identification of the voice we would go to the police; otherwise, we'd wait until I'd had a chance to see him. "We can't bring the police a theory about Elliott Martin's vocabulary, and Pirandello's plays," Sabina said. "They'd laugh us out of the station house. We need positive proof this man is Royce."

I knew the real reason that she was resistant to the idea of calling in the police was that she was afraid they might somehow scare Royce off, once they stepped into the case.

Reluctantly, I resigned myself to the inevitable.

There was nothing we could do but wait for a phone call to come from Elliott Martin. For days we hardly stepped outside the door of the apartment. By the fifth day we were getting on each other's nerves, and by the sixth, we were afraid something had gone wrong.

On the afternoon of the seventh, I was reading *War and Peace* in the bedroom with the door closed. I'd grown tired of watching Sabina pace back and forth, and I didn't want to hear any more of her theories about why Elliott Martin hadn't called.

Suddenly the bedroom door flew open and she appeared, wearing her coat.

"Vic!"

A new theory, no doubt. "What?"

"Suppose I've overlooked something!"

Just as I'd thought. "It could happen."

"Suppose Royce doesn't intend to call?"

I sighed. "Then why did he answer the ad?"

She shook her head. "I don't mean that. Suppose what he does is write a second letter!"

"Well—yeah. Sure, that's possible."

"Just because I asked him to call doesn't mean he will. Remember, he has to remain in control at all times. I'm going to the post office."

"I'll come with you," I said. At least it was a chance to get out of the apartment.

We found two letters in the box, and one of them was from Elliott Martin.

My dear Sylvia:

I can't tell you how pleased I was to receive your gracious note. Your lovely picture is before me as I write, and I see that when you penned the word "attractive" in your ad, you were not exaggerating. Am I wrong in assuming you are a lover of flowers? It just so happens that flowers are among my favorite things in the world. Maybe instead of going to the Wyeth museum you would prefer an excursion to Winterthur, a magnificent garden which is open to the public, since the weather is so unseasonably warm.

I propose that you meet me for lunch on Saturday at the

Wilmoral Hotel in Wilmington at 12 noon. If you can't make it, please write to me and we will arrange another rendezvous! I am eager to meet you in person, and am sure I will recognize you from your picture.

I hope you don't mind that I prefer to communicate by letter rather than telephone, at least until we get to know each other better. I warned you I'm old-fashioned! I happen to have an aversion to the telephone, although I use it in connection with my business where I have no choice.

> *Sincerely and with anticipation,*
> *Elliott Martin*

"Saturday—that's tomorrow," said Sabina.

"You won't change your mind about the police?"

She shook her head. "I'd rather wait until you've seen him and confirmed that he's the same man."

"But we're sure he is! Look at his letter—you send him a picture with flowers, right away he's a flower lover. This has got to be the guy."

"I tend to agree, but we'll still wait."

"I don't like you getting that close to him without a police presence."

Sabina frowned. "Victor, I've made my decision. The danger is negligible—I'll be carrying a gun, and you'll be right nearby." She put the letter in her pocketbook. "Come along, I want you to drive me to Wilmington. Immediately. I think we should take a good long look at the Wilmoral Hotel before my little rendezvous."

Thirty-two

On Saturday, I arrived at the Wilmoral Hotel an hour early and was greeted like an old friend by Carlos, the guy in the checkroom, who for a small consideration had agreed to let me stake out the lobby from behind one of the coat racks.

The Wilmoral was quite a few notches above the Deluxe Budget Motel. Concealed behind a couple of mink coats, I kept my eye on the spacious lobby, with its high ceiling, tall, gold-framed mirrors, and oversize antiques. The people milling around looked prosperous and confident, and there was no shortage of men about the same height and build as Royce.

I kept wondering if he was really going to show up. I didn't *think* we'd made any blunders; yet after six months on his trail I couldn't rule out the possibility that something—pure animal instinct, a phrase in one of Sabina's letters, anything at all— might arouse his suspicions and make him stay away.

Across the lobby, a tall man in a gray business suit lit a cigar. I stiffened. He gave a couple of puffs, shook out the match, and raised his head.

Just another guy who wasn't Royce.

I tried not to brood over the obvious fact that if Royce failed to show up we had no way to trace him. Sure, we could stake out the Wilmington post office, though I doubted even Donna would want to underwrite eight hours a day of surveillance, for an indefinite period, of a box Royce would probably never use again. Yet the box number was the only clue we had.

In other words, we had nothing. Nada.

At eleven-forty, twenty minutes before Sabina was supposed to arrive, I was trying to pretend an interest in some snapshots of Carlos's new baby, and to ignore the feeling of deepening pessimism that was creeping over me like a bad case of poison ivy. For what seemed like the hundredth time, I leaned forward to peer between the minks.

The man I'd met at Fran's house was coming through the revolving door.

Royce.

I could feel the hairs on the back of my neck prickle. Until that moment I hadn't believed he would show up.

"Cute," I muttered, thrusting the baby pictures aside.

Royce stepped into the lobby, looking as if he belonged there, in a dark three-piece suit, paisley silk tie, and freshly shined, Italian shoes. His blond hair had been cut a little on the long side—not too much—and nicely blow-dried. The first time I'd seen him, bare chested and in running shorts, he'd looked like a middle-aged jock. Today he projected a more conservative image, maybe a successful businessman or a corporate lawyer, with a six-figure income and political ambitions. On second thought, he was a little too handsome for that, his skin too smooth, upper lip too pretty, eyelashes a shade too long: a Chamber of Commerce type as dreamed up by Central Casting.

He was carrying a white rose, the son of a bitch.

He cased the lobby, the narrow dark eyes I remembered darting everywhere, a nerve jumping in the corner of his mouth. I was damn glad I hadn't decided to station myself on a chair behind one of the pillars with a newspaper, which I'd considered. He circled every pillar. He also peeked behind the massive flower arrangements on the mahogany tables, cased the phone booths, browsed through the aisles of the glass-walled gift shop, checked out the corridors, and finally disappeared in the direction of the Men's Room—not, I suspected, because nature had called but to see who was in there. The guy wasn't taking any chances, he must be hurting badly for cash or he'd never have started setting up a new victim, as spooked as I could tell he was.

I placed a red folding umbrella on the cloakroom counter. It was the signal Sabina and I had agreed on, and meant I'd recognized Royce.

A few minutes after twelve, Sabina walked through the revolving doors. She'd spent the morning in the beauty parlor and looked great. She was wearing a rose-colored silk dress with a lot of soft, lacy stuff under the chin that gave her an air of innocent vulnerability. Her gaze swept the lobby and took in the red umbrella. She started wandering around, the hem of her dress sort of rippling and floating around her long, slim legs, giving demure, ladylike glances at the men as if searching for someone. Royce was standing against the wall in an adjacent corridor, and when he saw her, the nerve jumped once in the corner of his mouth. Then his face became totally still. He watched her the way a cat studies a bird that is fluttering closer and closer.

Suddenly he smiled, and the two deep brackets I remembered appeared in the skin beside his lips. He stepped forward into the lobby and went up to greet her. She raised her chin and gave him a long, unsmiling, yet somehow welcoming look as their eyes met in a stare of mutual curiosity. He handed her the rose. She took it, acting pleased. Then he took it back from her, and her hand jerked as if she'd pricked her finger. With a look of concern, he seized her hand and raised it to his lips, murmuring something. Then he took the handkerchief out of his breast pocket and dabbed at her finger, saying something, while she stood there and smiled. After a while he released her hand. He snapped off a piece of the stem and carefully pinned the rose to her dress. She kind of played up to him, and then he took her arm and led her across the lobby in the direction of the dining room. They disappeared through an archway, her arm pinned beneath his, and I could feel anxiety churning in the pit of my stomach, though I told myself there was nothing to worry about. Sabina would be perfectly safe surrounded by people, and the dining room had no other exit, except for the door to the kitchen—we'd checked.

I waited on a stool behind the coatrack, reading a magazine the way you do in a doctor's office, checking the time and looking around every few minutes; after an hour I put the magazine away and kept my eyes on the archway that led to the dining room. We'd agreed that if Elliott Martin turned out to be Royce, Sabina was to make an appointment to meet him again, say goodbye when the lunch was over, proceed to the parking lot, and drive away. Fifteen minutes later, she was to return and pick me up.

After about an hour and a half, they came out of the dining room and crossed the lobby, arm in arm. She said something to him and he nodded. With a quick glance in my direction, she headed toward the restrooms, while Royce walked to the revolving doors and left the hotel. The way the two of them parted didn't look like they were saying goodbye.

I could see Sabina loitering in the corridor that led to the restrooms, and as soon as Royce disappeared I went and joined her.

"Well?" I said. "How'd it go?"

"Fine," she said in a low voice. "He's very charming." Her eyes scanned watchfully over my shoulder. Drawing me further down the corridor, she stepped into a recess where there were telephones, and I followed her. "Vic," she said. "There's been a change in plans. We're going to Winterthur—he absolutely in-

234

sisted. We have no time to talk, he's just gone to get his car. I know," she said, putting up her hand to forestall my objections. "It's not what we'd agreed, but he's on his guard every single minute, he's extremely nervous. I'm afraid if I let him get away, we'll never see him again."

"Sabina, you promised—"

"I know, but—" She shook her head. "The lunch went well, the weather's perfect. I had no good *reason* for refusing, and he knew it."

"Do you think he's suspicious?"

"No-o, not *particularly*, but he's walking a knife edge, I could feel it. You'd better get the car and follow us."

"Let me call the police first."

"It'll take too long, you'll have to do a lot of explaining. Just follow us. Call them from Winterthur—once we get there you'll have time. I'll stall him, I'll go into ecstasies over every leaf, believe me I'll keep him there until they arrive."

"Sabina—"

Firmly, she shook her head. "There's no *time*, Victor. Get the car."

I hurried outside. The parking lot was a big one, with islands of landscaping separating the rows of parked cars, and it appeared deserted in the wintry sunshine. Nothing moved. If Royce was out there, I saw no sign of him.

I'd left my car in a distant corner and I headed in that direction, hugging an evergreen hedge. As I rounded a group of trees, my eye caught a sudden flash of movement. I whirled. An enormous German shepherd was bounding toward me, fangs bared, growling ferociously. I barely had time to recognize it as Royce's dog, Wolf, when it caught up with me and sprang. I kicked out at it, and the fangs closed in the cloth of my pants leg. There was a ripping sound as I jerked away. I broke into a run, thinking, "There go my best gray slacks."

A voice shouted, "Wolf! Down! Down, boy!" I glimpsed

Royce running toward the dog. "Sorry!" he yelled in my direction. I kept on running—I didn't think he'd recognized me. Ducking behind a hedge, I doubled over, keeping out of sight and running hard. When I reached my car I jumped inside, took a couple of deep breaths, and waited, gun in hand.

Nothing happened. Nobody came.

Thirty-three

I followed them through the streets of Wilmington. There was enough traffic so it wasn't hard to stay out of sight, and my two-year-old blue Honda looked like dozens of other cars on the road. Royce was driving a silver Mercedes—the guy sure liked fancy cars—and the sun made a spot of brightness on the shiny roof that was easy to follow.

I kept brooding over the incident in the parking lot. I didn't think Royce had recognized me, but I wasn't sure and that bothered me. Why hadn't I remembered that Royce took his dog everywhere, even to funerals? It was obvious, now, that Wolf had been in the car while Royce had been wining and dining Sabina, and that afterwards he'd decided to walk the dog before picking her up. I didn't know if Wolf had attacked me because he remembered me, or because he didn't like my looks. Either way, it was a piece of bad luck.

Up ahead, Royce was weaving skillfully between the cars, yet staying within the speed limit. I followed him onto I-95, where he shot ahead in the left-hand lane. Traffic was heavy. I kept as many cars as possible between me and the silver Mercedes, without running the risk of losing it entirely.

I wondered how Sabina and Wolf were getting along. She definitely wasn't a dog person, in fact she'd told me once she didn't understand the point of dogs; and when I'd explained they didn't need to have a point because they were man's best friend, I could see she still didn't get it.

It wasn't until we passed Newark and a sign flashed by saying WELCOME TO MARYLAND that I started worrying about where we were going. Wasn't Winterthur north of Wilmington? If we'd entered Maryland, that meant we were heading south. I grabbed the map on the seat beside me and tried to read it with one eye while watching the road with the other, a procedure I don't recommend. In the process I almost lost the Mercedes, which slipped suddenly into the right-hand lane and sped off on an exit ramp without signalling for the turn. Tires squealing, I followed, irritating a few drivers.

At the end of the ramp, the Mercedes turned left onto a two-lane shunpike. Was Royce taking the scenic route, had there been still another change of plan, or was he aware I was on his tail? I wished I knew, but there was no way to find out. All I could do was follow him, staying as far back as possible.

We seemed to be heading in the general direction of the Chesapeake Bay. Traffic thinned out, and I dropped even further back, hoping he wouldn't notice me in his rearview mirror and feeling more and more unhappy about the way Sabina's date with Royce was turning out.

The Mercedes started making quite a few turns, until I finally lost my sense of direction completely except for a persistent feeling that we were going around in a big circle. A couple of times I thought I'd lost Royce for good, and I had to edge up closer than I liked to keep him in sight.

The area we were passing through was starting to look familiar. We were back in Cecil County—same mobile homes with stamped metal skirting, same rusty Dr. Pepper signs. Finally the Mercedes slowed down, and I pulled back thinking that maybe Royce had gotten to wherever it was he was going. There was nothing much to be seen though, except for a couple of horses in a field with a fence around it, a stretch of woods with a row of wooden beehives at the edge, a rundown house, and a sign that said HONEY FOR SALE. The Mercedes was dawdling down the road, and I was staying far behind it but keeping it in view, when Royce suddenly stepped on the gas and took off like a rocket. I floored the accelerator, but too late. Behind the tail lights of the disappearing Mercedes, a freight train came barreling down a railroad track that had suddenly appeared out of nowhere.

All I could do was jam on the brakes and sit stewing in the car, waiting for the damn train to go by. It was one of the longest waits of my life.

Royce knew about those tracks, on that I'd have bet a year's pay. He'd known when the train was coming and he'd led me by the nose around the countryside until the exact moment when he could use the train to get me off his tail. Which proved a couple of things: he'd realized—for how long?—that he was being followed, and he knew the area well, maybe even lived nearby.

But where?

Finally, the train passed. I stepped on the gas and zoomed across the tracks and down the road. The Mercedes, of course, was long gone. I knew that sooner or later the road would fork, and I'd have to make a choice without a damn thing to go on.

And while I was trying to find the Mercedes, what would be happening to my boss? She'd landed herself in exactly the kind of mess I'd warned her about; as I'd told her over and over, Royce was too tricky and dangerous to fool with.

Great, I'd been right. Now I could say, "I told you so."

It didn't give me a whole lot of satisfaction.

I reached a fork in the road. For no particular reason I turned left, and after a while came to a house where there was a man up on the roof, nailing shingles. I pulled over and asked him if he'd seen a silver Mercedes. He said, "No." It wasn't clear to me that he'd know one if he saw one, but anyway I made a U-turn and went back and took the right-hand fork, trying to tell myself Sabina would be fine—after all, she did have a gun in her bag.

I followed the right-hand fork over a bridge and another set of tracks, until the road I was on became the narrow main street of a tacky little town that showed a few signs of gentrification—a couple of antique shops, and an art gallery with duck decoys and paintings of waterfowl in the window. I cruised past the Inches Off Emporium, looking for a good place to stop and ask questions, and decided on the Mor-Valu General Store. Right across the street I found a parking space, outside an old red brick church that stood in the middle of a graveyard with an iron fence around it. The headstones had been there so long that some of them had sunk into the ground until only the tops showed. I noticed a pair of linked stone hearts bearing the worn inscription, "And I Gave Unto Them Eternal Rest." A sign said the church had been founded in 1714.

The Mor-Valu general store was jammed with merchandise that looked as if it had been gathering dust for fifty years. There was a small open space in the middle, and in it a gaunt old geezer sat in a rocker with his nose about a foot from a color TV that was playing a war movie. He didn't look up. The place smelled strongly of cat. Behind the counter, a heavyset man with tattooed forearms was talking on the phone. He acknowledged my arrival by hunching his shoulder so his conversation would have more privacy. Both men were wearing plaid flannel shirts and plastic mesh caps with visors in front. The old man's cap said COORS BEER, and the younger man's said, MINE IS LONGER THAN YOURS.

I figured with an attitude like that I'd get further if I didn't interrupt his phone conversation. He took his time about finishing up. The old man continued to ignore me, in fact I wasn't sure he'd noticed me come in. There was a wooden box lined with newspaper in which a mother cat was nursing a litter of kittens. I waited.

"Do fer ya?" The heavyset man was off the phone.

I gave him a friendly smile. "I wonder if I could ask you a few questions."

He shrugged. "Figure you know that better'n me."

"Yeah, well I'm trying to locate somebody."

"Who'd that be?"

"I think his first name is Royce, but I'm not sure that's what he calls himself."

He looked at me suspiciously out of little black eyes sunk in a doughy face. "Don't sound like you're no friend of his."

"You know him?"

He shrugged again, and picked up a stub of pencil that lay on the counter. "Plenty people named Royce. Listen, you a customer or ain't you? This here's a store. You don't want to buy nothing, I got my work to do." He picked up a grungy invoice pad with a couple of rubber bands around it. There was a burst of machine gun fire from the TV.

"I don't need anything," I said, and took out my wallet. "Except information. I could buy that."

"How much you paying?"

I had his attention. Slowly I took out a bill. "Ten."

His little eyes clutched greedily at the money, and there was regret in his voice as he said, "Trouble is, I don't know no Royce."

"Sure?"

"Sure I'm sure." He sounded a little hostile, as if I'd called him a liar.

"You ever see a silver Mercedes around?"

His eyes caressed the money. "You mean like one of them Mercedes *Benz*? Sure I seen one, there's a feller has one." He added, "I don't know the feller."

"You know where he lives?"

"What'd you say you're offering?"

"Ten." I waved the bill.

"Aw, I don't know if I could remember for ten."

I took out another ten. "I might go twenty."

He said shrewdly, "How about thirty?"

I put the bills back in my wallet. "Twenty's my limit."

"You want to know or don't you?" He was grinning, and I could see he needed to win. Competitive guy.

"Okay, thirty. But that's it."

"I'll take it." He held out his hand.

"Wait, first let's hear what you know."

He turned away and said sullenly, "I don't know nothing for no money down."

"Okay, suppose I give you ten now and twenty after."

He thought it over and decided to do me a favor. "Guess that'll do." He held out his hand again and I laid a ten in it. "Guy owns that Benz has a trailer off of Marsh Road. Doesn't use the place much, comes here just to hunt, I guess."

"Where's Marsh Road?"

He pointed toward the street outside the store. "You take this road a mile and a half, turn left by a green house, left again first chance you get, then watch for a dirt road going off to the right into the woods." A sly look came into the little eyes. "There's a sign says KEEP OUT. I don't know as I'd drop by without an invitation. Gimme the twenty."

I gave it to him.

Thirty-four

The words KEEP OUT had been splashed in white paint on a big rock. I saw the sign before I saw the road, because the road was nothing but a couple of ruts heading into the woods. They ran straight for a few hundred yards, then curved and disappeared behind the trees.

I turned off the main road onto the track. A small animal, a rabbit or squirrel, lay in a squashed heap in one of the ruts. It had been run over recently; the blood was still shiny. I swerved to avoid it.

When I reached the bend in the road I stopped the car and got out. There were no houses around. It was very quiet now that I'd left the main road—so quiet that anybody listening would definitely hear my car. I decided it would make more sense to proceed on foot. Trouble was, I had no idea how far I'd have to go. The trailer could be a mile down the road, and the idea of leaving my car so far behind made me edgy. What if I needed to take off in a hurry?

Gun in hand, I walked cautiously around the bend to reconnoiter. But all I saw were trees and more trees, leafless and bare. I began jogging down the narrow, curving track for what seemed a long time, until the bend started to straighten out. Then I slowed my pace and left the road, cutting into the woods. There wasn't much cover—the underbrush was as leafless as the trees. I kept moving ahead, parallel to the road. Every time the wind picked up I could smell the Chesapeake Bay.

Finally I caught sight of a narrow clearing up ahead. Half hidden behind weeds and bushes stood an ancient trailer. Out front, the silver Mercedes was parked alongside a heap of rotting boards. I ducked behind a tree, tightening my grip on the gun.

The trailer had been there a long time. Long enough to collect a lot of rust, long enough for moss to grow on the sagging roofs of the sheds that leaned against it. Was Sabina inside? She had to be somewhere around—at least I hoped so.

I crept toward the clearing, keeping low, and was almost there when the damn dog started to bark. I backtracked as fast as I could until the barking stopped. After a while I started cautiously circling around the clearing at a distance, studying the situation. There was a creek in the back. I headed for it, hoping the sound of the water would cover my approach.

As I neared the creek, I could see a rotting shed on the bank. There were piles of rusty chain outside, and shreds of netting, hung from a frame. Moored to the bank was a battered rowboat. The door of the shed hung open.

In the doorway, Royce's dog stood on guard, head raised and ears pricked up alertly.

What was he guarding?

Sabina?

I tried to think of a way to get close enough to find out without the dog barking up a storm. I knew Royce had to be around somewhere.

Suddenly something cold and hard jabbed me painfully in the spine. A voice snarled. "Drop the gun!" I jerked my head around, and the voice said, "Don't move! Drop the gun or you're dead!"

It was Royce, with a rifle in his hand. He'd come up behind me without making a sound. I could smell the reek of his sweat and I knew he was scared, as scared as I was, scared enough to pull the trigger if I made one false move. I opened my hand and let the gun fall to the ground. "That's good," he said. "That's better. Start walking straight ahead. Slowly—don't make any sudden moves." I took one step and then another in the direction of the clearing. He followed, prodding me with the barrel of the gun. He said, "So it *was* you in the parking lot. At first I wasn't sure. But Wolf knew."

"Yeah, I figured, when he took a bite out of my pants."

He gave an unpleasant little laugh. "Fran's precious Vicky."

"Vic."

"Vicky, the suburban sleuth. You know, you seemed like a nice guy. No mental giant, but okay. Why didn't you mind your own business, Vicky? I never harmed you."

I looked at him in amazement. "You really believe that? Fran was my friend."

He shrugged. "Come on. That old bag. Well, I bet you're sorry now you stuck your nose in. You shouldn't have come after me, or did you think I was some kind of punk? Some dummy? Did you think you were smarter than me?"

"I'm not smarter than you?"

He jabbed me painfully in the ribs. "You? Coming after me was the biggest mistake you ever made in your life. I'll tell you something, I've known a lot of smart people, Vicky. Educated people." He laughed again. "So how come I always stayed one step ahead of them?"

I figured I better keep him talking. "How did you?"

"I have a high I. Q." The fear I'd sensed in him earlier seemed to have drained away. "I'm a genius, actually. Fact. I've had more tests than you could possibly imagine. They all showed the same thing. Hundred and eighties. Genius level."

"A hundred and eighty I.Q.? I'm impressed. Do you have a college degree?"

He prodded me forward. "I've taken courses. You don't need

degrees." We entered the clearing. It was littered with old tires filled with muddy water, rusted metal drums, a defunct refrigerator lying on its back in the weeds. The dog looked up and growled but remained motionless in the doorway of the shed. "Take a look around." Royce motioned me toward the stream, the gun still pointed in my direction. He was an incongruous figure in that setting, with his three-piece suit and blow-dried hair. Not a strand of it lifted when the breeze blew. Half lowering the rifle, he stroked the barrel absently and eyed me with a sly little smile. "You're one of the few who've seen my, shall I say secret kingdom? The very few, you should feel honored. This creek runs right into the Chesapeake Bay. Ducks, geese, you name it—or maybe you don't hunt." His smile broadened into the grin of a man pleased with his own cleverness. "Don't hunt *birds*, I mean. Right? I've got twenty acres, on both sides of the creek. A beautiful spot—right?"

"If you like substandard housing."

"Why you—" His face twisted into a mask of fury as he leaped toward me, raising the rifle. The barrel slammed into the side of my neck as I ducked, knocking me to my knees. I shook my head to clear it and the dog charged toward us, growling ferociously. It landed on top of me and I went sprawling. Royce grabbed the dog by the collar and yanked him away. "Stop it, Wolf! Stop it!" He gave another yank and the dog backed off reluctantly, baring yellow fangs and growling. Royce stood looking down at me. He shook his head pityingly. "Vicky, Vicky. It's not smart of you to be a wiseguy, under the circumstances. Let me give you some advice—make an effort to appreciate what you're seeing, because you're not going to see a whole lot more of this world. Wolf! Calm down!" He grabbed the dog's collar again. "Don't think I'm keeping Wolf off of you out of the goodness of my heart." He smiled. It wasn't a reassuring smile, and the narrow eyes were cold as he said, "I'd rather not have any toothmarks on your body when they find it, that's all. After the accident. Attention to small details is a sign of a superior intelligence."

246

"After what accident?" I shook my head to clear it. The blow had left me dizzy.

"The one you're going to have."

I swallowed. "An accident on the railroad tracks, like Fran? Like Ruthann Duncan and Sondra Turette and a few others I could name?" His smile stiffened but he showed no other reaction. I said, "Isn't that idea getting a little stale? There are people who know about it by now, aside from us." I added, "People who know we're—"

"Here?" His eyes narrowed still more. "Oh, I doubt that. For instance, if you'd gone to the police, *they'd* be here, not you. You're bluffing, Vicky. Anyway, that's not the kind of accident I had in mind. An ordinary highway smashup would be much better. The kind that could happen to anyone—say, tonight when the fog rolls in from the bay. I know several places where the curves are quite treacherous, and the visibility—" He shook his head. "Really, the authorities ought to do something. But so far they haven't, fortunately for me and unfortunately for you." The dog growled softly and Royce threw him a glance. "Poor Wolf, he doesn't understand these subtleties. All he wants to do is tear you limb from limb. He had the same problem with your friend Sylvia, or whatever her name is."

I stumbled to my feet. "Where is she?"

"You'll see her soon enough."

"Where is she, Royce?"

"What makes you call me that?" he said sharply. Suddenly he gave the dog a vicious kick in the ribs. "Wolf! Didn't I say, 'Stay!'? Didn't I say, 'Guard!'?" He pointed to the shed and the dog retreated, whining, and resumed his position in the doorway.

"Isn't that your name?"

He studied me. "Well, well. Perhaps you're brighter than you look. How'd you learn my name? I think I need to know." A nerve in the corner of his mouth jerked a couple of times.

"Tell me where Sabina is."

"Is that her name, Sabina? It suits her better than Sylvia.

Sylvia's a weak name, and your friend is quite a little tiger. Fortunately, she's been declawed." Reaching in his jacket, he pulled out Sabina's Sterling pocket gun. He dangled it for a moment on his index finger, watching me, and then dropped it back in his pocket. "All right. I want to hear what you know about me."

"First, where's Sabina?" I said stubbornly.

He raised his eyebrows. "You're in no position to bargain, Vicky, in case you hadn't noticed." He shrugged. "But since you're so curious, she's in the shed."

"Let me see her."

"Why not? Go right in and I'll follow. But please don't do anything stupid. I admit I wouldn't shoot to kill, not yet, not unless you give me no choice; but I understand a shattered kneecap can be very painful. And I happen to be an expert shot."

"If you don't want toothmarks in me, you don't want bullets, either."

"Clever, clever. I can change my plans if necessary, so don't provoke me. After all, where there's life, there's hope. Right? You might catch me off guard—right?"

I didn't answer. The bastard had read my mind.

I stumbled toward the shed with Royce behind me. I wasn't as groggy as I was pretending to be. Wolf growled as we passed him, but remained on guard outside the shed. We went inside. Royce closed the door behind us.

There was a smell of mildew. Light slanted in through cracks in the walls. As my eyes adjusted to the dimness, I caught the gleam of glass all around me. From floor to ceiling the walls were lined with framed photographs.

Then I saw her. She lay huddled on the dirt floor at the far end of the shed, her eyes closed, her face covered with blood. She was tied hand and foot. "Sabina!" I cried, and took a step toward her.

"Don't move," Royce barked.

I froze, and my head jerked in his direction. "Is she alive? Is she—"

"Don't get excited, Vicky. She's not dead."

. "What did you do to her?"

"Just a little tap on the head. To keep her quiet—nothing fatal. After all, I wouldn't want her dying before the accident. Rigor mortis would be too advanced. Perfection is in the details—you know who said that?"

"You scum!"

He smiled. "Sticks and stones may break my bones— Did the kids used to tell you that, when you were growing up in Bowie, Vicky?" He pulled Sabina's gun out of his pocket. Then he leaned the rifle against the wall of the shed, about ten feet from where I was standing. I saw that all the photographs on the wall were of trains—trains shot from up close, distant trains like toys snaking through valleys. . . . Royce trained Sabina's gun on me and, bending cautiously, picked up a coil of rope and a length of two-by-four that were lying on the floor. It was a hefty hunk of wood and he looked at it gloatingly. "Sticks and stones," he whispered, and his eyes grew sick with excitement. As he moved toward me, I knew beyond a doubt that the two-by-four in his hand was going to come crashing down on my skull in a matter of seconds, unless I managed to distract him.

"Did they say that when you were growing up in Baltimore, Royce?"

He stopped. The excitement in his eyes seeped away a little, and craftiness took its place. "You know so much about me. I should be flattered." He tossed the two-by-four aside, and I stepped back as if involuntarily, which brought me a little closer to the rifle. "I forgot. How could I? I forgot we have to talk first. Lie down."

"What?"

"Lie down! On your stomach." He raised Sabina's gun and pointed it at my head. "Remember, I can always change my plans." I got down on the dirt floor. It stank of mildew and long-dead fish. His eyes scanned the shed and stopped at a thick, rusty hook low down on a wall. He went over and tied one end of the rope to it. "Now crawl over here," he said. "But stay low. Don't make any sudden moves." I didn't budge, and he said, "Or if you'd rather, you can have a bullet in the brain. It's your choice. Freedom of choice—that's what this great nation's all about, right?" I started squirming slowly in his direction. "That's better. Now. I want you to tell me everything you know about—Baltimore."

My eyes were on the two-by-four. It wasn't that far away. If he was planning to tie me to the hook, there would have to be a time when his attention was distracted from the gun in his hand. If at that moment I could manage to kick his legs out from under him, or at least knock him off balance, and grab the two-by-four. . . . I said. "I know that's where you grew up. I know you were in foster care most of the time. But you didn't stay anyplace long, did you? Those families couldn't get rid of you fast enough. Not that I blame them."

"Why the fuck should I care? They were nothing to me. Stupid fools."

I edged closer. He was holding the gun in one hand and nervously twisting the rope in the other. "And your real parents—" I had only a few feet left to crawl. I tensed the muscles in my legs. When I got close enough I would spring, knocking his knees sideways with my shoulder while I went for the two-by-four.

"What about them!" His voice was harsh.

"Your father locked you in a closet and left you to die. I guess that shows how much he thought of you." The nerve was twitching in the corner of his mouth again, and he twisted the rope tighter. I tensed. "Too bad you *didn't* die!" I cried, and sprang. He sidestepped, trying to aim the gun, but he was slightly off balance. I could feel my fingertips graze the two-by-four. I grabbed at it while managing to give one of his legs a kick. He yelped, and as my hand just missed the two-by-four, he fired. The shot went wild. Outside the shed the dog was barking and leaping against the door, which rattled in the frame, but stayed shut. Royce shot again, and a white-hot flame seared the flesh of my forearm. I reared up and tackled him. He staggered backward. I swarmed all over him while he tried to bring the gun around, and we grappled. Outside the shed, the dog was going crazy. Royce was strong and in top condition, but I was younger and I kept myself in good shape. We were well matched, even with a flesh wound in my arm. I managed to get a hold on his wrist and forced his hand backward until the gun dropped on the floor; I kicked it away and he stomped heavily on my foot and we fell to the floor, rolling over and over together in the direction of the two-by-four.

I snatched at it but he managed to grab it first.

The last thing I remember seeing was his face above me, contorted with rage, and the arc his arm made as he swung.

Thirty-five

"Vic! Vic, wake up!"

Something was jabbing me in the ribs. The pain was no big deal, compared to what was going on inside my skull; still, it was annoying and I wanted it stopped. I mumbled, "Quit that!"

"You're conscious! Open your eyes!"

I tried to roll over and found that I couldn't. I blinked, and found myself staring straight into the headlights of a locomotive that loomed over me. . . .

My heart started to hammer.

I shook my head.

I was lying on the floor, trussed up like a turkey. On the wall in front of me hung a photograph of an oncoming train, blown up to mural size.

Memory returned, of Royce, the two-by-four, the shed . . . of Sabina huddled motionless in a corner. . . .

I opened my eyes and, with an effort, kept them open. Ropes had been crisscrossed around my body. The arm that had been winged by Royce's bullet was aching, but I didn't seem to have lost much blood. I could hear Sabina whispering urgently, "Vic! Vic!"

She was lying on the floor behind me. It took a while for me to figure out that the thing that kept jabbing me in the ribs was her elbow. "Quit it," I said thickly, and lifted my head as enormous bronze bells bonged in my skull. I saw these Japanese monks on television once, bonging a bell with the end of a timber so thick it took two of them to heft it. That's how my head felt. I screwed my eyes shut, waiting for the bonging to die down.

"Quick!" she whispered, jabbing me in the ribs again. "There's no time to lose."

I turned my head, and blinked to bring her into focus. She, too, was tied up, and she looked a mess—hair matted, face streaked with dried blood. Her eyes, though, were alert and determined. I said thickly, "What do you mean, 'quick'? Quick, how? *I'm* tied up. *You're* tied up." Outside, the dog growled, and I lowered my voice. "How'd you get over here, anyway? Weren't you over there?"

"I crawled. It doesn't matter. Vic, how numb are your hands?"

I flexed my fingers. "A little stiff. But not numb."

"That's lucky. I can't feel mine at all." Craning my neck, I saw that her hands had been tied behind her back. She began doubling up her body and then straightening it out again.

I said, "What are you doing?"

"Trying . . . to turn," she grunted. "So you can . . . grasp my heel."

"Your what?"

"Sh!" She kept slithering around on the floor until she managed to position her feet close to my hands. She said, "Try and reach my feet." Slowly and painfully I tilted my body until my bound hands touched her. "Good!"

"Now what?" The dog growled louder, disturbed by the sound of our whispers.

"Grasp the heel of my left shoe."

"You have a reason?"

"Yes."

"Might I ask—"

"Just do it!"

"I can't reach it."

"Wait." She squirmed closer. "Try now."

My hand closed around one of the high, smooth heels of her patent leather pumps. "This is the left one?"

"Yes. Now untwist it."

"Untwist it?"

"For heaven's sake, will you stop repeating my every word? Untwist it!"

I twisted the heel as hard as I could with my stiff fingers, but nothing happened.

"Try the other direction."

"Hey!" The heel began to unscrew smoothly in my hand, and after a moment I was able to detach it from the shoe. "What do you know! Now what?"

"Let me back up. All right. Feel for a tiny switch in the seam, and flick it with your nail. And whatever you do, don't drop that heel and lose it!"

I felt for the switch and found it, concealed in the seam of the leather. It was about a quarter inch long. I slipped the nail of my forefinger under it and pried it up. The heel gave a sudden little jump in my hand, with a sound like the springing of a trap. Outside Wolf growled again, a longer, more threatening growl, and then barked. One bark. We froze. If Royce came to investigate . . .

But nothing happened. Cautiously, I slid my fingers down to the tip of the heel and encountered a cold, narrow shaft of metal that hadn't been there before. The whole damn thing was a switchblade knife! "Well, well," I said. "Where'd you get that?"

"From Mr. Kim." Kim is a Korean on the Rockville Pike who sells ordinary electronics as well as not-so-ordinary devices for surveillance and other special purposes.

I said, "Why didn't you tell me about it before?"

"I wanted to surprise you."

"Okay, you succeeded. Now shove your feet over here so I can start cutting you free."

Her feet landed against my hands. The switchblade was razor-sharp, and it didn't take me long to sever the ropes that bound her ankles. "What a relief!" she said. "I can move my legs. Now do my hands." She swiveled around again, and soon I had freed her hands. "My fingers can't feel a thing," she complained, and began swinging her arms up and down to restore circulation.

The dog growled threateningly.

"Cut me free!" I said. "Hurry!"

She tried to take the switchblade in her hand, but it fell uselessly from her slack fingers. "I can't! I can't hold it!"

"You have to! There's no time—"

"Maybe with my teeth?" Her face dove into the dirt.

"Don't cut your face—"

"Does it matter?" She had the heel between her teeth now. Bending until the blade was close to my bound hands, she mumbled, "Saw!"

I pressed the rope that was wrapped around my wrists against the knife, but I was afraid to saw too hard and hurt her.

"Harder!"

The dog was still growling. I knew she was right—we had to hurry. I pressed harder. Once the knife slipped and she drew in her breath sharply, but all she said was, "Go on!"

Together, finally, we managed to free my wrists. I grabbed for the knife and cut away the ropes that bound the rest of my body. Then I stood up and pulled her to her feet. A thin trail of blood was trickling down her chin. "You're hurt."

"Never mind, there's no time!"

Outside, the dog burst into full-throated barking.

Quickly, we improvised a plan.

The dog began throwing his body against the door of the shed, which rattled and creaked under the impact. Sabina hobbled over to the door, braced herself, and then threw it open and retreated as rapidly as she could manage. Growling savagely, Wolf burst through the doorway and leaped straight for her back. I was standing off to one side, and as he sprang I brought the two-by-four down on his skull with all my strength.

Blood spurted, and he fell and then tried to get up again, dragging his hindquarters on the ground but somehow managing to turn and face me with bared fangs. Lurching forward, he collapsed and lay still.

"I hear Royce!" said Sabina. Running footsteps were crossing the clearing. She threw herself on the floor where she'd been lying originally, while I flattened myself against the wall behind the door.

Royce came pounding up to the shed. Breathing hard, he stopped on the threshold. Through the crack between the door and the frame I could see his movie-star profile, and the gleaming barrel of the rifle in his hands. He'd changed into a red T-shirt and jeans, and the powerful muscles in his arms rippled as he swung the rifle from side to side. "Wolf?" He peered into the dimness. The spot where I'd been lying was off to one side, but Sabina was right in his field of vision, at the far end of the shed. Between her and Royce lay the heap of fur that had been Wolf. I could hear the blood dripping from his muzzle to the floor, where a small puddle had begun to form.

Drip.

Silence, and then: Drip.

"What the hell is—" Royce took a few steps into the dimness of the shed, and then he froze. "Ah, no—" he cried. I edged silently from behind the door. At the sound of Royce's voice, the dog slowly raised his head and gave a strangled little whimper. Then his head dropped with a thud to the ground. "No, Wolf . . . please, no. . . ."

Suddenly, Royce seemed to remember where he was, or maybe he heard a sound as I came up behind him. Whirling around he raised the rifle just as my arms reached out to grab him. I slashed down with the switchblade across his hand, cutting the fingers so deeply that the rifle tumbled out onto the

256

floor. As I snatched it up he pushed past me and raced out of the shed, holding his wounded hand. I fired, but the shot went wild and he kept on going.

Sabina jumped up crying, "Stop him!" I sprinted from the shed into the clearing, dropping the switchblade for Sabina to pick up. Royce was heading for the trailer, but when I fired two shots that pinged off the rusty metal he veered toward the woods. I swerved after him. Behind me Sabina yelled, "Don't let him get away!"

I pounded after him, and saw her out of the corner of my eye, running in her stocking feet toward the Mercedes. Royce crashed into the woods and I followed, shouting, "Royce! Stop or I'll shoot to kill!" I didn't think he'd stop, and I was right—instead he ducked behind a big pile of firewood.

It was late in the day, and the wintry shadows were lengthening. Soon night would fall. I knew if I didn't corner him fast, there was a good chance he'd lose me in the woods—this was his turf and he must know it by heart, the way I knew every cul-de-sac in Bowie.

Suddenly he sprinted from the far end of the woodpile and darted back into the clearing, this time heading not for the trailer but the Mercedes. I followed, the undergrowth slowing me down.

"You bitch!" I heard him shout. "Fucking bitch!" Sabina was backed up against the Mercedes, holding him at bay with the switchblade in her outstretched hand. Behind her, the car settled as the tires she'd slashed deflated. "Bitch!" He heard me coming and as I paused to aim he ducked behind the car and raced into the woods on the far side of the driveway. I chased him, and Sabina followed.

We headed deeper into the woods. Royce ran steadily at first, but after a while his pace began to slow. He was getting winded, and the loss of blood from his wounded hand must have weakened him. Still, the distance between us kept lengthening. With all those bells ringing in my head I wasn't in what I'd call top shape, and Royce knew how to slip through the underbrush, it didn't seem to hold him back the way it did me. Branches kept clawing and catching at my clothes and whipping my face. Even so, I managed to keep the red T-shirt in view most of the time.

How far could the woods extend? This was settled country, not wilderness. I had no idea where we were in relation to the town where I'd asked for directions, but sooner or later we'd have to reach civilization. Until then, all I could do was keep going.

Before long, I started to see sky up ahead. The woods were thinning out. Could we be coming to a road? The distant red speck that was Royce's T-shirt had picked up speed.

Then it vanished.

I kept running toward the place I'd last seen it. I started hearing something, but my head was pounding and my breath was so loud that I couldn't identify the sound.

Abruptly, the trees ended. Ahead of me, a big field sloped downward, with a dim white line in the distance that looked like a fence. Above, the sky was red and full of dark, piled-up clouds. Something raced across the shadowy field at the foot of the hill.

Royce?

No. Too large for a man.

I stood squinting down. The running thing was a horse. It came to a stop and grazed.

Somehow, the place looked familiar. The field, the horse, the fence . . . Hadn't I passed it earlier in the day? Hadn't there been honey for sale—a sign, a row of beehives?

Halfway down the slope, a man was crawling slowly toward the horse. Crawling in a zigzag path. Waving his arms around.

Screaming.

It was screaming that I'd heard.

Behind me, Sabina was stumbling around in the underbrush. I peered down the darkening slope. I saw the beehives. One of them had been knocked over. It lay on the ground.

I hesitated. Sabina burst out of the woods, panting. "Vic! Vic! Did we lose him?"

"No." I started down the slope and she trailed after me. "He's down there. See him? Looks like a swarm of bees got him."

"If he reaches that horse— What's that noise?"

The screaming was becoming words. "Help! Get them off me! Somebody help!"

I broke into a run, peeling off my jacket as I ran. Sabina limped after me.

When we reached him we found him kicking and flailing, covered with bees and trying frantically to get rid of them. He saw us and cried, "I'm allergic to bees!"

I threw the rifle on the ground and started swatting the little devils away from him with my jacket. It didn't make me too popular with them, and they showed their displeasure the way they knew best. Pretty soon I had bee stings all over. Sabina, flailing away with a branch off a pine tree, got her share.

Finally, most of the bees were gone, or dead. Royce was a swollen mess, gasping for breath and buckling at the knees when I tried to haul him to his feet. He managed to wheeze, "House over there," and wave his arm weakly. "Hospital . . ." He looked like a very sick man.

"Go for help," said Sabina. "I'll stay with him."

"Do we really want to—"

"Yes," she said. "Or why did you get the bees off him? Go, Vic."

It was night now. Not far away, lights were burning in the windows of a house. I started toward them, leaving Sabina, Royce, and the rifle behind me.

Thirty-six

The beekeeper, a slow-moving, heavyset guy about my age who was in the middle of supper when I knocked, picked up his jacket and came with me as soon as I told him what the problem was. I sat beside him in his big Ford pickup truck, and we jounced through a gate in the fence, across the field, and up the grassy hill. We found Royce lying on the ground with his eyes closed. Sabina was standing next to him.

"He's unconscious," she said. "Better hurry, his pulse seems very weak."

We hauled him up onto the flatbed. His skin felt cold and clammy. I covered him with a blanket that smelled of horse, and rode to the hospital beside him, while Sabina sat up front with the driver. I had the rifle but I knew I wasn't going to need it, judging from the look of him and the sound of his rapid, shallow wheezing.

It took us twenty-three minutes to get to the hospital. Just before we pulled into the grounds, the wheezing suddenly grew loud and harsh and then tailed off into a rattle; by the time we pulled up in front of the Emergency Room, Royce had stopped breathing.

I ran inside and told the nurse what the problem was, and a couple of men in white jackets appeared with a stretcher and rushed him away through a pair of double doors. The receptionist wasn't happy when I informed her that, not only was I unsure of the patient's name, I had no idea whether or not he was insured. "Are you *positive*?" she kept asking. "Don't you have *some idea*?"

I joined Sabina in the waiting room. People were staring at us, which wasn't surprising considering how we looked. She told me she'd sent the beekeeper home. He didn't know Royce's name, though he'd heard someone lived in the trailer off and on; Royce wasn't the neighborly type, which wasn't surprising. There'd been speculation among the locals about the source of the money that paid for the fancy cars—most folks figured it had something to do with drugs, the beekeeper told us.

We waited. A nurse gave us both an antihistamine shot.

We waited some more. Sabina said, "Do you think they'll pull him through?"

I shook my head. "I'd be surprised. He wasn't breathing when they took him in."

For a while she was silent. Then, "Maybe it'd be better that way."

Finally, after an hour and a half, a doctor came out and said he was very sorry, but Royce had been dead on arrival, and all their efforts to revive him had failed. The doctor was explaining to Sabina about anaphylactic shock when I slipped away to find us a cab.

The taxi dropped us off next to our car. Sabina paid the driver and we watched him drive off down the dirt road, his tail lights dwindling, until he reached the big rock with "Keep Out" painted on it, and turned into the main road.

Then we got in the car. "All things considered, it's better this way," Sabina said after a while. "It's a kind of—rough justice. Not the manmade kind, perhaps, but a trial would have been quite an ordeal for Ms. MacNiece."

"Not to mention the other families."

"True."

We sat without speaking. Finally I said, "What now?"

"Back to the trailer."

"Back? Why?"

"I left my pocketbook in the Mercedes." When I didn't say anything she said, "Well? What are you waiting for?" Reluctantly, I started the car and headed down the dirt road, deeper into the woods. Sabina turned on the roof light and inspected herself in the rear-view mirror. "Heavens, I look ghastly. Do you have a comb?"

I handed it to her. She started tugging it through her hair.

I didn't want to go back to the clearing, and I wasn't sure why. There was nothing to fear—Royce and Wolf were both dead—yet I had this feeling of dread, and it kept getting worse as our headlights tunnelled through the darkness, illuminating the naked trunks of the trees.

We rounded a bend. As the trailer came in sight, I saw that light was spilling out the open door. Instantly, I killed the motor and the headlights.

"What is it?" said Sabina. "Why did you stop?"

"Someone's in there!"

"Don't be ridiculous, there's no one here but us."

"There's a light on!"

She turned to look at me. "Vic, what's making you so jittery? Calm down! Royce must have turned it on while he was still in the trailer."

"It wasn't on before."

"I'm quite sure it was. We simply didn't notice, because it wasn't completely dark yet."

"I guess you're right. Sorry." I restarted the motor and drove the rest of the way.

As I parked, Sabina took a flashlight out of the glove compartment. "Leave your headlights on so you can see," she said. "Fetch my bag from the Mercedes while I get my shoes from the shed. They cost me a pretty penny."

"Do you have the switchblade?"

She nodded. "In my pocket."

The bag was on the rear seat of the Mercedes. When I'd retrieved it I got back in my car and turned it around. Sabina reappeared with the shoes in her hand and I drove away, while she carefully screwed the heel back in. Then she started rummaging through her bag. We'd almost reached the main road when she suddenly cried. "Stop! I forgot about my gun!" I stepped on the brake and we slid to a halt. "Royce took it, we'll have to go back for it."

Resignedly, I turned the car around once again, and we headed back toward the clearing.

"It's probably in the trailer," she said when we got there, adding with an expression of distaste, "I suppose we have to go in. It looks extremely squalid."

"I'll go, if you want."

"Good. You go."

I parked, and she stayed in the car while I took the flashlight and got out.

There had once been wooden steps leading to the door, but they'd half rotted away and cinder blocks had been piled in their place. I climbed up and was about to hoist myself into the trailer, when I heard voices.

I froze—then realized that what I was hearing was only a television commercial. Grabbing the frame of the open door, I pulled myself through it.

A large, state-of-the-art TV set was blaring away in the deserted trailer. The room was carpeted in dark blue shag—floors, walls, even the ceiling, from which the carpeting had begun to pull away at the corners. On the walls, enlarged, black-and-white photographs of trains had been crowded together and pinned to the carpeting. The gloomy shag seemed to soak up the blue glow from the television, as well as a reddish light I could see coming from somewhere off to one side. In the shadows were piles of junk—boxes, old magazines, pillows, empty six-packs. Velvet curtains had been nailed across the windows.

There wasn't much furniture, but along each wall a carpeted ledge had been built, which seemed to have served Royce as bench, table, bed—whatever. A halfeaten frozen dinner lay in a nest of dirty sheets on the ledge opposite the TV, as if he'd lain there eating, watching the tube, and waiting for darkness to fall, when he could carry out his plan for getting rid of me and Sabina. Above the ledge hung a rack of guns, but Sabina's Sterling wasn't among them.

I looked around and didn't see it, so I moved down the trailer into the kitchenette. Here, too, the window had been covered with a heavy curtain.

The kitchen was cleaner than I expected, and I soon saw why—Royce had used it as a darkroom. A red bulb glowed over the sink, and in the faint light I made out flat plastic trays on the sink and drainboard, some containing fluids with a chemical odor. Bottles of chemicals were crowded on a shelf, together with tongs and a timer; an enlarger occupied most of the kitchen table.

In the dimness at the far end of the trailer, a counter ran from one wall to the other, with drawers below it and shelves above. On the counter lay something with the gleam of metal.

Sabina's gun? I switched on a lamp with an aluminum shade that had been clamped to a shelf and, blinking in the sudden brightness, went over to check it out.

Yes, it was the Sterling. I picked it up and dropped it in my pocket, and was turning to go when I noticed something.

A length of clothesline had been strung from wall to wall above the counter, and there was a strip of negatives clipped to it with a clothespin.

Royce's last project, hung up to dry?

I don't know what made me take the strip off the clothesline and hold it up to the lamp.

I saw: a woman's huddled body lying on the floor; a close-up of hands bound at the wrists with rope; a face I recognized—Sabina's; a man's body and face—my own. There were other shots too. All were of us; a roll of twenty-four, taken from different angles.

While we'd been lying in the shed, unconscious, Royce had photographed us.

I don't know why the idea made my flesh crawl, but it did. Maybe it was because he seemed to have done it so calmly, in such a leisurely way, judging from the number of shots he'd taken, and the various angles he'd tried. Very businesslike he'd been about it, apparently.

As if he'd done that kind of thing before.

I started hunting through the drawers underneath the counter, sorting rapidly through their contents and throwing them on the floor. I found blank photographic paper, more pictures of trains, a thermometer, boxes and boxes of loose photographs, pages torn from the Personals column with certain ads circled—these I folded and stuffed into a pocket—a box of zoom lenses. . . .

Outside, Sabina honked the horn impatiently.

How long had I been inside the trailer?

I looked around, and my eye fell on the bookshelves above the counter, behind the clothesline. There, on a shelf above a complete set of the Encyclopedia Britannica, and flanked by books on railroading and photography, stood eight identical photograph albums with black leather covers, each labelled neatly on the spine.

I leaned closer and saw, with an absence of surprise that felt almost like inevitability, Fran's name on one of the labels. Taking down the album, I laid it on the counter and began leafing through it.

After that, I didn't move for quite a while.

"Vic! What's *taking* you so long?" Sabina hauled herself up into the trailer. "It's freezing in the car and the heater is broken, in case it's slipped your mind. Did you find the gun or didn't you?"

"I found it."

"Well? Let's go, we have to get in touch with the police." She came bustling over. "What a hideous place, it's like the den of an animal—" She saw my face, and broke off. "Vic! Vic, what's wrong?"

Her eyes went to the album that lay open on the counter.

"No, don't look—" I said, and tried to close it.

Her strong hands pressed the album open. "Why not? Don't be ridiculous . . . my God!"

Together we stood looking down at a picture of Fran.

She was sitting tied to a wooden chair. It looked like one of the chairs from her kitchen, only she seemed to be in the garage. Across her mouth, a gag had been strapped tightly. Above it her eyes bulged out in absolute terror. Terror—horror—pleading—I don't know how to describe it, only it was the kind of expression you'd never, ever want to see in the eyes of someone you love.

"Don't look at any more!" Sabina commanded, clapping the book shut. "Go out and sit in the car!"

"It doesn't matter," I said, and my voice sounded strange. "I've seen it. I've seen all of them."

"It does matter!" she said crisply. "Go straight outside and sit in that car. I want you to start forgetting—right now!"

I stumbled from the trailer, shivering, and got back in the car. I sat there and couldn't stop shaking.

I'd seen all of them. The one of Fran's body in the car—alive or dead, I couldn't tell—with her head lolling back against the seat; the one of the car on the tracks, the one of the moment of impact, and all the ones in between. . . .

I'd seen them all.

Thirty-seven

"Royce claimed it all started in 1981 with Sondra Turette," said Sabina to Donna. "After he'd met her at Johns Hopkins and married her. He insisted that *her* death was an accident."

The three of us were in the cloister. Sabina was standing with her back to the herb garden, the fountain splashing musically behind her. I sat straddling the low wall of the colonnade while Donna perched nearby, leaning back against one of the columns.

"I'm inclined to believe he was telling the truth when he said that," Sabina went on. "Even though he'd been a pathological liar since childhood—at least according to old Mrs. Becker, who'd been the social work supervisor at Hopkins when he was a client there, and who probably knew him better than anyone. In fact, I believed *most* of what he told me about the murders, because he had no reason to lie. He was planning to kill me." She paused, looking embarrassed. "He'd taken away my purse, with my gun in it—I'm afraid he simply grabbed it and threw it in the back seat, while we were stopped for a red light. It was right after we'd left the Hotel Wilmoral, and he took me completely by surprise. I had no way of knowing that he'd seen Vic in the parking lot and recognized him. But he had; and he remembered that Fran had mentioned Vic worked for a detective agency run by a woman. After he put two and two together he realized who I must be."

"He was shrewd," I said. "In fact, according to him, he was a genius." I closed my eyes for a second. I hadn't slept well since that night in the trailer, and I had what felt like a permanent headache, though the doctor had assured me it would go away in a week or two.

"I doubt that he was," said Sabina. "But he was bright—and he loved boasting to me about how clever he'd been, once he had me at his mercy. Of course I tried to retrieve my bag, but that vicious dog of his was in the back seat and wouldn't let me, and then it jumped over into the front seat and spent the rest of the trip sitting in my lap, glaring into my eyes, ready to sink its fangs into my throat at the slightest word from Royce."

"It must have been terrifying!" said Donna.

This was the first time I'd seen her since the day I'd bailed her out of jail in Stony Brook. She sat crosslegged on a Chinese cushion, wearing skinny pants made of supple black leather and a jacket she'd told me was the creation of a "fabric artist," explaining that this person had cut up a bunch of men's silk ties and fitted the scraps into this intricate pattern, sort of like interlocking butterflies, and then quilted the whole thing. I've always hated to throw out ties that have a spot on them, and now I know what they're good for. I liked the jacket, at least on Donna. The colors set off her blond hair and creamy complexion. She was paler than I remembered—the tan she'd brought back from Italy had faded.

"It was certainly unpleasant, and the dog had very bad breath," Sabina replied. "For the rest of the trip, the conversation was a monologue by Royce. In fact"—she shook her head, and a hairpin fell out of the bun at the back of her neck and landed on the flagstones with a clink—"and this I must say I find extraordinary, he told me he'd always wanted to write his autobiography! Only he hadn't worked out yet how to guarantee that his identity would remain a secret, and he seemed to be hoping I would give him some suggestions! Can you imagine? I've known some arrogant criminals, but Royce's grandiosity was of a different order of magnitude." She shook her head again. "His autobiography! He was convinced it would make millions!"

"Why not?" said Donna. "Just look at the authors on the best-seller list—plenty of them are crooks!"

"The wages of sin *used* to be death," said Sabina severely, "which I consider *much* more appropriate. And of course Royce did die in the end—he was dreadfully allergic to bee stings. He'd almost succumbed to them in his teens, according to Mrs. Becker, when he overturned some beehives belonging to one of his many foster families. That time he did it deliberately, but this time was accidental—he was in a panic, running for his life, and it was getting dark."

I said, "It's a good thing *we're* not allergic to bees." My face and body were still swollen and blotched, despite the shot I'd been given. Also my head was bandaged and my arm was in a sling. Otherwise I looked great. Donna had murmured a few words of sympathy when I'd met her at the door, but I had the feeling that after one glance she'd wondered what she'd seen in me.

"True. But to get back to Royce. I'd suspected the death of Sondra Turette was an accident, because she had no money and therefore didn't really fit the pattern, even though her age and profession were right. Sondra lived in a commune, and she'd had to take out a loan to go to graduate school. Obviously, she had nothing for Royce to inherit.

"According to what he told me, he met her one day when he happened to be passing through Baltimore and impulsively decided to visit Johns Hopkins, where he'd spent so much time as a youngster. She was sitting on a bench outside the clinic during her lunch hour, and they fell into conversation. At first he didn't know she was a social worker, and he didn't inform her he'd once been a patient at the clinic. She did find out eventually—Mrs. Becker saw them together, and warned her against getting involved with him—but Sondra, who was a bit of a rebel, didn't pay any attention. In fact, Royce was attracted by that quality in her, and when he learned she was a social worker he was 'even more intrigued. As he explained it to me, social workers had had enormous power over him when he was young—that was how he'd perceived it—and now here was Sondra, fascinated by him, and the shoe was finally on the other foot. That intrigued him, or he'd never have bothered to date her once he found out she had no money.

"They got married. Sondra had no way of knowing that Royce already had a number of wives scattered up and down the eastern seaboard, women he'd met through the Personals column and then defrauded. These 'wives' of his were still alive, if Royce can be believed—he claimed that up to that point he'd never killed anyone, though he'd been a very successful confidence man. However, no amount of money was ever enough for him; as soon as he'd get his hands on it he'd go on a gambling spree until he'd lost it all—a common pattern, I understand, with compulsive gamblers. He'd been in debt more than once to some very unsavory people, and this worried him. In fact, that was his situation when he answered my ad in the *Grapevine*."

Sabina paused, and plucked a leaf from one of the herbs. "He told me about one woman he married, who agreed to move with him to another state. She entrusted him with her life savings, including the proceeds from the sale of her house, and he went on ahead, ostensibly to buy a new house and to wait for the arrival of her furniture. The poor woman shipped it, and as soon as it arrived he sold it and skipped town, leaving her with nothing. Imagine! Not even a stick of furniture!" She shook her head. "He laughed when he told me about it, as if it was the greatest joke in the world. There was no remorse whatsoever, not the slightest trace of concern over what might have become of her!"

Rolling the leaf between her fingers, she held it to her nose for a moment and then continued. "The question is, of course, why did Royce, who'd been a con man for many years, suddenly change? Why did he start to kill the women he defrauded?" She frowned. "Probably the full answer will never be known. I doubt that Royce, himself, knew it. But it was somehow connected with the clinic at Johns Hopkins, where he'd had that endless succession of social workers—a new one every year, so he could never form a genuine attachment."

"Don't you think the origin was earlier?" I objected. "I mean, look at his childhood! His mother was institutionalized; his father locked him in a closet and left him to die—how traumatic can you get?"

Sabina nodded. "All that is true. Nevertheless, the clinic was crucial. After all, it was the one stable element, the sole fixed point, in a totally chaotic childhood."

"Are you saying he *liked* the clinic?" asked Donna.

"That's an oversimplification, Ms. MacNiece. He had mixed feelings. He certainly never showed any appreciation for the kindness of the young women who dealt with him there, or for their efforts to help him. Nevertheless, he seems to have had a certain sentimental attachment to the place, a twisted kind of nostalgia—mainly for the idea of himself as a younger person, I suppose. Royce was quite incapable of caring about anyone but himself. He was attached to his dogs—he'd had others before Wolf—but doubtless what he appreciated was their total devotion to *him*.

"His marriage to Sondra Turette turned out to be stormy. From what Royce told me, I gather she soon realized she'd made a mistake. One rainy night she packed her clothes and left him—drove off in her car, and was killed when it stalled at a railway crossing.

"Royce wasn't exactly heartbroken—he thought it served her right for leaving him, which had been a blow to his colossal ego and his image of himself as irresistible to women—but her death had a powerful effect on him. He told me that all at once he couldn't stop thinking about his childhood, although he'd managed to repress those early memories almost completely for many years. Suddenly he was flooded by terrible thoughts, thoughts that tormented him. He couldn't get rid of them. And then—he found a way.

"He'd spent his entire adult life preying on women. Any woman would do, he wasn't particular, as long as she had money. Now, that changed. Now he had a more specific target. Social workers! Social workers like Sondra Turette, like the ones who'd pretended to be his friends when he was a child and then abandoned him; even, perhaps, like the ones who'd failed to help his mother. He felt an overwhelming, a murderous rage at them, he blamed them for every bad thing that had ever happened to him.

"Defrauding them—raising their expectations and then betraying them, taking their money—of course he was going to continue to do *that*. As he said to me, sounding quite self-righteous, 'I had to live, didn't I?'

"But that wasn't enough, not nearly enough. No—they also had to die."

Donna shuddered. "What a twisted mind! No wonder I had such a violent reaction to him at Ruthann's funeral." She shook her head. "Poor Ruthann, I guess she was so lonely she took him at face value."

Sabina nodded. "And she wasn't the only one, far from it."

I said, "The social workers were really just a stand-in for his parents, don't you think? Unconsciously? I think it's what they call 'displacement.'"

Sabina nodded. "Possibly. Who can tell how much of anyone's motives is unconscious and how much intentional? Of one thing I'm sure—Royce had managed to convince himself that he was doing his victims a favor, in a way."

"A favor?" said Donna. "You're not serious."

"I am. He said they'd all lived terribly dull lives before *he* appeared on the scene, like Prince Charming, and swept them off their feet." She paused, and her lashes fluttered, veiling her blue eyes. "In fact, he—*was* very attractive. I felt it while we were having lunch."

Donna looked at her with amazement. "You mean, *you* found him attractive?" There was revulsion and disbelief in her voice. "Even knowing he'd killed all those women?"

A tinge of pink came into Sabina's face. "To be honest, I'd have to say yes. He was one of the handsomest men I've ever met, but it wasn't just that, it was something more."

"I couldn't stand him," said Donna emphatically. "I certainly didn't find him attractive. Good-looking, yes, but—"

"You met him at Ruthann's funeral, Donna. The circumstances were completely different. He wasn't focused on you, trying to charm you; there were other people present—you can't know." She sighed, and shook her head. "There was just something that flowed from him. A responsiveness, a sympathy, a sense that he was a wonderful listener, that he appreciated me, understood me deeply—better, even, than I knew myself." Suddenly she laughed. "I know! He was like a good shrink! That's what it was!"

"He should have been good," I said. "He was trained at Johns Hopkins."

"Well, he was. And he knew it. He said he made a study of each woman so he could fulfill her particular fantasy. He brought excitement into his victims' lives."

I nodded, remembering Fran's words: "This man's exciting, he's a doer. . . ."

"Royce felt that knowing him had been the highlight of each woman's existence, and if she'd paid a high price for the privilege"—she shrugged and raised her hands, palms up—"so what? He was sublimely self-centered, remember."

"But he wanted them to suffer," I objected. "Now you're saying he thought he was giving them a treat."

"It's possible for both statements to be true, Vic. As I said, he had mixed feelings. He did feel rage, but he also had a desire to charm and to please, and he took pride in doing it well."

She paused.

To charm and to please. Right.

I thought about the pictures of Fran in the album I'd found in the trailer—as a matter of fact I'd spent most of my time thinking about them since I'd seen them. According to Sabina, the ones of Ruthann and the other victims, which she hadn't allowed me to see, were similar.

Sabina claimed not to have been totally surprised by the existence of the pictures. She said she'd suspected Royce might have photographed his victims, at least while they were on the railroad tracks, because of something Henry Freulinger had said about having seen flashing lights when he was trying to stop the train. I'd assumed he was talking about the blinking red signal lights at the crossing; actually he must have meant the flashbulbs used by Royce.

Donna spoke up. "Why did Royce choose that particular method? Was it just because he wanted all the social workers to die the same way Sondra Turette had? I mean—it seems so complicated. What if someone had come along and seen one of the cars, after he'd left it on the tracks? What if one of the engineers had been able to stop in time? It would have given everything away."

Sabina and I exchanged a glance. This was a point on which we'd disagreed. Sabina thought we had an obligation to tell Donna everything, but I felt strongly that no mention should be made of the pictures Royce had taken of his victims' final hours, or of the fact that he'd kept them where they were easy for him to get at, to look at, to gloat over—in other words, that it was obvious he'd gotten some kind of a sick thrill out of the way they'd died.

We'd removed the Fran and Ruthann albums from the trailer, and left the others for the police to find. I doubted Donna would ever learn about them—after all, the case would never come to trial—and I saw no reason to mention them to

274

her. I'd told Sabina so, in no uncertain terms, and after some discussion she'd agreed with me.

Sabina said to Donna, "Sondra's death, of course, gave him the idea, but also he was fascinated by trains."

"He was a railroad buff," I explained. "It was his hobby—that, and photography. There were books on both subjects in the trailer where he lived, and the walls were covered with photographs of trains. He knew the ins and outs of railroading, he knew that if he called the office of the chief dispatcher he could find out exactly when a certain train would reach a certain spot. We were able to learn that someone who said he was a photographer called the dispatcher of the Old Dominion lines the day Fran died, and asked when the train would be passing through the place where she later died."

"That *was* Royce—I asked him and he confirmed it," said Sabina. "He'd picked out an unguarded crossing near a curve in the tracks, so the engineer wouldn't be able to see too far ahead. He'd worked it all out ahead of time. The fact that it wasn't easy gave him an added satisfaction."

"It was an ego trip," I said.

"And he did the same with all the others, he admitted it." She paused. "Not admitted. Boasted."

Afterwards we had tea in Sabina's office.

Donna said, as she set down her second cup, "I really don't know how to thank you, Sabina. I feel enormously better. I know I'll always miss Ruthann, but at least now I can come to terms with the fact of her death."

"You're very kind to say so."

Donna shook her head. "It was terrible, knowing the man who'd killed her—and I always believed he had—was walking the streets, enjoying himself. Now that feeling's gone." She paused. "So I've brought you something."

"Oh?"

"A little surprise. A present. It's out in the car, maybe Vic can help me get it. Though—" She looked at me with consideration. "On second thought, with his arm in a sling—"

"I can help. It's just my left arm."

Sabina's eyes gleamed. She didn't tell Donna she shouldn't have done it; she adores presents. "My goodness, it must be a *big* surprise."

"You'll soon see. Stay right here."

We went out to the driveway.

I said, "It's been good seeing you again, Donna. You're looking terrific."

"Thanks. I wish I could say the same for you. I hope the injuries are only temporary."

"That's what the doctors tell me."

There was an awkward silence. Donna said, "Vic. Maybe I owe you an apology."

I didn't answer.

"I gave you mixed messages."

"True."

She pushed her hair back out of her eyes. "Well—I'm sorry. You've been decent."

"For a man."

"For a man, right."

We'd reached the driveway. I said, "So maybe we'll see each other some time?"

Smiling, she shook her head. "I honestly doubt it, Vic. Not for a long while, anyway. I've decided to go back to Rome and study with the same sculptor. He's been great for my work."

I felt a twinge of disappointment. Somehow I'd thought that Donna and I might give it another try, once she was no longer a client; maybe the next time we'd do better. I said, "Well, Donna—it's been memorable. But don't you have to hang around until your trial?"

"Oh, Dr. Levesque decided not to press charges, after my lawyer threatened him with a malpractice suit for advising

276

Ruthann to put an ad in the Personals. Not that I think we'd
have won it, but I guess he didn't want to have to deal with it."

"I see. Well, that's good but even so, take my advice and
don't commit any burglaries while you're in Europe."

She grinned. Then she put her arms around me, gently because my arm was in a sling, stood on tiptoe, and kissed me on
the lips—not passionately but in a friendly way. It was nice and
I was glad she'd done it.

Her car was a big, cream-colored van. She opened the doors
and jumped inside. "Okay," she said. "Let's start hauling this
out." I saw a big pile of scrap metal that looked like junked auto
parts. She hooked a wooden ramp onto the floor of the van.
"Climb in," she said. "Grab it with your good hand and we'll
get it on the dolly. Then we'll slide it down the ramp."

"What is it?"

"A sculpture, what do you think it is?"

"Isn't it, ah, rusty?"

"That's the patina. Actually, it's a fountain, you couldn't
know that. To replace the simpering maiden in Sabina's
cloister. It'll look great, with the light spilling down from the
skylight."

"Yeah, well. You made it?"

"Yes. And I very seldom give my work away. Think she'll like
it?"

"I'm not actually sure it's her taste."

"She'll get used to it," she said briskly. "Sabina's a wonderful
woman, but she needs a little updating. This happens to be the
twentieth century." She squatted next to the fountain and
grabbed the humongous thing around the base, while I got a
grip on a protruding whatchamacallit. Together we wrestled it
onto the dolly and rolled it carefully down the ramp.

Out in the open with the sun shining on it, the thing had
more of a shape. Or maybe I mean a rhythm, the way the big,
knobby joints kind of spiraled around it—I don't know how to
talk about this stuff. What I'm trying to say is, it didn't look that
bad. Still, I couldn't imagine Sabina wanting to stick it in her

herb garden, where she'd have to see it every time she was doing a piece of heavy thinking.

. Donna was studying the thing, leaning back with her arms folded. "I kind of hate to part with it," she said, smiling at it fondly, like a mother about to leave her kid on the first day of school. "Oh, well. Let's bring it in."

Sabina heard us coming as we rolled it into the waiting room. She was still in her office. "Is that you?" she called. "Can I see it now?"

"Not yet," said Donna. She gave the dolly a quarter turn and then stepped back to judge the effect. "Okay," she called. "Come and get it!"

Sabina's heels tap-tapped on the flagstone floor of the cloister as she headed in our direction.

Donna grabbed my good arm. "She's coming, Vic," she said, and gave an excited little wriggle of anticipation. "I can hardly wait to see her face!"